Good I̶̶̶̶̶̶̶ ̶̶̶̶u

Anton Marks

Marksman Studios
London, United Kingdom

Marksman Studios
123 Navigator Drive
Southall
London
UB2 4UU
www.antonmarks.com

Publisher's Note: This is a work of fiction. Names, characters, places, and incidents are a product of the author's imagination. Locales and public names are sometimes used for atmospheric purposes. Any resemblance to actual people, living or dead, or to businesses, companies, events, institutions, or locales is completely coincidental.

Ordering Information:
Quantity sales. Special discounts are available on quantity purchases by corporations, associations, and others. For details, contact the "Special Sales Department" at the address above.

Good II be Bad/ Anton Marks. -- 1st ed.
ISBN 978-0-9562660-2-6

*To My Wife Yvonne, for Enduring the Nightmares &
Celebrating the Successes.*

The night was meant for people like us. For people who use it to get away. For people who see themselves in the city lights and for those who lose themselves in the long walks home.
The night is where the gentle madness is, my friend, and that is where people like us belong.

-R.M. Drake

1.

DI John 'Shaft' McFarlane knew better than to be sitting in a car with the Guardians of the Light without expecting the unexpected. These three women who were comfortably seated in his vintage Jaguar were like mystical lightning rods that attracted the supernatural and the otherworldly as a matter of course. It was surprising they were here. But who was he to deny these sisters-in-arms, who had saved his life on numerous occasions, an opportunity to help him with a case?

"It looks like your boy has just arrived, G." Patra said indicating to the approaching car with a lift of her chin. It crawled to a stop, about a hundred meters away. Shaft nodded quietly acknowledging the American woman whose beauty bellied the fact she was a brawler in bar fights and had a knack of emerging unscathed from the most, dire of situations. She hated to be called lucky, but she was.

"What is he doing just sitting there?" Shaft asked not expecting an answer.

"The dude looks spooked," Patra added. "You sure he don't owe you money."

Shaft snickered.

"We need to have met for him to borrow money from me. He's so skittish, I'm amazed he's here. But he knows I can't protect him if he doesn't come in." Shaft leaned forward drumming his fingers on the steering wheel, thinking. "You know what? Let me go get him. He's the one who insisted we meet in this dump in the first place. What's with the cloak and dagger?"

Shaft huffed and released his seatbelt, as a soft but unusually strong hand gripped his shoulder from behind. Suzy Wong leaned in from the back seat; her perfume subtle; her presence strong for such a petite woman.

"Yuh bettah mek we do that detective. Someting... is a bit off."

Shaft didn't argue with Suzy's estimation. The Chinese Jamaican's empathic abilities had saved them too many times to mention. Besides if it wasn't for her this meeting would not have taken place, and the Guardians of the Light wouldn't be here. Shaft leaned back into his seat.

"Just keep the engine running detective," Y dark skinned Londoner spoke from behind him, leaning close to his ear, their skin almost touching, and a crackle of electricity passed between them. Her tone was measured and calm as was her way. She was the de facto leader and strategist of these amazing women. Shaft had difficulty concentrating around her. For a ten-year police veteran, an anthropologist turned Detective Inspector, Shaft should at least have the discipline to be professional, but he couldn't help himself. Y's smoky voice alone made his heart quicken and his knees weak. The great thing was, she was into him. The challenge? There were no rules for romancing a woman like Y and maybe there never would be.

"Did he drive his own car?" Y asked.

"Uber," Shaft responded.

"Text him." Y said. "We'll escort him over."

Shaft let his fingers do the talking, and the three women exited the car. Suzy had sensed something about this case was unusual. They had insisted they be here. A ride along, Patra had quipped. Shaft felt flattered they would take time away from a successful Celebrity Bodyguard business and their mystical responsibilities to be here. Unless they too thought it was important. Shaft thought about it as he watched them through the window. All three wore casual jeans, fitted tops. Y had what looked like a Louis Vuitton snooker case over her back. Patra had both her hands in her fitted leather jacket while Suzy the shorter of the three, swung her shoulders, her left arm showcasing an angrily beautiful Chinese Dragon wrapped around her biceps and forearm.

Bad II the Bone walked shoulder to shoulder. The name they gave themselves in the early days of their relationship felt comfortable and meaningful.

It had stuck with them.

It became the name of the Celebrity Bodyguard company they had established with a millionaire friend. That was their day job. They were ordained for much greater things, and their unique abilities were respected and feared in the supernatural circles that they slowly were being introduced into. The Guardians of the Light have walked the earth for millennia. Always three, always women and always chosen by the *Powers that Be* to redress an imbalance in the shifting landscape of good and evil. London was becoming an epicenter of that imbalance, and their powers were required again.

Suzy took the lead, her sensitivity best suited up front. Her eyes sparkled as she absorbed and interpreted the forces. The man who had arrived in the minicab opened the door but did not step out as they approached.

Suzy stopped and put her hand to her ears.

"Yuh hear dat?" She said.

Patra shrugged and kept advancing.

Y stopped.

Almost on cue, an angry growl of engines echoed off the disused buildings surrounding them.

The girls reacted immediately.

Suzy pointed to where the sounds were coming from despite the acoustics bouncing off the crumbling walls. Y started running towards the minicab. Just as three motorbikes rocketed into view, their riders in shiny black helmets, bodies covered completely with leather and all three trailing glinting swords in their hands.

"I'll get the informer; you two deal with the rest," Y called out.

Y was running full tilt towards the minicab, reaching back to unclip the Katana strapped to her back in the Louis V snooker bag. She felt the comfortable and reassuring hilt touch her fingers and she yearned to have it in her hand.

Use me it whispered.

The informer stepped out of the cab, unaware of what was coming, looking at Y as she gesticulated wildly at him. The riders were bluish-black contusions on the landscape, unconcerned about obstacles and debris, pushing their machines to the limit, dust billowing up behind them. In a choreographed movement, the two end riders peeled off allowing the middle rider to slice down the middle.

Suzy and Patra took a bike each. The Jamaican had no weapon, and that was cool. Patra had a transparent gauze bag attached fashionably to her belt, filled with a selection of oversize marbles and ball-bearings she called her cats eyes. She emptied three shiny balls into the palm of her hand and prepared.

Once Shaft heard the growl of motorbike engines echoing off the building, he bailed out of his Jaguar, leaving the door open as he scuttled behind the girls and towards the parked Uber. He reached under his jacket and smoothly pulled his weapon free. He held his Sig Saur in a two-handed grip and started sprinting towards the speeding bikes. He tried to absorb the situation as he moved; his instincts were telling him this was about to end in disaster, but it had to play out whether he wanted it to or not. Three motorbikes were heading towards them, eating up the distance with every aggressive rev of their machines and giving Shaft less time to react with every heartbeat. The girls were moving quickly, but even they couldn't intercept in time.

He had no chance.

The bikes parted gracefully. One rider headed for the Uber and the other two giving their biker friend room to work. The informer seemed to be frozen and confused. Y was waving at him, and the biker behind was bearing down on his position. Shaft stopped, lowered his center of gravity, watching as the scene unfolded, took aim at the biker heading towards his snitch and emptied his clip.

Shaft's informer knew something was wrong. He turned awkwardly, registering the sound coming from behind him. Then he saw the black woman running at him – one of the detective's colleagues, wildly waving her arms. The informer's body language shifted from curiosity to panic as the ominous black-clad rider beared down on him. He heard the Crack! Crack! of gunshots and instinctively ducked, his focus now on survival. He savagely attacked the taxi door trying to get back to the safety of the interior. Nothing else mattered. The door swung open, he stepped up, then glanced back.

The dark rider was on him.

His fear heightened senses registered an onyx streak and before he could process the significance, there was a silver flash and his world ended.

The man's head arced off his body in a shower of arterial blood. The Uber driver was screaming as his car was splashed in human claret. The informer's fingers still tried the door handle before nervous impulses stopped and the body slumped to the ground. The rider hurtled past the taxi without pause and in a fractured heartbeat, Y and this crazy rider would clash at 70 miles an hour.

Y stopped, braced and anchored herself, bringing her Katana up and at right angles to her body, as she channeled some of her life force into the forged steel and breathed. The rider whose visor was tinted red expertly swerved out and swiped with its blade, hoping for a repeat of the decapitation, but Y anticipated the move and came up with her blade to block it. The spirits of the Japanese blacksmiths rejoiced as the Red Visors blade shattered against Y's weapon. And without pause, the rider flashed past her.

Patra flung three silver balls in the direction of the rider with the tinted blue visor, bending probability, cause and effect to her advantage.

One hit the gas tank the other went wide. The third ball wedged into the spokes of the motorbike doubling its velocity from the centrifugal force of the wheel then releasing. The silver projectile shot up like a bullet, firing into the rider's helmet. His head snapped back sending him toppling off the bike, flinging it from under him and cartwheeling it into a skidding exploding heap. The rider rolled, a disjointed, ungraceful and painful looking tumble. The rider slammed into some debris and came to a sudden stop.

A moment later Blue Visor got up and dusted himself off.

"Motherfucker!" Patra spat in surprise. "You a Power Ranger or something amigo? You should be dead dawg or hurting." The rider didn't agree and except for a scratched and banged up helmet, he was no worse for wear. The superhuman stood up and turned to face Patra and then started to run towards her.

Suzy heard the explosion when she was in mid-air, avoiding the bike and the blade of the third rider with the yellow tinted visor that had attacked her. She hit the dirt gracefully, tumbled and came up to a fighting stance, snapping her head back to see where Yellow Visor had positioned itself in the shifting landscape of the conflict.

The bike slowed down, made a doughnut in the dust and headed back towards her.

"Rass!" She cursed and tensed.

Yellow Visor came hurtling back in her direction, and Suzy locked into a Tiger's claw stance, ready for what was to come.

The rider swung sharply around her, the reflexes required for that last-minute maneuver were lightning fast. Suzy spun, trying to follow it hurtling by her only to see the red taillights blinking and realized she was no longer of interest. One of the trios of riders was without a bike, and Patra was facing down that threat in the distance.

Yellow Visor was making sure no man was left behind.

What was behind that goddamn helmet? Patra thought with annoyance, dodging left and right as the blade from Blue Visor threatened to dismember her. It made a sound through the air like a swarm of angry hornets and was moving so fast only her enhanced senses could track it.

Patra moved backward, her stance perfect, slipping under a cut from the blade then coming up to block its return swipe. Blue Visor adjusted, testing her skill with some deft almost cocky swordplay. Patra anticipated every move as the rider changed tact, discarding flamboyance for savagery. Patra parried, but the force of the attack took her by surprise, and she stumbled backwards. Patra rolled away, but Blue Visor was relentless and kept thrusting at her as she rolled, cracking the concrete as she kept moving away, its attempts to skewer her to the ground failing.

It did not stop thrusting at her, but Patra was too quick. The dark rider held the sword in both hands this time and plunged. Patra slid back and spread her legs, the blade wedging into the concrete between them. Blue Visor tried to pull it free, but Patra corkscrewed up from the ground kicking the blade.

It thrummed and snapped.

Lucky thing she had stumbled.

Patra lunged with a Muay Thai spear knee thrust, to the solar plexus but Blue Visor brushed it aside almost disrespectfully countering and delivered a rapid flurry of elbows and fists. Patra managed to deflect most of them, but then an explosive punch that came from nowhere shattered her defenses. She rolled with it, but the blow smashed into her shoulder and popped it clean out of its socket. Patra spun to her knees and grimaced.

"Fuck!" The pain lit up her senses like a systems overload. In seconds she sprang back up, shrugging her dislocated shoulder back into place and ignoring the ex-cruciating pain. But before she could resume where they had left off, Blue Visor was skilfully picked up from the incoming bike that had snuck up on her. Both killers picked up speed and lowered themselves into the slip-stream on acceleration, disappearing in the acoustic growls of the bike's intakes and exhausts.

"Son-of-a-bitch!" Patra flung her arms in the air in frustration then grimaced with pain.

Shaft finished talking to his department calling in the murder. His mind was already constructing a plausible report that would either include the girls or not. He wanted to see what the CSI team discovered. He would embroider his story around the science.

He looked at the girls flabbergasted.

"What the hell just happened?" Shaft asked both hands on the back of his neck massaging the headache that was about to emerge in all its painful glory. He surveyed the carnage and shook his head again.

"What happened is your contact just got fucked up," Patra added her expression deadpan.

"Thanks," Shaft said. "I've gathered that much."

"Just checking." Patra said.

"How did they know?" Y asked.

"My exact thoughts." Shaft said. "Why, how and who?"

"I don't tink dem human," Suzy said matter-of-factly.

"Definitely not." Patra rubbed her shoulder. "They hit like a motherfucker."

"Their reflexes were off the charts too," Y observed.

Suzy shook her head in tense agreement.

"When I was close to one of deh riders, I felt nothing from him like a dark swirling cloud, hunger, and anger. My mouth tasted like ashes." Suzy shuddered.

Y moved closer to Shaft, and without thought, the detective held two fingers of her hand reassuringly.

"Why did he want to meet you here of all places?" Y asked.

Shaft sighed.

"What you don't know," Shaft began. "Is our deceased friend, was the most uninformer-like informant I've ever worked with."

"Uninformer-like?" Y asked, the corner of her eyes crinkling.

"Work with me here. I'm stressed." Shaft said. "Did you see what they did?" His voice raising as he went off on a tangent.

"We saw." Suzy confirmed.

"They shrugged off nine-millimeter rounds." Shaft shook his head, hoping what had just happened would settle into rationality.

"I dislocated my shoulder," Patra mentioned as if it would help.

Shaft chuckled at the absurdity of it all.

"I digress." The detective considered his next words, then said. "Mr. Duncan Harris did not want to meet up at night. He wouldn't have it. He told me he had been hired by an international client who he claimed had murdered two of his competitors and he would be next. I checked him out, and he was kosher. He was respected by his peers. A Chamber of Commerce member for fuck sake." Shaft exhaled harshly. "When I got the file on my desk, and he called the office from a burner phone, he had been on the run for months. The man was a wreck. His business was in tatters, and his wife had left him. I followed it up." Shaft smoothed down non-existent hairs on his chin. "Suzy got in contact soon after, scaring me

shitless. Saying I needed to be careful. You were right."
Shaft considered his own words in silence for what felt
like a drawn-out moment. "He had something to show
me. Something was coming he said, and I had to be
ready."

"Well, whatever that something was, it didn't want
you finding out about it." Y surmised. "They really want
to keep it a secret."

Shaft turned away from the women and towards the
taxi driver still in shock.

"I fucking hate secrets," he mumbled.

2.

1 Year Ago, London - Solar Eclipse at 14.36

It was mid-week, and London felt as if it was the beginning of the weekend. The impending solar occultation had Londoners uneasy or excited. Some were curious about a celestial event that happened last over a hundred years ago. And they celebrated the wonders of the world. For others, it reminded them of their mortality and what they could acquire or squirrel away in the moment. A select few saw opportunities and the possibility for chaos.

The man entered the bank twenty-five minutes before the celestial event was to occur. He had a spring in his step, a smile on his face and a twinkle in his eye. It was hard to judge his age by his face or posture, but there was something about him that spoke experience, a hard-won ancient experience that had figured out existence required laughter to give it meaning. He strode past the three lines of people waiting for tellers, whistling a tune dressed in a bright mustard suit, green waistcoat, black broad-brimmed trilby with a peacock feather in its band. He carried a cane that was made from gnarled wood that was polished to a brilliant shine and had the most exquisite carvings on its shaft. For every four steps he took, he stylishly twirled it and let its metal tip touch the tiled floor with a clack. His very dandyish presence brightened up the dull day, and for a moment he captured the attention of everyone in the branch, some more than others, depending on your susceptibility to the powers of the old ways.

He walked past the customers waiting at the ATM's his whistle carrying with it the flavor of the Caribbean. He continued on his way to the stairs that led up to the personal advisor's office and the waiting area. He did a little shuffle and turned stylishly. He mounted the steps, two at a time and within seconds he disappeared from view, only his whistles of a Calypso tune, Rum and Coca-Cola echoed downstairs.

Solar Occultation 14:30

Cleopatra Jones pulled her Suzuki onto its kickstand just before a mini coupe had an opportunity to pull into the space and smiled at the frustrated driver. She looked up to the sky and then her surroundings as twilight came early – seven hours early. It had been a spur of the moment decision to come to the bank. She had a great shift at the Pink Kitty Kat last night. Both male and fe-

male punters couldn't get enough of her unique brand of
pole dancing and banter. Strip Clubs were fickle like
that. She was lucky to be a consistent high earner and
respected every cent from her hard work. Today was
supposed to be a lazy day in. What had changed her
mind? It was nothing spectacular. Patra had suddenly
woken up earlier than normal. Strangely she could not
resume sleep, and the two-thousand-pound cash she
stashed in her gym bag was demanding to be taken to
the bank. But first, she did go to the gym and shadow
box, circuit train and had a Sauna. Her insecurity at having so much money laying around her apartment
gnawed at her, so she rolled with it and let intuition
guide her. The High Street was busy - she could never
understand why the Brit's called it that.

Main Street sounded so much better. Patra had mis-
takenly felt this Solar occultation would have had Londoners inside or huddled together watching the
astronomical phenomena from the safety of their mobile
phones. She couldn't have been more wrong. The Dunkirk spirit they called it. Keep calm and carry on. This
wasn't a disaster situation, but for Londoners, this was
business as usual. Patra placed her predator helmet under her arm, she secured the Superbike and clothed in
her curve-hugging leathers ambled up to the bank. Patra
checked her watch realizing that she had about thirty
minutes before closing time and picked up the pace. She
came to the glass doors briefly perusing the interior.

"Goddamn it!" she said. "You people ain't got homes
to go to." She reached to push the door open, when a

dark hand bedecked with gold sovereign rings beat her to it. He clicked his fingers and motioned her inside with a flurry of hands.

"After you daughter," the voice said, its tonality Caribbean and filled with amusement. "And be careful of dat nasty hump in the doorway. Wouldn't want to see you fall."

Patra smelt the whiff of Old Spice aftershave before she turned to acknowledge the gentleman.

Daym!

Old dude, carefree smile and dressed like a Detroit pimp from back in the day.

"Thanks, playa," she said smiling and entered carefully avoiding the brief hazard. The pimp nodded his appreciation and followed in behind her, whistling some Calypso tune with a sweet melody.

Solar Occultation – 14:36

Y stood in the queue with the takings from the Nail Bar for today and yesterday. She was wondering all the way here, why her boss wanted her to drop off the money to the bank. Normally, Sandy Brewster took the time out herself not wanting any of her underlings to have any contact with her finances, but fear had replaced paranoia today. Y was still in shock from her promotion from A+ Nail Technician to security courier, when it dawned on her. She was five customers away from the teller, when she understood, the reason she was in the bank and her boss was cowering in the nail salon on Merchant Street.

Superstition.

Ms. Sandy Brewster believed that her destiny and the destiny of every man, woman, and child on the planet was preordained in the stars. She read her astrological charts religiously and frequently got her palms read. Y guessed that an eclipse with its omen of new beginnings would be a good thing. But Y's boss tended to lean towards 'the worst always happens' brand of fatalism. So, the coward that she was, decided not to tempt fate and allow a patsy to handle what misfortune could befall anyone caught in the spider web of this celestial event.

Just for the hell of it, Y thought to tell her she had been robbed. The imagined look on her face was precious. Y chuckled to herself not understanding how a cynical businesswoman like Sandy Brewster could be so gullible. Y tapped her feet to an old Calypso song she may or may not have heard from her mother's music collection. Suddenly the tune was playing in her head for no rhyme or reason. The lyrics, and the melody were as clear as day. Instinctively Y turned to look behind her as if the origin of her sudden memory would show itself. Instead, an older gentleman in smart but garish attire tipped his hat at her and winked.

"Can yuh feel the winds of change? The man said. "Don't fret; this is what you were born for."

"Excuse me?" Y asked. But the man had not spoken except for the twinkle in his eyes. The man kept on walking without losing a stride.

"Strange," Y thought.

Solar Occultation – 14:38

Suzy Wong walked into the bank and kissed her teeth under the SecureX protective helmet. The small bank was filled with customers, and although it was a short shuffle to the deposit shoot, just the thought of wading through people with her bulky Impact Box just grated on her nerves. Her other stops had been routine and without incident. She felt good physically; her blue and grey SecureX uniform was crackling with static electricity, from the charged atmosphere outside, shocking a few people on contact and making her skin tingle. It was her mental state that was dark. This Bank was her last drop-off on her route and then it would be back to the depot to collect her things for home. She walked past customers who instinctively gave her way due to her grey and blue uniform. Suzy pulled up to the reinforced door beside the bunch of tellers and absently looked at the buzzer that was supposed to gain their attention. With her hesitation came an overwhelming need to look behind her. And with it came a rush of memory or déjà vu that struck her pleasantly like a pillow fight. It wasn't a specific recollection but more like a smorgasbord of happy, sun-soaked sensations that wiped away her foul mood like a light wind through the mist. And the focus of this maelstrom of good vibes was a spritely old boy of

African or Afro-Caribbean descent, she couldn't accurately tell, and neither could she estimate his age between fifty and seventy, dressed elegantly like a garish dandy in bright yellows and greens with a black fedora with a peacock feather in the band. He reminded her of a performer and storyteller who had visited Immaculate Conception Prep school in Kingston. He had spun tales of Africa and the Caribbean that enthralled her young mind. His skill was such that she had never forgotten him and this man whistling melodiously to himself and strutting with his fancy walking stick brought it all back. Suzy wondered if the man had also triggered a keen olfactory sense, as her salivary glands were pumping in anticipation of something delicious. She could taste avocadoes and Bulla - a kind of small ginger cake popular in Jamaica, cascading over her taste buds. As the magic man came up beside her on his way to the other side of the bank, he stopped tipped his hat and winked at Suzy.

"I miss the sun too," he said. "But the people, they make me who I am. They never forgot me." And he was on his way with a merry smile. He left a subtle whiff of old spice, and Suzy wondered if the strange man had just read her mind.

The magic man was perched comfortably on the upper deck of the manager's office, surveying the bank floor below through glass walls. He massaged his ancient back into the supple leather of the Wrexham chair and straightened the pens and papers on the Bank Managers ornate desk. He knew the manager wouldn't be arriving on time. He had been threatened, tortured and tied up with his family. He would be safe. Anyway, he was required to have the best seats in the house for him to witness a spectacle of cosmic proportions. He crossed his legs showing a sock with a monogrammed spider smiling rakishly. The magic man steepled his fingers together impatiently waiting for the next ingredient that would complete this special brew for him. It was like watching how two people fell in love, mad love and prepared for the arrival that had consummated the union. Beings such as himself had to play by the rules. These tenets were older than he was, older than mankind itself, older than the birth of the cosmos. They were built into the machinery of the universe like the teeth in many, many cogwheels; numerous, ubiquitous but essential from the smallest subatomic interaction to the forming of an event horizon in a black hole. This was a cosmic countermeasure for what was to come by the Powers that Be, but for him, it was much more than that. Call them what you will the magic man was as proud as a doting father to see his three daughters become. He watched the matrices of probability that thatched their way around human existence with his ancient eyes. The patterns were made clearer with the event of a solar occultation. He propped his story cane on the side of the desk and got more comfortable. The carved images animated, perpetually telling their tales. He took off his Trilby placing it on the desk, his peacock feather pointing up and searched the interior folds of his dress jacket. He produced a cigar that he stuck in his mouth. The magic man snapped his fingers, and the cigar's end ignited. He took a deep pull on the Cuban.

"Anytime now," he said.

Ramesh Parkram was relieved when the branch manager told him to lock the doors because for him that signaled the end of a long and busy day. The sooner he placed himself at the main door, the better so he could prevent more customers walking in to extend his clock off time.

He had places to go.

Ramesh quickly walked over to the main doors juggling the keys between his fingers. Miscalculating where his forefinger was positioned in relation to his thumb, the bunch fell at his feet a stretch away from the front door. Ramesh sighed, reached down to pick them up and saw a pair of leather loafers on the pavement outside. He stood back up to give the customer the bad news; his eyes followed the trousers, belt, jacket, latex werewolf mask, and shotgun! The man used the butt of his weapon to ram through the gap in the door, breaking Ramesh's nose and sending him backward, a whip of blood trailing him to the ground. The Werewolf stepped through and over Ramesh's body, followed by two other men similarly dressed in latex masks of classic monsters. Frankenstein throws a small box to the floor and presses a switch in his hand. The man with the mummy mask is almost marching towards the four lines of customers his gun pointing to the ceiling, Ramesh's collar in his hand being dragged unceremoniously from the door now locked from the inside, blood streaming over his white shirt. The Werewolf discharged two rounds above his head and captured everyone's attention in a moment.

"Ladies and gentlemen this is a robbery!" A voice boomed from the man in the Werewolf mask. "Could I kindly ask you to lie on the floor right where your standing or my colleagues will kill you."

The werewolf spokesman continued as panic took hold.

"If anyone has any ideas of using their mobiles, don't. Frankenstein monster here has just disabled all electronic equipment with his nifty toy."

In seconds the mummy and Frankenstein had placed five packages on the five counters. They suspiciously looked like bombs.

"For the banking staff, the five items on your windows are explosive devices which will be used as plan B if we are not readily given access to today's taking. And if you didn't know we've disabled the silent alarm and phones lines all courtesy of Mr. Branch manager and my behind the scenes colleague Dracula." He paused dramatically. "Now in an orderly fashion start handing my monster colleagues today's takings."

The Werewolf barked orders, his weapon more than adequate in corralling the customers on the floor and circling him as if he was the chosen one. Everything was going according to plan except for three things: Patra, Y, and Suzy Wong. They stood proud and strong, unmoving from where they originally stood, unrepentant, unflinching.

The three women were hyperaware of everything happening around them. It was if a universal feed was tapping into everyone's senses and then plugged into them. Something amidst the shouting, gunshots, and panic threw a switch in their heads. It wasn't a fear reaction why they ignored the demands of the gunmen. Instead, it was a universal power they tapped into, a choice that all living things had at their disposal and could use as they saw fit. At that moment, they had decided not to be told what they should or should not do. All their life they had been asleep and at this moment they had woken. They were ancient warriors, gifted with mystical powers that have been passed down for millennia. They were the Guardians of the Light, called upon to maintain the delicate balance of good and evil. Always three, always women.

Today they were to be reborn.

The magic man eagerly stared down from his vantage point in the manager's office and swelled with pride.

"They are taking to their responsibilities like ducks to water." He said and took a deep drag on his cigar. He held his head back and puffed out doughnuts of smoke. Then he paused for a moment at what was yet to come.

"They haven't communicated yet" He clapped his hands together gleefully, ash falling on the desk and carpet. "Now that is going to be a sight to behold." He walked around the desk wanting to get a closer look from his vantage point and watched the story unfold.

The three women triangulated each other visually. A closed loop of communication was established between them, and the lead was given to one of their number with the heart and mind to take control. Y squared her shoulders and gave them the slightest of nods, these women, these cosmic sisters knew with every cell in their bodies, what they had to do.

"Are you fucking nuts?" The man in the Werewolf mask pulled the breach of his shotgun with a Clak! Clak! He pointed his weapon at Suzy Wong and Patra nervously, in turn. "Get down on the floor now bitches, don't let me say it..." He hesitated then quieted himself. There were three women weren't there? Someone touched him on his shoulder, and he jumped. The pretty woman who had been in the white uniform in front of him was now behind him. He knew it was her from the perfume she was wearing. She couldn't have moved so quickly, surely.

"I think you better put that down," she said from behind him. It may have sounded like a request, but it was, in fact, a demand. Y was not familiar with the social norms of dealing with criminals so that she could be forgiven.

The man in the Werewolf mask grunted and swung his weapon around, hoping to connect with Y's stomach, but she blocked it without effort. The Werewolf stepped back pulling the trigger in almost a seamless arc that should have put a round into Y's chest. Instead, in a blur of movement, Y gripped the weapon, pointing the barrel up and discharging it into the ceiling. In another flurry of hand movements his eyes could barely register, Y had dispossessed him. He looked at his empty hands and wondered what had just happened. Y had complete control of what a moment ago had been impossible odds. Effortlessly she swung the stock of the shotgun in a trajectory that ended smashing into his forehead and sending the Werewolf to his knees. Before he could gain any semblance of composure, he was on his ass, starring into the barrel of the shotgun, cranked and ready to blow his brains out by the pretty girl in the white uniform.

"Bravo! Bravo!" The magic man jumped to his feet and was applauding wildly. "This was something special, special I tell yuh."

Suzy had the Mummy unconscious and slung over the counter in five moves. A crushed Adam's apple and a mild concussion ended his preoccupation with a crime. Frankenstein fared no better with a broken nose and dislocated arm being led around like a puppy by Patra, ever so often twisting his good arm to the breaking point. The magic man grabbed his story cane and grinned broadly, doing a little jig around the manager's table and then plopped down into his chair, his demeanor more serious. He reached for his hat and put it on. He lifted his story cane to his eyes and peered into the dimensions of what could be, what was and what must be.

"No stories for you yet. Soon there will be plenty." He stood up again and wondered over to the wall of glass and looked down at the surprise and confusion on the bank floor. The victims in shock and relief. And so were the victors.

"Hard times ahead my daughters, but I'm proud. You are the ones to maintain the balance. Some of the Powers that Be were not sure; maybe this performance will sway dem."

The spider God picked up the remainder of his stoogie and shoved it in his mouth. He rolled it around on his lips until it was comfortable. He then drew in the aromatic smoke and exited out of the Bank Managers Office, stopping before closing the door. The light from the room rendered a shadow of a big spider in the hall before him.

"I'll be watching. Yuh can rely on me my daughters; you can rely on me."

He closed the door behind him, tapped his cane thrice and before he got to the stairs the spider God disappeared. You could hear him whistling faintly.

"Day'o, mi seh day'o. Day deh light an mi wah go home. Come Mister Tally man, tally mi banana. Day deh light an mi wah guh home."

3.

Negril, Jamaica. Jungle Nightclub

Two Months Ago

Their chariot awaited. The two couples stumbled out of the nightclub and were met by a dapper and smiling chauffeur – double-breasted suit, matching cap – the whole nine yards. He motioned to a squat black Mercedes Benz with gleaming metalwork and tinted glass on the other side of the dual carriageway.

It was a balmy night out at the seaside resort.

"Congratulations," the chauffeur said a full set of white teeth on display. "My name Is Mr. Opoku, and I will take you to the great House for champagne, Hors D'oeurvres and your prize, compliments of Pheare Plaza, Ocho Rios."

The driver sounded like an Irie FM advert and to their ears that was a good thing. Neither of the couples had ever been the recipient of a prize such as this before. They contained their excitement very well. Eddie held onto Shanice's, hand, squeezed and kissed her.

"Didn't I tell you tonight would be lucky for us baby. Didn't I."

"I'm lucky for you." Debbie corrected. "I was the one who bought the raffle ticket, so I'm deh charm."

Desmond chuckled and playfully slapped Debbie's ass. She squealed.

Desmond said.

"I paid for that rass ticket, what does that make me?"

They all laughed making their way across the road to the luxury car.

"Lucky too." Debbie said, "And I'll show you how much later."

Desmond grinned hungrily.

"What about some double trouble?" Eddie asked sheepishly hinting at the prospect of two-way action in the back.

"Yuh mad?" Shanice blurted out to everyone's amusement but only Eddie knew that if he played his cards right tonight, he might have a shot of getting between those sexy broad hips and thick thighs. Standing beside the Mercedes picturing Shanice between the sheets with him, Eddie absently observed how the paintwork grabbed the moonlight and hungrily trapped it in its surface. Its dark opalescence seemed almost alive. He didn't know why it did that, but it made his skin crawl. Eddie reached out to gingerly open the door, but the chauffeur deftly appeared and ushered the ladies in first, leaving the door open and retreating to the driver's side. Eddie and Desmond slid inside and closed the door to the outside world.

The drive took an hour or so and try as they might in their excitement to talk to the driver they couldn't. The Mercedes was custom built. The interior was luxurious and smelt of leather, cigars and vintage rum. The driver and passengers were partitioned into what felt like two separate and self-contained areas. Communication between the two was facilitated by a handset that was positioned on the opposite panel facing the seats. It didn't work. They had tried. Not that anything they had to say was of real significance. They were just giddy on the experience and alcohol. If they had paid attention to the competition rules, they would have known that they would receive their prizes at the Miranda Pheare great House. Home to one of the oldest and richest business Dynasties in Jamaica. Also, a place of historical interest that was preserved from the pre-colonial era. Pheare Mansion was also the subject of many tales and stories that were popularized by books written on the subject. A few were required reading for many High schools on the island.

"What do you think the first prize is going to be?" Shanice asked the question as the car slowed to a stop at the end of a lavish driveway with an orchard of oranges on both sides. The car stood in the shadow of the magnificent great House that looked as good as it did in the seventeen hundreds.

"Whatever it is," Eddie commented, "It's going to be quality. I can feel it."

"Feh real man," Desmond said. Then moonlight flooded the interior. The chauffeur ushered both couples to the front of the great House up the sweeping stone stairs to a set of imposing doors. The chauffeur stopped dramatically and made a point of highlighting the detail on the two massive doors.

"What do you think?" he asked. The design was exquisite and looked like it was depicting a battle with soldiers, casualties and animals that resembled wolfs and dragons dripping blood from their fangs. There was a coat of arms too with the image of a female with piercing eyes and a rose between her lips dripping blood.

Intrigued, Eddie said:

"A real craftsman did this. Look at the detail." He ran his finger across the sculpted depiction. He shuddered involuntarily in the warm night.

"It is just over two hundred years old." The chauffeur turned-guide told them. "Made from Wallachian Cedar, from the foothills of Transylvania. Very valuable", he continued and reached up to the dragonhead knocker and slammed it down three times. With an intake of breath, the doors swung open silently. The chauffeur nodded his head crisply towards his guests and they entered the candlelit interior.

"I bet the servants back in the day nevah entered through here," Debbie said.

"Yuh know," Desmond agreed in a whisper.

"And they were never greeted like this either," Eddie said. "Wow!"

The interior had a high ceiling reception area and a central staircase split the space in both directions as the style of the times dictated. As they entered, they saw that the staff of ten women and men had formed a kind of hospitality gauntlet. They applauded curtly and nervously as the couples smiled and walked towards them. The chauffeur coaxed them on, and they walked through the servants to another door and down a candlelit staircase. At the bottom, they entered a banquet hall with a sumptuous spread of food and drink to feed twenty couples. Instrumental reggae was playing low in the background.

"Take a seat and relax," the chauffeur said. "Let me introduce you to our host." He bowed again and left the room.

It was minutes after the chauffeur left them that both couples took stock of their surroundings.

Desmond was first to comment.

"It looks like we first at deh party?"

"The very first," Eddie added.

"I'm feeling cold," Debbie said hugging herself, the action making Desmond reach around her shoulders and draw her into him.

"I can't have that," he said and squeezed.

"We could just eat some food until whoever coming next turns up," Eddie reasoned. "What yuh say, baby?" Shanice did not hear him. She stood staring at the end of the banquet hall and the darkness that occupied that space. How it sat lurking in anticipation, readying itself to devour the light and anything else it fancied.

"Baby, yuh alright?" Eddie asked again touching her shoulders gently. He broke the spell.

"I'm fine," Shanice lied, "I want dis over an done with. I want to go home."

She kept staring into the darkness that was untainted by candlelight.

"But we just got here," Desmond complained. But Shanice did not explain. "What yuh looking at Shany?" Desmond asked.

Shanice said nothing.

Eddie looked at her weirdly.

"Yuh scaring me Shany. You okay."

Slowly Shanice turned around to her friends her eyes wide and distant as if tiredness was finally a night of raving. She spoke almost in a whisper.

"Can't you hear it?" She asked, "Over there." She pointed at the end of the hall.

Everyone looked to the inky darkness unable to distinguish anything in its depth.

"Can't hear nothing," Desmond said.

"Duppy," Eddie grinned sheepishly.

"From the earth we came, and so shall we return."

"What?" Eddie asked.

"Her words," Shanice continued, "Can't yuh hear it?"

Desmond shook his head but suddenly could not take his eyes away from that spot that had Shanice spooked.

"Let's go look?" Eddie blurted, regret at his outburst came too late for him to back out. "Yuh with me?" He looked over to Desmond, and the bigger man nodded.

Shanice looked up to the vaulted ceiling, and all eyes did the same. A collective internal thermostat turned anticlockwise as a coldness burrowed through their flesh and into their marrows.

"Jesas Christ," Debbie said.

Eddie opened his mouth but nothing, no words emerged. It was a bas-relief of intricate detail, stretching from one end of the hall to the next. The whole ceiling depicted scenes of bloodletting that stretched across history and locations. From plantations, sugar cane fields, World War I, civil uprising, political rallies, World War II, men, women, and children were being gutted and massacred as one figure looked on.

A dark-skinned woman.

Both men walked down to the end of the hall shoulder to shoulder their breathing strained, the effect of that ceiling still had them shook. Desmond with his mobile phone in hand was the only one who thought of the diminishing light from the candles could not light there way and hoped his phone was bright enough to suffice. But the closer they came to what they thought must be the end of the hall the more suffocating the darkness became. Desmond stopped abruptly, and Eddie followed suit. The light from the mobile phone was dying.

"It's cold, an getting colder," Desmond said looking longingly from where they had come.

"Yuh have a lighter, king?" Eddie asked, his voice a tremor.

"Yeah man," Desmond said, producing a Bic Lighter. He flicked the flint three times watched the sparks tumble to the floor, then on his fourth attempt, it ignited. The flame stood steady unperturbed by draught or movement. They preceded forward the shadows threatening to engulf them. Then they saw what Shanice felt and with it came the faint smell of blood. The coppery taint became stronger as they approached something that was revealing itself every step; they took towards it.

They stopped as if they had hit a wall.

A large sarcophagus of exquisite design sat there. Thick herbaceous vines grew out from the moist walls and held the ornate coffin in a protective grip.

"What deh fuck are we doing here. What the fuck is dat doing here?" Eddie took a step back an invisible barrier of dread erected immediately. His instep was still off the ground when Desmond brushed passed him.

"I can see something on top of it. I'm going to check it out."

"Yuh mad. Mek wi leave dis place. Right now!"

"One-minute Eddie, just... a minute."

Desmond stepped closer, straining to see. Closer still and then, he knew. With his mobile phone held high, strobing as it lost power, the intricately designed tomb much easier to see, he could make out the thing on top.

A pig was gutted from throat to crotch and its blood spilling over the edges of the sarcophagus, seeping into the cracks and fissures, soaking into the stonework, like a sponge, the vines leaves splattered with blood and entrails. Heat issued from the lifeless carcass shimmering into the vault-like it was on a griddle. That was not normal; this situation was not normal.

Desmond made a gurgling sound in his throat, the contents of his stomach unstable. He retreated in haste, his footfalls ringing in his ears as he hurried to his woman.

Debbie hugged him.

"What did you see, baby."

"Nothing to worry yuh little head about. Let's just go."

Eddie was way ahead of them, one hand on the big door that led them out of the banquet hall and the other holding Shanice's hand reassuringly. The door would not budge.

He tried with both hands and his shoulder.

"It's locked," Eddie hollered, "The rass door's locked."

"Let me try," Desmond said rushing over with a conviction he thought was missing from Eddie's attempt.

The effect was the same.

"Fuck!" He spat, looking beaten, trapped and fearful. Another sound accompanied his harsh breathing. A dull vibration at first, then a louder, more intense hissing issued from darkness at the halls end. From the sarcophagus. Then came a thunderous pounding. They all looked at each other barely comprehending what was happening. Something trapped inside was trying to get out with a desperation bordering on madness. The pounding reverberated through the hall reaching a crescendo then stopped suddenly.

Silence descended, punctuated only by the murmurs, sobs and pounding of Eddie, Desmond and Debbie trying to get out of this massive crypt.

Another sound rendered everyone immobile. A sound like a lid on a very large pot, sliding off to the floor centripetal force eventually steadying it. Silence again was replaced with a wild scratching that got louder, more defined. It became many scratching appendages on the floor. And the many became thousands, tens of thousands.

A fowl torrent of black, hungry cockroaches streamed forward. They moved as one, a disturbing hive mind holding the tumultuous swarm together. A surge of foul air proceeded them with thousands of empty pupae shells carried like tumbleweed. A screeching roar lifted to the ceiling, and suddenly the insect tsunami's forward motion was interrupted. The writhing black mass filled the hall from ceiling to floor, throbbing like a heartbeat. The writhing insect mass became calm for a moment and then the surface stretched to accommodate a female form pushing against it from the other side. The woman that emerged, eyes flashing, stretched, her entire body was covered with anthropoids. The different species of cockroach formed a kind of gross exoskeleton protecting every curve of her from head to toe. The woman's eyes fell on the hapless group and it was as if they were dirt on the soles of her feet. She sneered at them and a primal understanding that she was the top of the food chain was delivered in no uncertain terms. Desmond panicked and ran for the door again at it in desperation. The armored woman made a gesture in Desmond's direction, a stream of insects hitting and engulfing him.

The man screamed.

Debbie was gibbering incoherently, trying to get away on her hands and knees. But she was struck dumb by another wave of roaches that filled her mouth, entered through her nose, down her throat and exploded her head.

Eddie stumbled away from the unfolding horror, grabbing Shanice by the arm but she was riveted to the spot, stopping him in his tracks.

Fuck dis!

He ran without her and for his chivalry a stream of weaponized roaches bored through his back and spectacularly burst out of his chest.

He was dead before he hit the ground.

Walking through Viscera and blood, with every step her insect armor disassembled. The roaches scurrying away from her, leaving behind a beautiful African woman. Bald, flawless skin, red lips, ultrachic dress, long, long legs, and stilettos. Her eyes were flecked with flame, a fire she could ignite with a gesture. She cleared her throat and revolved her neck.

"Welcome to my banquet Shanice; my name is Miranda Pheare." She smiled, and her extended canines gleamed Ivory and needlepoint sharp. "Do you believe, that deh blood is deh life?"

Shanice, the sole survivor, stared at her unblinking, eyes wide, mouth open.

"Virgin blood is particularly special," Miranda continued, the shadow of a forked tongue flickering in the dark cavern of her mouth. "Come to me pickney and Let me show you."

4.

Central London, Present Day

They say history is written by the conquerors and Mr. Walter Opoku knew even vampires could massage the truth of history as well as, if not better than any human could. But in this case, the truth was a virtue of survival of their kind. He was always excited to be on these trips because he was seeing vampire history created first hand. Mr. Opoku could not help wondering even with his Mistress sitting beside him as they drove through the heart of London whether the accounts of their exploits could be massaged or embellished. The Chronicles of the Wamphyri, a historical account of every vampire Lord and Lady that ever existed was as accurate as the most researched and tested, historical text a human could ever compile. This tome of vampire life would never be seen by human eyes, not in its entirety at least because it wasn't written to tablet or papyrus but stored in the great vampire consciousness, accessible to every vampire mind of higher blood. But sometimes a familiar such as him were given the privilege to study the history of their mistress or master in written form.

It was impressive reading and if his esteem for his mistress wasn't high enough, the facts he had absorbed on her rise and domination had sent his adoration for her to stratospheric levels. Popular opinion in vampire circles would talk about what made the vampires powerful, usually citing the supernatural gifts of immortality or their superhuman strength and senses. But Mr. Opoku knew it was neither of these things. In his estimation, it was their adaptability to almost any environment. It was that uncanny ability to walk in the footsteps of their Lord and Lady ancestors with every sense impression vividly recorded as if they had been there themselves. The question remained, would they lie to themselves about an unfortunate incident they would prefer to forget? Mr. Opoku was a patient man with potential at least his mistress felt that way. But he was still human mostly, he wasn't nocturnal or required blood to live, but his life span was extended by his mistress. One day he would be experiencing the sublime beauty of immortality himself and a lust for the life force which is blood. Until then he still had questions. That did not take away from his purpose to serve, and he was honored to do so. His mistress had done so much for him. She had opened his eyes to the true nature of the world, and he was forever in her debt. All these thoughts were swirling around in his head, but on the surface, he calmly sat beside his mistress, looking straight ahead as the driver of the Mercedes S class expertly weaved through the night-time streets of central London. The vampire Queen beside him was quiet, but he knew her calculating mind was absorbing everything. Her eyes glistened rhythmically, flitting from left to right without moving her head. A light turned green in the passenger compartment, and the nervous voice of the driver came through the speakers.

"We are ten minutes away from the Hellfire Club, ma'am."

Miranda Pheare nodded then Mr. Opuko felt her powerful hand on his leg. At her invitation, he turned to face her.

"Who am I?" She asked her voice husky and rich.

Mr. Opoku controlled himself, stifling a smile. Their journey from Jamaica on the SS Ceres had taken two weeks. The mistress had been hibernating in her custom-built sarcophagus filled with soil from the parish of St. Anne where she had been born as a mortal. London was her first port of call and the most important destination on her European tour. Her clan extended from the islands of the Caribbean to London, Paris, Milan, Barcelona, and Berlin. Over 200 years she had been busy. Her family had been busy, and she was eager to see what was done in her name. For fifty years his mistress had come in contact with nothing but her food and that didn't have much to say, above its screams for mercy or quick release. Five decades had passed, and his Mistress had no contact with anyone while she slept. Even her image was lost to her. She could not see herself on any reflexive surface. Mr. Opoku tried to imagine never seeing himself for hundreds of years.

He couldn't.

Every other lord and lady handled that dilemma in their own way. Miranda had her unique take on it, a ritual they shared.

He had been her mirror for the last hundred years.

Mr. Opoku cleared his throat and felt her reach into his mind. Sharing his nervous system and seeing what he saw.

He spoke because this was important to the process too.

"You are a beautiful African woman. You have green eyes, full lips, prominent cheekbones, and dark, luscious skin."

Mr. Opoku could feel his words reinforcing the shared impact of seeing herself through his eyes.

He continued.

"You are physically perfect, curvy and tall, the envy of men and women alive or dead." His voice was rhythmic, hypnotic to even his own ears. "Your dress sense is impeccable, and your taste and style are 2nd to none. You chose this ensemble mistress Pheare. An off the shoulder, burnt orange, Karl Lagerfeld creation with matching Luxus Pigalle heels. You are the definition of Vogue."

Miranda nods her head slightly in agreement or with a sense of rightness to all she was experiencing.

The black Mercedes S class and the accompanying black Mercedes van pulled up to the exclusive and mysterious Hell Fire Club loading area and waited.

Entry would only take a moment.

The unseen mystical barriers lowered first and then the corporeal ones sometime later.

Mr. Opuko could feel his mistress's mental tentacles gently pull away from his mind, and the connection they shared was severed. His breathing was labored after the intrusion. With difficulty he kept his eyes focused on her unfathomable ones that had the power to suck you in whole and devour you. The vampire Queen closed her eyes or was it an extended blink for show. When they opened again, they blazed and the certainty that was missing earlier returned.

"I am Miranda Pheare." She said.

"You are mistress," Mr. Opoku agreed. "You are."

5.

Shaolin Temple, Shaingz District, Peoples Republic of China

Suzy Wong came thrashing and screaming out of her nightmare soaked in sweat and remembering some of the terrors that had stalked her into the realm of consciousness. The images melted like bee's wax, but the fear and her panic remained. She tasted blood on her palette and smelt the faint waft of its coppery taint. Suzy knew whatever had been shown to her in this nightmare had been a massacre, an orgy of savagery.

In the early Chinese morning, the pangs of loneliness overwhelmed her like hunger. She sat up on her hard hay-stuffed mattress; a thick prickly sheet draped over her shoulders, a candle flickered on the verge of extinction for lack of wax, throwing jagged shadows on the roughhewn walls of her insubstantial stone room. It wasn't that her hosts were not gracious – having a woman studying with them was unusual in itself – but Abbot Chen Shu and the other monks accepted her humbly into their family, especially after testing her to substantiate if she was truly a Sheng-Chi gifted warrior. She figured the real reason for her melancholy was that she missed her sisters and being away from Trevor did nothing good for her frame of mind either. This time in the morning she found herself feeling alone and vulnerable. Thoughts of her family in Jamaica, her mom, and dad, still working in their sixties, in the rough parts of downtown Kingston. Her brother and his growing family - she was an aunt to two cuties, and it all made her yearn to be with them.

That was the nature of sacrifice.

Being here was important and a part of her journey as a Guardian. For months Suzy and her sisters had been navigating there calling using instinct alone. That changed when Maw Ching the Siamese cat woke her up at the Mansion with a message in its collar. Once she got over the shock of an intelligent feline that could bend space and time, she read the invitation to attend the temple for her ongoing training. Suzy shivered from the chill of the room or was it a residual disquiet that had followed her like a stray puppy into the waking world. If she were reckless and tried to ignore it, the premonition would scream its presence from every cell of her body until she acted. The warning was like a message written in invisible ink. When she applied the heat of her reasoning mind to it, the message began to percolate and make sense. The process wasn't something she could rush, but she knew the Guardians of the Light were at the center of it. She would have to break the bad news to the Abbot and prepare for a swift journey back to London. Suzy just hoped whatever was flexing its psychic muscles did not decide to begin its carnage before she got home.

It made sense to call ahead, but the Shaolin Temple was way off the beaten track, no cell reception, no telephones – except for an ancient landline in the Abbot's office, basic water supply, and limited electricity. Thirty minutes into town on a donkey, forty-five minutes by foot, and almost a day into a city with an airport.

Suzy stared at her two Samsonite suitcases beside her bed.

"I don't know whether I should Laugh or cry," she thought grimly.

The suitcases were virtually untouched for her stay. Toiletries and underwear were the only things she needed; the temple provided it all. Looking at it now she could have packed much lighter.

The Maw Ching sat almost on guard watching Suzy wake from her nightmare vision and struggle to decide her next move. Its opalescent green eyes intensely looked beyond Suzy. Peering at the place she was coming from, making sure nothing came out with her to play in the land of the living. The feline was unmoving, unblinking for uncomfortable moments. Then she broke the spell by meowing and cleaning her whiskers. She jumped on the bed to nuzzle Suzy, giving her new-found friend some love and once her job was done, strolled out of her room and back into the stone walkways of the temple.

A teleporting cat, she mused.

Suzy would break the news to the Abbot after her first exercise in a few hours from now. In the meantime, she made plans.

In the Shaingze foothills, banks of fog conjured imagery of a fantastical kingdom in the clouds, while whitewashed buildings seemed so close to the heavens, they could cut the sky. Far from civilization, Suzy was unclear this Buddhist temple existed on any map or the ordinary realm of reality. Not that it mattered. Her new reality was teleporting cat's and being the honored guest of the Abbott of the Shaolin Temple. She had been working for the last five months to improve the channeling of her chi, something she discovered had been charged to differing teachers of all spiritual persuasions and locations to help guide the Guardians. Suzy sat in a lotus position, eyes closed, her steady breathing appearing as white streams with a lacquered wooden box in front of her. Standing a step behind her elderly teacher Weng Wei.

Suzy reached out with her mind, meticulously piercing through what her mind was persistently telling her could be a figment of her rational thought. Reality was a frame of mind after all. In her head, she peeled away a sense of resistance and saw something.

A lychee fruit was within the box.

Sitting beside the fruit was something else, but she saw it as a nebulous mass that her mind could not peel away.

Her frustration must have been obvious.

"Are you extending your consciousness into and beyond the box in front of you or are you back in England."

The old monk spoke English well, taking pity on Suzy's abominable mandarin when they trained.

"You see into me too well, teacher?"

"What is troubling you, Suzanne?"

Suzy smiled.

Only her father called her that outside of these walls.

"One of the fruits in the box was a lychee, right?"

The teacher nodded.

"The other?" He asked.

"I'm afraid, I'm not deh most focussed of students. Teacher Wei."

"On the contrary, you have thrown yourself into your training and have an unusual grasp of the principles."

"I should be here, but I am not," Suzy said.

The monk was wrapped in a thick brown woolen shawl protecting himself against the biting cold. Suzy was on the frosty flagstones in leggings and sweat top. She was controlling her internal body temperature to such a degree she was surrounded by a damp patch having melted the frost.

"Let us walk and talk," the old monk said.

Wrapping herself in a woolen shawl that was bungled up beside her, Suzy gracefully rose up and walked in step with the teacher.

The Shaingz Temple was an architectural wonder of brick walls, soaring towers, and graceful roofs, wedged into the hillside like a mountain climbers piton. They walked along open-air corridors centuries old and took steps that plunged earthward like a waterfall into a circular garden populated with hardy winter flowers and surrounded by hard, austere seats of granite.

"Sit, sit." Weng Wei said motioning to the rough-hewn seats. "And tell me what troubles you."

Suzy clasped her hands and leaned forward towards her teacher.

"My sisters are in danger Teacher Wei. I have to leave."

6.

Platinum Exhibition Centre, Westminster, London

Patra & Y sat beside Mr. Christoph Holtz in a co-coon of luxury as their limousine glided to the curb. Anyone seen around this German business luminary would have their moment in the media spot-light. Patra and Y knew this but didn't care. They had a job to do. The billionaire was renowned for his love of women, his stock trading genius and being an eligible bachelor who could almost have any of the capitals sin-gle or even married beauties beside him. This was one of Mr. P's mystery gigs. From time to time Mr. Patel, the business mind behind Bad II the Bone's Personal Securi-ty Services would offer the girls a job that came directly to him and had nothing to do with his extensive market-ing efforts. These jobs consisted of show business or

Internet business types who needed protecting not just from threats to their person but possible assaults of the spiritual kind. Bad II the Bone's presence, could dissuade most normal attacks but what of the supernatural? Mr. Patel was somewhat of an enigma himself. A multi-millionaire who was known by some heavy hitters in the film and music industries across the world. They never figured out how he became so connected. All they knew was after helping Mr. Patel with a gangster problem; this devout Hindu was indebted to them and backed their vision. But he never pried into the weirder aspects of their life. He believed in them, and Mr. Patel had an uncanny sense of when standard bodyguards would not do.

You could be certain that the tabloids would be curious about Y and Patra, but that came with the territory. Two beautiful but unknown women would keep them guessing. The driver almost sprinted out of the warmth of his cab to open the doors for his occupants. The gleaming black stretch was just as or even more impressive than his peaked hat and his grey starched and sharp driver uniform.

Patra exited first just as a call came on Y's mobile. Y smiled into the phone, her excitement obvious. But as Patra watched snapshots of her sisters conversation, Y's smile slowly diminished into a grimace.

Mr. Holtz would not know that something had just changed, he was too focussed on his lovely escorts. They led the way, both wearing glistening evening gowns that he unreservedly approved of. Patra's Louise Perring Creation had a split to the side showing her long toned legs. While Y's cream St. Cruz dress had a plunging neck and back that stopped deliciously before the mound of her booty. Mr. Holtz with his shoulder-length blond hair, athletic physique, and a thousand-watt smile, came next. The girls took his arm and proceeded up the steps of the Platinum banqueting hall. When the party reached the top of the stairs, Mr. Holtz turned to them and said.

"I feel like I am wasting your time here ladies. Time is the reason I do what I do. And I'm not living up to my philosophy by abusing yours."

"You are a paying us, right?" Patra asked with a gleam in her eyes.

Christoph smiled sheepishly.

"Of course. But I feel silly about having you protecting my person at a non-profit organization fundraiser."

"Mr. Patel seems to be determined we accompany you tonight." Y said. "There are only a few people I would go out on a limb and say they are selfless. And he is one of them. Whatever his reasons, tonight we have your back."

"Dienkeshen." He said bowing slightly to them both. Their discussion had taken them to a group of Organisation reps with tablets confirming attendance. A huge double door stood behind them that showed brief glimpses of inside with the strains of excitement, boisterous exchanges, and pop music squeezing through as the door opened and closed.

"Mr. Hans Christoph Holtz and a party of two." The young woman announced altering the words and smiling at them. "I hope you have a fantastic evening ladies." Mr. Holtz nodded. They were ushered towards the swinging doors that were opened on both sides by two large men. The evening began with an explosion of color and razzmatazz.

Y looked around an urge to check out the place, satisfying her natural wariness.

"Can you to manage without me for a moment, sir," Y asked.

"Of course." Mr. Holtz said. "I will be safe with Patra. And call me Christoph. I insist."

"Christoph." Y nodded trying to keep an air of professionalism, but Patra had disarmed the billionaire from within the stretch limo, and they were fast becoming budding pals. Poor Christoph didn't know what he was signing up for.

"Swing by the roulette tables when you're done. We'll be parked there." Patra said. Then much lower. "Watch your back boo."

The call she had taken in the car had come from Suzy in China. She was panicked, and almost incoherent which had freaked her out on its own. Suzy had sensed a malevolent force taking residence in London and preparing to strike. She couldn't say where exactly, but there was a massive tug-of-war between the balancing forces around tonight's event and those seams were tearing.

Her sister was a Zen master of calm at the worst of times but whatever she had seen had spooked her to such a degree, she wanted to come home.

Y felt a hazy bundle of emotions centered in her gut that could switch from calm to panic depending on the circumstances. That early warning system that they shared enhanced their performance in situations like this. It was alerting her, now. But to what end. Y controlled her breathing regulating her pounding heart. This kind of situation was Suzy's forte, picking up inconsistencies in a situation, discerning the truth of an event, job, gig. And she was damn good at it. Y had promised she would take the client home and call it a night, but she wanted to find out more. She didn't want to explain to Christoph that his night of fundraising and fun was to be curtailed because of a paranormal threat they could not establish. No, she would mingle while Patra had the client covered.

Y sashayed through the banqueting hall smiling as she went, her clutch bag in one hand and her free hand nibbling on hors d'oeuvres or sipping on Christal as she passed through. Her senses were sharp and were anticipating the mood of the patrons sitting around tables, eating, talking or dancing. Everyone was upbeat, and so it should be. At five hundred pounds ahead, the event was to raise funds to build high-tech schools in third world countries. Y imagined the vibe would change after the Celebrity raffle in twenty-five minutes when the demands of some of the spoiled rich would be met.

Everything here was as expected. What had Suzy seen that could have broken her focus at the temple? With the faith, she had in Suzy's talents, she kept observing. Y recognized a few of the celebrities and some of the business people and entrepreneurs. Mr. Patel had insisted they become familiar with their market of high net worth individuals of which Mr. Patel was a part himself.

Y stopped for a moment and shifted her focus from the big view to taking mental snapshots of the huge affair. Y slid over to a table fully occupied with well-dressed men and women watching with rapped attention as an illusionist entertained them.

Whimsically Y wondered if he was a real and not an entertainer.

Her gaze fell on a group of men in a tight circle brandy in hand; the discussion seemed deep. Further to the north facing wall a young woman in a tight-fitting clown outfit, her red shoe ten sizes too big was deafly juggling multicolored balls and batons and pratfalling much to the delight of an audience at two tables.

On the complete opposite side of the hall, a small crowd was forming. Y immediately thought of toilets, but this was no concert venue, the ratio of toilets to patrons would be high. Her next thought was the smoking area. Y felt she needed to check it out. Why not? Nothing had peaked her attention so far, so she spun on the balls of her feet, eyes towards where she was heading and moved off.

Y stopped suddenly.

The thought came sharply in a voice that was not her own. And like a bullwhip snatched her attention, she pulled up instantaneously. She nearly smashed into a waiter if not for her reflexes. Y stylishly adjusted the exquisite control she had over her body to avert disaster. In doing so, something became abundantly clear. She wasn't the only one with refined reflexes. The waiter was carrying a tray with four champagne flutes filled with the bubbly liquid. In his haste, he had not seen Y but when he did it was too late. They toppled forward beginning to slide off the silverware, but the waiter moved with such uncanny speed and unbelievable dexterity he tracked the falling flutes and positioned the tray in four different positions in one fluid move, catching them all. He stood up from his crouched position, the four glasses still on the tray, the meniscus of the liquid almost steady. He smiled sheepishly, his teeth white, his eyes were deep-set.

"Sorry, ma'am," he said quick stepping away, his posture perfect.

Y caught her breath.

"What just happened?" Y said to herself.

She watched him disappear through the swinging doors into the kitchen. Of all the people who shouldn't be taken aback by the unexplained or the fantastic, she was, the one.

And yeah. That was strange.

If Mr. Fantastic, the waiter, was anything like her, what had just happened wasn't something he would forget especially after seeing Y watching him. Everything fell into a haze as her focus narrowed to the silver tray staff who were scurrying around her, going about their business. Y's attention fell on one young woman who was clearing a table of its plates and glasses. Her movement was clipped and precise, posture impeccable and her sense of balance effortless. The table attendant turned suddenly to look at her, sensing Y's stare. The young woman's unblinking gaze carried with it a dark intelligence that crawled over Y's skin and when it had enough, snaked back, her focus elsewhere again.

Y shivered.

She was nowhere near as sensitive as Suzy, but she felt that. What kind of person is attuned and sensitive enough to feel someone watching them from across the room? Y looked away a cold chill running up and down her spine like liquid nitrogen. Y was nothing but thorough in situations like this. She let all the disparate strands of facts and speculation mix in her consciousness, and as that stew bubbled away on medium flame, she headed for the ladies.

The dominant sounds of excitement, joy and general tomfoolery was taking place at the intersection of fine wine, exquisite food, unlimited finances and a game of chance. There were two blackjack tables, a bank of six slot machines and two roulette wheels. Patra was in her element in more ways than most could ever comprehend. But she resisted the urge to gamble on the job even if it was for charity. Her level of professionalism wasn't as militant as Suzy exhibited, but she still had her standards. And anyway, why would she want to take the shine away from her charge. Their table was being mobbed by guests who were attracted to Mr. Holtz good fortune.

"You are my lucky charm." Christoph gushed not knowing how true that was, rattling the dice in his face. And placing his chips on twenty-three.

"It's all for a good cause, Christoph, my man," she said.

"You got it, all for a good cause."

Patra was positioned behind him watching the people on both sides of the table cheering him on. Christoph wound up to deliver the twin dice down the satin runway like a baseball pitcher. Patra grasped his hand for luck, and Christoph let them rip. The dice bounced twice and hit the end border deflecting back onto to the die runway to reveal twenty-three.

Sonofabitch Patra thought, he's going for the whole enchilada. The table junkies erupted into celebration. Christoph pumped his fist and turned to Patra with a glowing grin. They high fived. The croupier pushed the winning chips in Christoph's direction then she saw the tattoo on the fleshy web between his thumb and fourth finger.

That was a weird ass ink.

Patra felt the tingle of excitement all the way to the tip of her clitoris.

"Damn." Something was hinky.

The tattoo was a geometric form with lines angling out from it. A strange place to have ink in the first place. Patra's interest piqued, and the croupier's nails came next for her scrutiny.

How come I never noticed that before?

The croupier's nails were long for a man. He was an androgynous looking dude with a wide smile that showed portions of pearly white teeth. Christoph collected his winnings and neatly stacked chips he had collected from his short stint in the Devils Game.

"I could eat a horse after that," Christoph said. "But I will settle for some pastry and one more toss before I retire."

"Sweet tooth?" Patra asked. Christoph motioned to a hostess pushing a trolley stacked with confectionary, and she came over. Patra watched the reaction of the brunette as she approached. It felt like a video file had been cut and pasted from an innocuous scene of a woman pushing a trolley and placed on the desktop of her mind for analysis. Without a missed heartbeat Patra knew why her luck factor was so keen to make a point of this. As the hostess moved with the grace of a cat, sensual and powerful at the same time. Patras thoughts shifted from how sexy she was to something that stood out and was beginning to annoy the shit out of her. The collar of her white dress shirt moved up and down her neck as she navigated the obstacles of the hall. The funky geometric shapes were tattooed to her jugular vein. It looked strangely like the one she had seen earlier.

Was this some kinda gang shit? Patra shrugged.

Y pushed the door open and immediately took a mental snapshot of the interior of the ladies' toilet. She headed straight for a free mirror of which there were two. Y placed her clutch bag at the side of the ample marble counter that allowed space for a shiny porcelain basin. Two women were beside her, one applying lipstick, the other straightening her eyelashes with a liner.

She turned the gold-plated taps on.

The mental image she was composing in her mind's eye was like a crime scene re-enactment with some pieces missing. She turned casually, just glimpsing behind the swing of the door.

Y knew she had missed something.

A woman sat beside the table filled with expensive perfumes, paper towels, steam towels and what looked like a filigree style dish filled to the brim with coins and notes. Y looked away casually and filled in any missing details to her mental picture. With the image clear in her head she washed her hands and checked her lips. Y tried to get a better look at the woman managing the perfume stand, but it would prove to be difficult especially if she didn't want it to seem obvious. She positioned herself, so that she could see the reflected image of the woman. Y blinked, eyebrows raised. The image of the seated woman was a nebulous blur that approximated her posture and position but was unrecognizable as a person. Y plucked a few tissues from a quilted box and wiped the surface of the mirror. She looked up at the mirror again, and the amorphous hazy cloud persisted. Confused Y turned around and looked at the woman. She was in her early thirties, slender but sinewy, pale white skin and red hair with shocking red lipstick. A toilet flushed, and a woman walked out of a cubicle, checked herself quickly and approached the table. The red-haired woman smiled broadly said something and made an open palm gesture for her to try whatever she fancied.

The other woman did.

When she wasn't looking the red-haired woman threw her head back and sniffed the air around her like a ravenous animal. Y looked back into the depth of the mirror and what should have been the redheaded woman, was an agitated cloud of light distortion where her physical presence should have been. Y popped her compact into her clutch bag and gathered it up under her arm. Suzy had been right, again.

Y had seen enough.

She casually walked out smiling at the redhead and wondering what big teeth she had.

Patra smelt Y's perfume before her warm skin touched hers.

"Whaddup sis?" Patra asked her eyes wandering, her hand on her shoulder.

"Somethings up." Y said.

"No shit." Patra snapped back with a smile on her face. "Didn't I tell you to leave the sexy g string panties to those of us who can rock that shit."

"You wish, bitch." Y retorted. "It's something else."

"Suzy spooked us?" Patra asked.

"And how many times has she been wrong?" Y added.

Grudgingly Patra agreed then said.

"There's something off about the silver service. They creeping me the fuck out."

"You and me both."

"Did you see that cute guy with the dreadlocks?" Patra asked.

"He is hard to miss," Y said.

"You feel me." Patra agreed. "He swung by our table earlier, and he caught my eye."

"Easily done." Y said.

Patra chuckled and let the barb pass.

"I stood up right in front of him. How tall am I?" Patra asked.

"Just under six feet give or take in heels."

"Well this dude was a shade over six foot, so our eyes met on a level, and they locked." Patra paused and shook her head in confusion. "Look at my outfit, stunning right? Cleavage banging, sleeveless body forming, showing off the curves, the booty, my waist and splits showing my legs. And I'm centered with Coco Chanel's latest joint."

"And your point is?" Y sounded exasperated.

"My motherfucking point is," Patra lowered her voice. "I'm hot, and he didn't react, at all to me. Nothing. Nada."

Y opened her mouth to say something and Patra cut her off.

"And he's not gay if you're thinking that. A Gay man would react. On a different level maybe but some sort of reaction. This cat looked dead into me, smiled politely answered my half-assed question but was cold. That shit ain't normal." Y checked out Patra again as if confirming the merits of her assets.

"You have a point."

"And what about the tattoos on the eyeballs?" Patra asked.

"Ouch," Y said. "You noticed that too. I thought it was a trick of the light."

"No trick and no bloodshot eyes either. Regular, and symmetrical like a number. It's a tat or contact lens."

"Now that's commitment." Y said.

"Oh, yeah! Whoever these dudes are they are committed. It feels like gang bangers and don't get it twisted they come in all persuasions."

"London street gangs are less intense than our cousins across the pond. It's something else."

"Do we give a fuck?" Patra asked. "All we need to know is Christoph could be in danger. His safety is our priority then we can start breaking shit down later."

"Agreed," Y said. "Let's move him out."

"Now you're talking."

"Oh, by the way. You can give him the real-world excuse for us leaving a charity event of the year for no apparent reason." Y smiled slightly.

"Don't you worry your pretty little head about that. I have got a story that's all wrapped up nice and neat with the bow on top."

With the decision made, they were beside Mr. Holtz in moments rousing him to his feet. He complained light heartedly on his way to the limousine, but he trusted their instincts. Once they were safely in the back of the stretch and pulling away from the curb, Patra looked at Christoph and said.

"That sexy blonde you were talking to earlier. She a good friend?"

Christoph looked puzzled at the question.

"Yes. We studied together in Switzerland. She's a Social Media entrepreneur."

"Call her." Y said finishing Patra's thought. "And tell her to get the fuck out of there, now."

Christoph looked at them intensely, his mouth twitching from an unasked question, unnerved from the serious looks that were chilling the interior of there ride. Without another word said he dialed a number into his Vertu mobile.

7.

Platinum Exhibition Centre, Westminster, London

Death and an ancient evil was mingling amongst the rich and famous tonight and only the very sensitive amongst them would see it coming. Diamond Back security had covered this event and others like it for nearly ten years. They were trusted and professional and understood the intricacies of doing business with this type of clientele. They thought they had seen it all but there were still stories yet to be told, and this would prove to be the strangest of them all.

The premature departures from the Fund Raiser began with the two celebrity bodyguards hustling the German billionaire into the night. They seemed to be in a hurry. A consistent trickle of other guests departed early too, some looking frightened or bewildered. There were a few arguments as partners wanted to stay but others desperately wanted to leave.

The Platinum Exhibition Centre was of contemporary design and kept to the stringent building regulations of central London, so it was curious seeing a viscous mist like substance rising through an air circulation vent. It quickly spread across the floor silent, odorless and ankle height. If it was smoke the automated front doors should have opened to let guests out and allow the substance to do the same. But the door was shut tight. The security team tried to contact colleagues positioned inside and around the event. But the radios crackled uselessly. The dank mist was making its way into adjoining rooms creeping up the stairs as it poured from subterranean levels. In minutes the mist had risen to their knees, its chill fingers making brave men begin to question whether they should abandon their posts. They stood their ground for now.

Alex Flint, the Diamond Back team leader felt something rub against his leg, that startled him. He reached down to feel for what was moving through the thick mist like a fish. He moved his hand about the faux stream, that was rising steadily, leaving eddy's as he would in any true liquid. His hand bumped on something, and he grabbed for it. Whatever it was, did not want to be caught. Alex reeled backward his hand shooting up from the swirling mist dripping in blood.

His blood.

Alex stumbled, his heart hammering, his breathing ragged, unable to scream, his eyes wide with surprise as he looked at his gnawed and missing fingers. His next impulse was to run, but he violently buckled to his knees as something snagged him, dragging him down into the rolling mist.

There is a moment of silence, his team looking on in mute horror then his head breaks the surface. It's like he's gasping for air, a grotesque whistling sound coming from a throat ripped to threads and his frantic breathing coming as scarlett bubbles from what was left of his ruined windpipe. He stops struggling, his will drained and is dragged away below the currents.

The lobby team disbanded in a crazy dash of swearing and shouts. The higher ground of the stairs became like the promised land for some of London's toughest men. From the vantage point of the sweeping stairs, the lobby now looking like a dangerous morass filled with unimaginable creatures from the wildest drug-fuelled nightmares and it was rising, and they had to tell the others. Not that it would matter not that they had a chance of survival.

When the frantic men burst into the main hall, they are met with the mist too, but it seemed the revelers thought it was part of the entertainment. Blissfully ignorant of the horrors it contained. The remainder of the security team tried in vain to alert the partygoers of the terrors in store, but they were relegated to a sideshow that did not hold anyone's attention.

And the mist kept rising.

The waiters and waitresses were abandoning their post with crazy elation, their eyes glowing with an inner light that got more pronounced as the lighting failed. They disappeared into the mist never resurfacing. The spread of panic amongst the guests was getting more pronounced. Some were leaving the main hall now; the mist was at waist height everywhere and rising. Anything electrical that encountered it was snuffed out. The sound system gave out a shrill burst of feedback and died, leaving only the murmurs, gasps and strangled screams for entertainment. Performers had stopped performing, the gambling machines and card tables were unmanned and abandoned as people left their posts to escape or simply disappear.

Something was coming.

The sense of expectation was palpable; a foreboding hung in the air amidst the panic. A silent master of ceremonies had made its introduction, and the audience was waiting for the main act to appear on stage. Everyone felt it on a primal level, and everyone knew the arrival would be gloriously horrible. The murkiness parted as she came forward, skittering away from her presence as if it was a creature scared or respectful. The light was low, but her presence was clear. The bald, high-heeled, alluring fashion sense of Miranda Pheare strutted into the midst of the chaos. Her dark skin contrasted with the snowdrift of mist and her beautiful face transformed by a monstrous grin and a mouth filled with a grotesque array of teeth that could only serve one purpose. As her smile widened, droplets of blood and saliva ran over her bright red lips.

She was transfixing.

A tremulous wail from one of the patrons rooted to the spot could have interrupted her grand announcement, but she was patient. That horrific smile appeared again and so did the shadow of a flickering forked tongue in the cabin of her mouth.

The woman's voice boomed without a microphone.

"Welcome," she said her voice sweet and feminine. Miranda exuded absolute authority. "As yuh know by now, there is no escape. And why would you want to? You are my guests after all." She paused for thought. "You have been invited to deh party of a lifetime." Her eyes watched keenly, the panic in some and the resignation in others. "This is a celebration deh blood, the legacy of a great man Lord Byron Byefield, my lover and progenitor, whose reign was cut short by you and your kind two hundred years ago." Her tone was more passionate this time. "You have the privilege of paying for dat injustice." And unsettling shout from someone in the throng made Miranda shake her head. "Accept it. We will drink you dry and honor our loss. Never again. This will never happen to a high-blood vampire. That is a promise, and your carcasses will be a testament to dat."

Miranda stooped and ran her hand through the mist, like she was beside a river testing its coolness. Taking her time, she plunged her hand into the shifting mist. When she pulled them free, they were no longer human hands but powerful talons gripping a human ankle. With ease, she lifted the unfortunate man up and dangled him while he thrashed and screamed. For a moment the shifting shadows made her look introspective. A fleeting sense of memory or sorrow that momentarily dimmed the burning hunger in her eyes.

It did not last, and her savage vampire nature became dominant again.

"Mek deh party begin," she pronounced.

Without a hint of effort, the man she held upside down by his ankles, was flung into the air. She transformed into her true monstrous form, lept up an incredible height to meet her victim in mid-flight. Her powerful jaws unhinged, teeth like razors unsheathed, grabbing and ripping the throat out to the spine. When she came back down to earth, the bloody body of her victim slamming into the wooden floor boards, she drank the life-giving blood to her fill, her minions already emerging from the mist, suited and booted, wreaking bloody havoc.

8.

Chase Estates, South East London

Amanda Walker sat at her window on the seventh floor of a block of flats in the Chase Estates. She looked away from the email screen of her mobile phone and stared down at the demolition site below. She smiled although really, she shouldn't have especially after stepping out of her comfort zone. But it felt good taking decisive action, and she had not expected such a speedy reply from the ladies of Bad II the Bone. It had been a shot in the dark but through their entertaining podcast where Cleopatra Jones talked about relationships and the supernatural. It was a weird combination, but it worked. Amanda had emailed them about a valuable family heirloom that was reputed to have mystical powers. As well as being bodyguards, the ladies were supposedly curiosity and antiquity collectors or had contacts in that world. They were glad to talk to her in person, so she needed to make the arrangements.

Anytime soon her stay here would be over. And the new life she was planning would begin. Amanda was a part of a group of nine tenants who remained, waiting for rehousing and would not move until the council had made appropriate arrangements for their relocation. Everywhere around her were signs of change and the destructive power to make that change happen. The atmosphere was hazy with cement dust, piles of rubble made of concrete and metal-formed mounds like zuggarat's in ancient Sumer. Instead of a burying ground for kings and noblemen, it felt like the final resting ground for the blighted and forgotten.

"Please don't do that," Amanda rapped on her window. It's a replica baroque you Philistines." She shouted, but the workmen tore down the sculpture anyway. Amanda was one of the few residents left to be rehoused. And as the destruction took place around them the nine inhabitants of the Wentworth Tower, Kentchester Tower and Blackstone Tower, looked on from their vantage points like trapped animals. Even if it was their choice. They were fighting this on her own.

Her boyfriend had moved out due to the endless arguments about what she wanted, what she should be doing with her life. They still talked but they both agreed some distance was the best thing for them. She looked away from the scene outside and sauntered over to the kitchen.

"No Ambition," she said. It hurt when her boyfriend had said it but coming from her Mum and Dad; it stung even more. She flipped the kettle and peered at the red light and watched the water through the transparent body quickly reach boiling point. She added a bag of Chamomile tea to her "Fuck Deh Police" cup and stirred in the honey. Why could no one understand she wasn't driven by the demands of a dying Industrial revolution? Amanda's degree in World History with a two-year unit in archaeology had prepared her for adventure. But instead, she was a P.A at a Canary Wharf Finance Company. The pressure she had been experiencing from her boyfriend and parents was because she had turned down opportunity after opportunity to start her ascent up the corporate ladder. An ascent she preferred not to take, Terre Firma was more appealing. She did need the money - living in a council estate was not her idea of ideal but she could not bring herself to waste her life in some vapid corporate culture when bigger things were demanding her attention.

Calling her.

She just didn't understand its language, not yet. With her steaming beverage in hand and her feet firmly in her furry slippers, she headed into her bedroom. This was her favorite room in the apartment. It wasn't the biggest, but it had a wide window on one side that featured a panorama of South London that was breath-taking. Sometimes when she slept, she dreamt the room had no intervening walls and windows, just an open concrete platform hundreds of feet in the air, exposed to the stars. She didn't feel that now. Amanda carefully placed her cup down and sunk to her knees beside the bed. She felt around the metal slats underneath, her fingertips brushing on the familiar wooden flat trunk. She grabbed the rope handle and dragged it out.

Her legacy and the path to her new life was contained in the box.

She was descended from a Victorian-era Monster hunter.

Amanda couldn't help breaking into a cheesy grin when she thought of it. The box and two other items were passed down in her family for over two hundred years. None of her ancestors had done anything with it but kept them safe, for Amanda, the firstborn of her father. She didn't believe for a second her ancestor Ezekiel Walker was a bona fide monster hunter. But from his accounts, diaries, notes, and diagrams he certainly believed in it. Her second Great Grandparent may have been born to parents who were slaves, but he was a shrewd and forward-thinking man, way ahead of his time. And maybe a bit crazy, to Amanda's thinking, she had been gifted a historical asset that she could use to raise money and explore her ancestry. She was in the process of corroborating the authenticity of nine phonograph records shaped like copper rolling pins, made by grandfather Ezekiel in his own voice relating to his exploits. That alone was gold. Her ancestor took his position seriously, and some of his stories were wild nightmare tales. Readers would lap this up and especially the compiled and documented evidence. Then the crown of all this was the heirloom that had been passed down to her.

The Heart of Ares was supposedly a weapon designed by a mad man or a genius. It was worth a fortune because it was made by a German alchemist and inventor around the time of Galileo. It included diaries and drawing from the crazy man who designed it. Grand Father Ezekiel believed it could momentarily give you the power of the God of War. And to think that story meant so much to him he made sure it was passed on to her centuries later. On her twentieth birthday she was given a key to a safety deposit box at Lloyd's of London. In it contained the Heart, the inventor's notebook and a weird looking stone. Amanda had time to research her plan. That's why she had contacted the ladies from Bad II the Bone. She wanted their expert opinion and maybe some guidance. But whatever happened, next week she would test the market and see what would come of it.

She was excited.

Amanda lifted the box on the bed beside a Tablet that was open to a high-end auction site. She had bookmarked a page with an item that looked like a steampunk inspired Rubik cube. Its 8 sides adorned with intricate rune symbols made from silver and copper. Another contraption built by the same German Alchemist that had constructed the Heart of Ares and the bid price was beginning at a high six figures. This was her way-out of mediocrity, but it felt just too easy. Amanda sat down beside the box with her cup of tea in hand, took a sip and opened the lid.

9.

Platinum Exhibition Centre Crime Scene, Westminster, London

'One hundred and fifty-nine are killed in Terrorist Attack, in London's Chelsea District.'

In twenty-four hours, this headline would scream on every tabloid, every news blog and twenty-four-hour News Platform around the world. The details would be sparse, but that did not stop journalist theorizing on reasons and consequences. World leaders would pledge their support and condemn the actions of these men with the usual rhetoric. Londoners had been through this before and expected that all the pieces of this puzzle would begin to reveal themselves as time went on. Soon the men involved, the witnesses, the terrorist groups that claimed responsibility and the pain and suffering would reveal itself in a wave of morbid fascination, grief, and surprise. These were uncertain times, where the horrors inflicted on the citizens of the city were not unexpected, and it was just a matter of time before it happened again until then it would be business as usual. A numb expectation that more horrors from the UK's unfortunate foreign policy and colonial past would be heaped on the city

But it was all bullshit.

Yes, one hundred and fifty-nine people did lose their lives, and it was a tragedy, a sickening one, but this was not perpetrated by any traditional terrorist the modern world had come to understand. This was unusual, unexplained with enough of a cultural bent that the word supernatural was being whispered. And this was where Shaft came into the picture.

He was not looking forward to it.

Shaft parked his Jaguar four streets away from the crime scene, taking his time to lock his pride and joy. It wasn't the fact that he didn't trust where he had parked his classic Jaguar XJR.

That wasn't it at all.

He wished he was somewhere else. He wasn't sure he could face a situation like this, knowing that, if he had been given the resources, he could have prevented this from happening.

Jesus! Over a hundred people dead.

Shaft stopped and crouched as if his stomach had cramped up on him, the smell of the concrete wafted up to his nose. He felt nauseous for a moment, lowering his head and breathing deeply. Standing up again he habitually straightened his Hugo Boss suit and continued walking. This was the event his beheaded informant was warning him about; it had to be. As he walked over to the crazy police presence in the distance, his every step was painful; he knew Black Book, his fledgling department, was only called in because the brief investigation had run into a brick wall or found something inexplicable. They wanted results especially after considering the rich and powerful that had been slaughtered last night. This would be a public relations nightmare, and if he wanted to prove his department had a purpose, he had to put this atrocity to bed.

His thoughts flitted to Y and the rest of the Bad II the Bone crew. Had they heard what happened through their otherworldly connections? It didn't matter because they would hear soon enough from him. He just had to access the scene, kiss some ass, upset some colleagues and walk on water like Jesus Christ himself to get the results the Metropolitan Police brass required. If he didn't, he'd be lucky to be a special constable walking the beat in Harlesden.

The only good thing about the high-profile nature of this catastrophe was he would not be the Senior Investigating Officer. This was a team effort and could be nothing else, the investigation into this would be huge, and his department would be buried in the whole framework.

The top brass was depending on it.

Shaft knew that traditional police work would not end the threat or solve this case. This was outside of the Met's purview but to admit that they had not prepared for this eventuality would be tantamount to calling the Metropolitan Police Force clowns. Again, Shaft would enter this investigation from the back door and if he was right - and he had a gut feeling, Suzy's talents were rubbing off on him, that he was. Supernatural forces were required to counterbalance a supernatural threat. He was surprised they came to that conclusion so quickly, or the SIO was the openminded sort and wanted to surround himself with a good mix and spread of talent. If that was the case, who had recommended him to the team? Shaft thought about it for a moment, picturing the hierarchical structure of an elaborate crime scene in his head.

The Crime Scene coordinator had assembled the team, and that meant they were pressured into bringing him in or his witchdoctor reputation proceeded him.

The outer cordon was about three hundred meters from the building and surrounded it. About forty officers were protecting the integrity of the crime scene when he walked up. A mobile Incident Room was parked within the boundary and from experience Shaft knew a Major Incident Room was set up somewhere in the city. Shaft counted five SCO19 armed police officers, eagle-eyed and grim. He had never seen anything like this before. Shaft could see a multitude of staff and experts that he recognized in this circus milling in and out of the building within the inner cordon: forensic scientists, scene of crime investigators, photographers, and pathologists. But what was strange was the outer cordon which was unbelievably free from media and the public. Shaft headed towards the officer with the tablet and made eye contact. The constable walked over making sure he was at a respectable distance from the cordon when he stopped.

Shaft took out his warrant card and held it in the officer's direction.

"I'm DI Winston McFarlane." Shaft said. "I should be on your log."

The constable quickly scanned him up and down and then checked his tablet. His expression changed quickly when he found his name. The constable hesitated.

"Is everything okay, constable?" Shaft asked.

"Sorry sir, yes all fine. I just have a note that the scene of crime co-ordinator wanted a word before you changed into your clean suit."

"Lead the way."

"Of course," the constable said. "Just over here." The officer called over a younger policeman to escort him to a tent which was acting as the Marshal's office. Shaft ducked under the cordon and was met and escorted to the tent. Younger constable entered first without announcement. Waiting respectfully outside felt alien to Shaft and he was reluctant to alter the reputation he had built as a bastard with some of his peers, but this investigation would require finesse on his part especially if he wanted Black Book ever to be respected. In seconds the constable came out and ushered him inside. Shaft took in the small confines quickly and knew immediately who the Crime Co-ordinator was.

He had worked with her before.

Aideen McGuire. A smart and pleasant redhead in her late forties, who usually had an impressive grasp on the human resources and logistics needed for an investigation. This case would give her sleepless nights.

"Detective McFarlane," she came over smiling at him with her hand outstretched from one of the two tables in the tent. Shaft shook it, knowing her greeting was a genuine one but sensing storm clouds on the horizon.

"Would you like to sit?" She asked.

Shaft declined with a raise of his hand.

"I think the condemned man should stand. Don't you?"

Aideen smiled weakly.

"I personally requested you be a part of this investigation." She said. "As far as I'm concerned you have a set of unique skills that could be an asset to this investigation. But as you know this is a team effort and ..."

"And I'm not a good fit for the team. Let me guess, according to SIO Cargill right?"

Shaft put his hands in his pockets and breathed evenly, regretting he had not come into this situation mob-handed.

"We came to the same conclusion detective. It's in the investigations best interests."

"And whose interest was it for me to come all this way for you to tell me, I'm not wanted. A phone call would have done it."

That revelation made Aideen's eyes brighten, as she realized this was much more than an issue of teamwork.

"SIO Cargill thought it would be better to tell you in person. You'd appreciate the gesture."

Shaft smiled grimly then caught himself. He would not give these wankers more credit than they deserved.

"How considerate. I'll make a point to thank him when I see him next time."

Shaft shrugged then shook his head.

"Have a good day Ms. McGuire."

He turned and headed for the flap in the tent.

"I'm sorry detective McFarlane," Aideen called to him

Shaft stopped halfway in and out and looked at his colleague.

"You know in situations like this my grandma would say, the stone that the builder refuse, will become the head cornerstone."

Aideen nodded although she didn't quite understand.

Shaft managed a dry, cynical smile.

"I think you're going to need me Aideen and when you do, I want Cargill to call me personally." Shaft let the flap of the tent fall in place. His voice was muted, but Aideen heard his parting words.

"Only SIO Cargill."

10.

"**M**etropolitan police commander Cunningham was the only man Shaft respected in the higher echelons of this esteemed institution. It wasn't right, but that's how he felt. The Commander was given some slack because of a few important things. He was the only one out of the cabal of Metropolitan police brass who decided quickly and took responsibility pre-emptively for a problem that could become worse without some form of attention given to it. Shaft always pictured Commander Cunningham as a risk taker and strategist because he had been able to put a PR spin on some weird and embarrassing cases and emerged smelling like a rose. The commander was even forgiven for taking credit for some of Shafts completed cases including Enoch Lacombe's bloody rampage through London's gangland. Explaining how a Voodoo priest that could manipulate dark forces was taking revenge on his enemies and how three supernaturally gifted women stopped him, was not something you could present to your superiors with a straight face. For the Commander, a win was a win. He loved that about him, but Shaft was no mug. He understood the reasons for keeping his activities secret – Londoners did not need to know the barriers between realities was thinning, an imbalance in the forces of good and evil was threatening every man, woman, and child in the capital. What he would not stand for was the Metropolitan Police top brass showing disrespect for what he did.

Could they be warming to him?

A year ago, seeing Commander Cunningham, the Grand Wizard of New Scotland Yard would have been impossible. To police hierarchy Shaft was a crazy anthropologist turned detective, talking about curses, magic, and murder. If his last major case with the Voodoo grandmaster Enoch Lacombe changed how his superiors thought, then the Platinum Exhibition Murders would change everything.

He sat in the reception area, the sixth floor of the old Curtis Green Building and the Commanders fiefdom. New Scotland Yard had been radically remodeled. The elegantly curved entrance pavilion, rooftop pavilions and an expansion of the floor plan, made the working environment more open and inclusive for staff. Shaft easily resisted the urge to check his watch. The zen calm of the place was in stark contrast to the controlled chaos your local nick could exhibit. The Feng Shui practitioner they had secretly consulted while designing the renovation had done a great job.

Shaft sat alone in the plush surroundings, the sunlight streaming through, the beep of telephone connections, fingers tapping on keyboards and the hum of HVAC made him thankful he had left the outside world behind for a moment. He fingered his way through a neat stack of modern policing magazines on a table beside him, but nothing caught his interest. Looking out the window and below to the streets of Embankment and then to the Thames, it seemed so far removed from the horrors this great city could dole out on its citizens. He checked his mobile just as the middle-aged PA who sat guarding the entrance to the inner sanctum stood up and left her desk. Five minutes later she came back with a tray of coffee and cups. And then disappeared into the Commander's office. Returning, she sat at her desk, made herself comfortable then looked up at him.

"Detective Inspector McFarlane, Commander Cunningham is ready to see you now."

Shaft briskly stood up, grabbed the case he had beside him and headed for the double doors before his superior changed his mind. He felt like he was being called into Headmaster Donahue's office all over again but unlike his school days, he had a voice, and he was about to make it heard. Shaft stepped in and closed the door gently behind him.

"Inspector McFarlane come in. Take a seat or stand as you wish."

The office had not changed much from the last time he was here. The Commander had a thing for minimalist display and Shaft thought of it as kind of understated trophy room. The entire space was arranged to celebrate his awards, achievements, and accolades but in a way that made you want to focus on him and how capable he was. He wondered if the commander understood the motivations behind the designs in his workspace and why he was no different from the chieftain of a Palaeolithic tribe in the Congo. Shaft suspected Commander Cunningham would not appreciate the comparison. The smile remained in his head.

"Thank you for seeing me sir, I know this is a busy period for you, but this is important."

The Commander nodded.

"I have to admit inspector I was expecting you. I have a feeling our discussion will punctuate my day with some well-needed mirth."

'Mirth' shaft thought, do they still use that word.

"I'm glad I can be of help in that department, but I don't think it's gonna be fun, sir. This is definitely not going to be fun."

The commander shuffled in his seat.

"So, this is not a face-to-face where you moan about your lack of inclusion in the Platinum Exhibition murders?"

"You heard about that?" Shaft asked.

"I did, but a choice was made Inspector. My team is filled with competent people whose judgment I trust.

You and your theories could just prove to be too much of a distraction."

"How much of a distraction would I be if you have a hundred more bodies on your doorstep next week." Shaft said flatly.

The commander leaned back in his chair and gripped the armrest.

"And I suppose you have an answer to our dilemma?" The commander asked as if he was challenging him to ruin his day.

Shaft wouldn't be baited into an answer just yet.

"Can I be brutally honest sir." Shaft said.

"I'm a big boy. I can take it, Inspector."

Shaft sighed.

"I have reason to believe the murders at the fundraiser two nights ago makes it a Black Book designated case."

The commander closed his eyes briefly then planted his ten fingers tips on his desk. He eased himself up to a standing position. Shaft was regretting having sat down now.

"How much of a risk do you think I took by facilitating the creation of your unit?"

"A big one sir."

The Commander walked over to the window and looked out over metropolitan London.

"Correct. And it's proving to be the right thing to do. But... "

His eyes dimmed, he let the thought run from him almost, then recaptured it.

"... For our relationship to keep working your natural need for progression, that ambitious streak of yours must be controlled. That was the unspoken agreement."

"I didn't agree to anything." Shaft said without apology. "You felt it was in the interest of the Met and the public. We're past that now."

"So, you say."

"With all due respect, sir. Let's not fuck about." Shaft snapped standing up too. "You are over your head with this. The government is pissed; this has happened in the Capital. Counter-Terrorism and MI5 are snapping at your heels for results. And your dream team have no answers."

The Commander didn't answer, but his eyes brightened. The muscles of his jaw tightened and relaxed.

"One hundred bodies found exsanguinated with puncture marks and savage bites. Fifty-odd bodies are missing. No evidence found, not even a fingerprint or shoe impression. It was as if ghosts had done this." Shaft looked over to a picture he had on his desk of his wife and two children. His daughters took their mothers look and dark skin. "You are searching in the wrong places sir, and because the Met is not prepared to accept or can handle the possibility of the occult, you're wasting a lot of time."

"How do I know that this not an attempt from you to gain more credibility for your ideas?"

"Do you really think this is an ego trip. Some stupid pretense that will get my face in Modern Policing? Over a hundred people are dead."

Shaft gave him a look of bewilderment.

"So, the fact that this is a high-profile investigation headed by Chief Inspector Cargill has no bearings on what you are demanding?"

Shaft wanted to kiss his teeth, but the cultural gesture would be lost on the Commander.

"It has nothing to do with that," Shaft said coldly.

Chief Inspector Cargill was a prick and Shaft had numerous run-ins with him to confirm it. But this was his world and Cargill would begin to understand he had no hope in hell, navigating its ins and outs.

The Commander saw Shafts focus shift for a moment and pounced.

"It must be frustrating handling cases that will never get any recognition and not being able to head up and investigation with a team at your back."

The commander knew enough of him to push his buttons. But lacked the nuance to hurt him. Those weaknesses were in his mental lockbox buried deep from the probing of people like him.

The Commander continued.

"Never having your colleagues congratulating you down the pub for a job well done would eventually piss me off."

Shaft made a frowning face.

"I don't play well with others, sir." Shaft stood up and moved closer to his desk. "But if you can find anyone in the rank and file equipped to do this then have at it. I'll step down."

The commander cleared his throat and shuffled papers uncomfortably on his desk.

"What do you need?"

Shaft bent down to pick up his case. He placed it on the Commanders table, opened it and retrieved two items. He handed the commander a folder and the flash drive.

His superior took it hesitantly.

"This is the abridged version of a report, I compiled being blocked by your team at every juncture, but I got it done. I still have some love in the rank and file. "

Without further thought he pinned the commander with his eyes, the intensity making his boss uncomfortable.

"We have a clan of vampires who have just begun a killing spree. I don't know why or who but If you don't let me stop them, London could be drowning in the blood of innocents in weeks. And it's going to be on your hands."

11.

Heathrow Airport Terminal 5, London

W hat the fuck is going on?" Patra asked, looking at the headlines of the Metro newspaper.

"A hundred and fifty-nine people dead." Y sounded distant, almost diminished like the news had sapped her of energy.

Patra brought up a manicured finger to her lips before Y could continue.

"Before you say it, we did the best we could. Our responsibility was for homeboy Mr. Holtz. We couldn't have saved them."

"Did we try?" Y asked.

"Would they have listened to us? What would you even tell those people to get them out?" Patra considered her own words with her trademarked slow rub of her palms. "Don't forget Christoph's friend left with her entourage."

Y nodded, but the satisfaction of saving five people was hollow.

"You think Mr. P had a feeling this would happen?" Patra asked.

"I don't think so, but I'm sure he sensed something. That's why he sent us. Mr. Holtz was lucky." Y paused and shook her head. "They're calling it a terrorist attack."

Patra laughed, the sound of her amusement making some people in the Arrival hall look over to her.

"We know that's bullshit. When Suzy gets here, we'll have a better handle on the truth. Five-O must be tripping right about now. They ain't going to tell Joe public shit. They got to keep our world under wraps." The corners of her lips dimpled as she thought of something mischievous. "You heard from Shaft?"

Y narrowed her eyes, not sure if her sister was leading with that question for mature conversation or a juvenile examination of her love life.

"Not yet but he'll find us. He's a great detective."

"You know he can't do without seeing you for a week. That brother wants the pussy so bad or should I say needs it. But he believes in timing. I respect that."

"I'm glad you approve. I'm lucky to have him," Y corrected herself. "We're lucky to have him."

"Yes, we are, so stop teasing the homie and break him off a goddamn piece."

Y smiled.

"It's so easy for you isn't it? Even before we knew our true purpose, you weren't afraid to take those risks."

"What's the worst that can happen?" Patra asked.

Y nodded and thought about it for a moment. Her mind switching from her love life to the direr situation they found themselves in. Suddenly Y was aware of the bullet resistant travel case positioned between her legs. If Suzy hadn't demanded she bring it, she would never take it from the mansion. The Codex of True Guardian History was a mystical book that wrote itself, but its contents had to be accessed by all three of them. It was a hefty tome, quartz and jade cover and living papyrus pages that charted the Guardians history from the very beginning. A month after they had controlled the runaway train that was the dark Vodun Enoch Lacombe and the damage he wreaked on the city of London, the book had appeared in their home amongst the other impressive Artefacts they had in their possession. It helped to give them a sense of meaning, knowing the characters, the traditions, the universal struggle. Suzy didn't want to wait a moment longer to find out what they were up against and she thought that a history lesson in the Guardians of the Light could help them. Combining both mystical assistance with mundane police proce-

dural work from Shaft, they knew they had a problem
of the Nosferatu kind.

And these vampires had not come to play.

Y looked over to Trevor.

Suzy's boyfriend was intensely scouring the flight
times on the monitors. He had strolled away from Y
and Patra, the three having swopped funny stories
about growing up. Y thought of something profound
that made her tingle inside. Under the worst of circumstances, they were building something meaningful.
They were creating an extended family that blurred the
lines between blood and bond.

"Isn't he just the cutest?" Y said. Trevor's six-foot
five frame unconsciously shifted at their scrutiny, highlighting his impressive physique. He attentively
watched passengers walk from the baggage hall to the
arrival hall.

"Homeboy is missing his boo," Patra said matter-of-
factly. "I wouldn't want to be the mattress on their bed
tonight. Hell, I'm lying. I would."

Patra grinned.

Y rolled her eyes.

"That's for later; we've got things to do."

"You would deprive a bitch sex." Patra voice of incredulity wasn't bad.

"Yep."

Patra shook her head in disgust then an unusual veneer of seriousness snuck up on her.

"Suzy copped a good one. Big-sexy there, may want his woman to himself, but he understands, she's got a higher purpose. He's willing to accept that to be with her."

"He just doesn't know that choice could kill him." Y said coldly.

"You a ray of sunshine today, bitch."

"Sorry." Y apologized. "I'm still processing what happened at the Fund Raiser."

They stared at each other for a moment.

"I can't believe I'm saying this shit," Patra mumbled. "But it's better to have loved and lost than to have never loved at all."

"Wow!" Y perked up. "Alfred Lord Tennyson. You've been reading girlfriend."

Patra gave her the finger,

"If you really believe that sis, then there's no better way to live as far as I'm concerned." Y shrugged.

"That's the problem. I'm not sure I do believe." Patra's expression was thoughtful.

"You have a big heart Miss P." Y said. "In love, I may be slow to act, and Suzy may be boringly predictable, but you need to express yourself. Be vulnerable."

Patra acknowledged her understanding with the slightest nod of her head. Y had a way of calming the recklessness that bubbled up from Patra's personality, and in serious moments her advice came from a place of love, she knew that. But these heart to hearts made Patra yearn for Atlanta. Or more to the point, her Mom's.

Y checked the time again and looked up at the arrivals board.

"She should be coming out of the baggage hall anytime now." Y said.

"Let's go fuck with Trevor," Patra said with a wry smile.

Y thought about it for a moment and grinned too.

"Good idea."

12.

Hellfire Club, Central London

Reginald Peabody strolled down the gaslighted and silent corridor towards the Queen Victoria suite. His footsteps were muffled by the thick carpet, but he was still able to maintain a marching rhythm that any self-respecting military man would appreciate. Perfectly balanced atop the ceramic tray he carried was a bottle of three-hundred-year-old Jamaican rum spiked with fresh human blood and two glasses. He carried out his duties with this level of style and pride for all of their guests whether they be Shamans from the colonies or demi-gods. His posture was ramrod straight, his demeanor formal as was the way for the Chief handman. He had worked here for twenty-five years, his father before him had done the same – The Founders – appreciated generational obedience – and the benefits were second to none. He had worked his way up from the

Kitchens, to the Doorman, to a Handman and now the rarefied position he found himself in at present. Hard work and discretion weren't the only two characteristics you needed here. Absolute secrecy was what made the Victorian mechanisms of one of London's oldest and most obscure establishment tick. And it did because it must. The things he had seen here, would boggle the senses of even the most open-minded individual. But he had grown up understanding the world was not as it seemed and for most the veil that separated the realities remained firmly in place.

Here was one of the few places that did not apply. In fact, the veil separating the realities had been ripped apart allowing for the mixture of all mystical races, good, bad and indifferent, all protected by the esoteric rules that governed the Hellfire Club and the mystical universe.

Mr. Peabody stopped at the double doors of the Victoria Suite and cleared his throat. He knew the procedure well; he had served vampires before just not one of such high standing. No garlic for breakfast, his silver buttons had been replaced, and he had checked himself of any inadvertent symbols of the Christian faith.

He knocked briskly and said.

"Your refreshment is ready, Ma'am."

Miranda Pheare stood on the cantilevered glass balcony, looking over a bustling night-time London. The world she had left behind had been quieter. Most humans did not know how to embrace something as primal as silence. This new era was a ceaseless, booming sound box folded onto itself, at war, competing with the silence of the universe to be heard. It was a wonder that anything could be deciphered in this constant racket. She rolled her neck and took a sip of her blood spiked white rum turning away from the panorama of the city and entered her palatial suite. The ten thousand-square-foot space boasted ornate furnishing - calfskin leather, afromosia, Venetian velvet, Chinese onyx, Japanese silk all to her specifications. The suite glimmered in gold leaf, stucco, ivory, and Italian marble floors. Her main chamber was housed within a vault that could only be opened or closed from the inside. The crystal chandeliers still held candles instead of electric lights, a relic from when the Club first opened its doors.

In the centre of the lounge, an antique oakwood table held an opened bottle of seventeeth century Jamaican Rum from a batch thought to be lost at sea after mother nature broke and swallowed the vessel and its crew. Two glasses sat near a jade and marble chessboard. Its hand-forged, steel and bronze pieces stood in their respective places, ready to charge into intellectual battle. Mr. Opoku sat patiently waiting for her.

Miranda's eyes glinted cold and dangerous as blood soaked recollections scrapped across her memory. Chess was Lord Byefield's game. He taught her how to play, and taught her through it, to rule his nocturnal world by his side.

"Madam Pheare," Mr. Opuko said, quietly. His voice tremulous. "I have much to tell you, Madam. Sit for a spell."

Miranda sat elegantly in her chair, her posture perfect, her dark and long legs unstockinged but gleaming. In the time it took to be comfortable, her vampire mind was recounting how well her first sacrifice had gone. Quenching Lord Byefield's thirst across the spiritual divide would take much more blood from the human cattle. It had been her main purpose, her focus until now.

After Miranda's fifty-year repose, she had to catch up on the advancements in the human world. Mr. Opoku would make a wide variety of trivia or business information available to her for absorption. Knowing how the world has evolved was important, even though she planned on cleansing it. It was his job to alert her of any threats in the era she found herself. And it was a job he took very seriously.

Mr. Opoku placed both his hands on the table and focussed on her desolate, soul-sucking eyes.

"It's as we feared, mistress. The Heart of Ares was not destroyed. I'm in the process of finding it."

Her ears drew in his words, and her psychic abilities revealed snippets of his thoughts. Edmund taught her that if you give a familiar a significant leadership role, they will give you their loyalty. Mr. Opoku had been trained well; her probes to his mind were cursory.

The Heart of Ares.

Her body stayed cemented in the present, a physical placeholder, while her mind traveled back in time. Flipping through memories of her lover was the only way she could see Edmund, feel his essence in perfect detail. The portrait paintings were long gone. Who knows where they ended up after Miranda fled London?

She didn't have the time to arrange Edmunds estate. And even if she did, a black woman, a maid in Victorian England, vampire or not, laying claim to the estate of the aristocracy was impossible. And if a bad situation could be made worst the relentless vampire hunter who had destroyed her lover was now looking for her.

Miranda absently traced her finger around the edge of her glass; eyes flashed away from their soft brown to a shade of cruel, dark ruby. The corners of her mouth twitched, and her elongated fangs slithered from her gums. Edmunds death was a poor choice of memory. It was a bad place, and she knew better than to go there. Not while she was hungry, and not even when fed.

Mr. Opoku's Adam's apple bobbed up and down his neck, the strength of the Jamaican rum, not enough liquid courage for him to pry into the secrets behind those demon eyes.

Miranda's control of her body was exquisite, and she transformed her human hand into something monstrous looking with thick, sharp claws. Mr. Opoku's eyes widened his mortality exposed.

"Mistress," he finally managed, his voice controlled although inside was a storm of emotions. "Is everything alright?"

"No Mr. Opoku it's not." Her fangs stayed bare, the monstrous hand flexing on the table. "I want deh Heart of Ares and its present owner. Everyone else I want dem dead."

Mr. Opoku blinked, the relief radiating off him like waves of heat.

"As you wish. Mistress."

13.

Metal Works Gym, West London

The steam issued up from the activation basin, a wispy curtain of heated moisture trapped in a wooden paneled box of the sauna room in Metal Works gym. Y sat on the ground, her back on the wooden slats that made up the amphitheater style seating. She was wrapped in a white towel covering her bust and down to the curve of her bum. Her long dark legs ended in feet slipped into pink Brazilian beach slippers. Someone was humming a Bob Marley tune, but they were invisible for the moment, then the steam cleared, and the impression of Suzy Wong became clear, laid out on her back, on the first tier similarly wrapped in a white towel, her black hair in a ponytail. She rested her arms on her chest, her hands touching fingertips together in an intricate pattern. Dragon tattoo on her right arm. Water droplets fizzled and evaporated violently as they made contact with her fingers. Patra stood up and came closer. She was five feet eleven inches of lithe caramel skin. She has muscle rippling under her feminine curves as she moved. The steam twirled wildly around her as if she was charging the ionized air molecules. She flung off her towel and sent it twirling towards a set of cloth hooks on the wall. It attached neatly to the third hook out of the five.

"Show off," Suzy said with one eye open.

Patra was nude, legs wide and arms spread.

"This feels good!" Y said.

"I'm tingling all over," Patra said. "Inside and out." She added.

"When was the last time we were all together like this?"

Suzy shrugged and then thought about it.

"About two months," Suzy said. "It feels like we just parted ways deh other day."

"You freaky bitches just like getting naked when I'm around; that's all."

"Keep telling yourself that," Y smirked.

"It's the connection thing we share, I guess, keeps us linked up no matter where we are."

"I have it more than you, and a little bit extra too."

"Saved our lives more times than I'd like to mention," Y said.

"And have got weh rass in some trouble because of it too," Suzy added.

"True," Y laughed.

"I wish I shared our connection with Trevor though," Suzy said, her tone somewhat distant.

"He really missed you?" Y asked.

"The dude worries about you but he ain't going to front and say it."

"I know. I just wish I had a way to reassure him when tings nuh right. Just mek him know how much he mean to me, when I'm not around him."

"Is he having doubts about you?"

"No,." she said with certainty. "Not doubts. He just deserves the truth from me. And if I can't give him deh whole truth; Bad II deh Bone kinda truth. Then how do I reassure him."

"You've got a really good man in your corner Suzy. After that gunshot wound from the Darkman case, I thought..."

"Me too, baby," Suzy said. "Me too." She expertly changed the subject. "So how is Detective Shaft?"

Y paused for a heartbeat, Patra may not have noticed, but Suzy picked up the nuances both physical and meta-physical.

"He's a really good friend. I love being around him." Her voice lowered. "Maybe too much, and that's part of the problem."

"Don't be afraid, babe," Suzy said her posture un-changed and only her lips were moving. "I can't promise a relationship will work out, but I can say he won't deceive you. He's honest and true. But remember he's a man, suh go easy on him."

"Even sir Galahad can't wait forever."

"I'm not sure I should." Y said.

"What the fuck are you talking about?" Patra said, trying a sneak attack on Suzy, but even with her eyes closed, she blocked her sister's attempt at flicking her nose with two fingers.

"Yuh tink mi born big." She said

Patra sniggered and sat down beside Y, hugging her.

"Let me lay it out straight for you sister. He deserves some sugar from the honey pot, you know some pussy and you holding out on him. He crazy sexy and, you hot as hell. I know you two like each other. Let's get it on."

"That simple?"

"That simple." Y said.

"And what about you Miss Ting? How is deh relationship game treating you?"

Patra shrugged.

"It is what it is. Whether I'm hooked up or not, I'm good. I get mine as you know, but I'll let it happen in its own time. The universe has its plans. For now, I'm having too much fun with you bitches."

Suzy sat up applauding.

"Well said gal."

Patra bowed.

Suzy continued but more sombrely this time.

"Now on the point of the universe having its plans. Do you want deh good news or deh bad news?"

"Good news," they both chorused.

"Come look at dis." Suzy waved them over.

The girls huddled around Suzy, and she lifted the inside wrist of her left hand to eye level.

Y blinked then Suzy said.

"Mi notice it by accident."

"Motherfucker." Said Patra "I've got one too. A replica of that. Let me show you."

Patra sat beside Suzy and without a thread of self-consciousness, spread her legs. Her silver genital piercing glinted as Patra pointed out the design that had formed on the inside of her thigh a finger span from her intimate folds.

Suzy rolled her eyes

"Why does that not surprise mi?"

"Don't hate," Patra said. "My VJ is manicured, faded and tight. No loose bits. You feel me?"

Looking at Y, Patra continued.

"I bet yours is all neat, respectful and shit," Patra made a face. "I bet Shaft doesn't know whether to kiss it or write it a ticket."

"Ha! Ha!" Y deadpanned. "The last I looked everything was in order thank you very much."

"So, you do examine it," Patra said laughing. "What do you call her?" She teased.

"None of your damn business." Y said.

"Don't feel left out sugah, I'll loan you one of mine." Patra was grinning from ear to ear.

Suzy shook her head like a mum patiently waiting for the kids to settle down.

"Every woman should get know dem body. Pum-pum included."

'Amen sister," Patra extolled.

"Now can we get back to examining your crotch," Y said sardonically.

"Knock yourself out," Patra grinned. "I'm loving the attention."

"The symbol looks familiar," Y said gently rubbing the pad of her finger over the mark as if it would smudge.

Patra giggled throatily.

"So, you're telling me it just appeared spontaneously on both of you?" Y asked.

"And you too, babe," Suzy said.

"Where?" Y asked.

"It's not as bright because yuh dark skinned. Let me take a look."

"Can I close my legs now?" Patra chimed.

"Please," Y said laughing.

In the meantime, Suzy was inspecting Y's arms.

"You don't think it could be on my ass, do you?"

Patra's eyes twinkled.

"I'd put it on your ass if it was up to me."

Y's cheeks flushed.

"Ah, Thank you."

"I have it on my wrist." Suzy reasoned aloud to give her thoughts more clarity. "Miss Sexy over there has it beside her fanny and you Miss Sinclair..."

Her voice trailed away, and suddenly her face lit up.

"You sister Y..." Suzy gently started trailing her fingers through Y's hair as if she was looking for fleas, then turning her head, left then right. "Found yuh." Suzy exclaimed. She rubbed it with her thumb. It was the area between her neck and ear, just where smooth skin became thicker strands of hair to her scalp.

"What do you think it means?" Patra asked, her eyebrows rising.

"It's an eternity symbol?" Y said.

"Wid insect legs?" Suzy asked.

'I think they're spiders' legs."

"Hum!" Suzy considered that by twiddling the ends of her ponytail." Well, whatever it is and whoever is guiding us, seems to think it is important to mark us."

"Spontaneous tattooing, now that is some cool shit!" Patra said.

"Higher powers?" Y murmured.

"Power we may never fully understand," Suzy said.

"Do we need to?" Patra asked. "Personally, I'm going to enjoy the ride, kicking up a shit storm on the way." The girls glared at her. "A good kind of shitstorm," Patra added.

"I feel vulnerable," Y said, "Like I'm not fully in control. Something or someone could flip a switch and bend us to their will, and we wouldn't be the wiser."

Patra shrugged, and Suzy sighed deeply.

"I feel yuh, sis, but it's your personality to have a strong internal locus of control."

"She means control freak in the nicest possible way." Patra clarified.

Y gave her the finger. Suzy ignored them both.

"I see it as we've been given a path to tread, a job to do and whoever or whatever it is has our back. I have a good feeling, about this. But time will tell."

Suddenly faces darkened, the main threat they had been avoiding talking about required discussion. Suzy sat down looking tired and frightened.

"I saw someting in China; I didn't tell you about. A part of the vision that scared me to the core. A nightmare that made me want to haul my rass back, to London to be with you." She took another deep breath. "A swirling tornado of blood that butchered everything in its path and left the streets ankle deep in blood. It was teasing me, whispering for me to try and stop it. And we couldn't, not alone anyway."

"The Codex wasn't much help." Y said. "It seems throughout the Guardians history we've never had much experience with vampires." Y continued. "A new chapter will be written about this in the Codex then. Whatever happens." Patra said.

"What's going to happen," Patra said. "Is we are going kick ass and take names. We Bad II the Bone, baby."

Suzy held Patra's hand. Patra held Y's. A tremor from Suzy, that radiated from her core resonated with her sisters amplifying the darkness she was feeling.

Patra had to have the last word.

14.

Metropolitan Police Archives, Central London

Shaft flashed his warrant card at his colleague in the foyer and headed over to a small reception area. The young Somali woman was looking down at a computer screen below the level of the desk that sat centrally in the space. He'd known Aisha for three years and she may outwardly give him grief, she was one of his many contacts that made a difficult career bearable. Scanner doorways and X-Ray machines flanked her on both sides, and she was humming to herself as she perused Shaft's request. She suddenly looked up, her hijab sporting met colours and looked at him sternly.

"They've been pissing around with your application again, I see."

"And I thought it was just me," Shaft said.

"It is just you Inspector. How many times have you come down here, trying to charm your way in without completing your form properly?"

Shaft started counting on his fingers with a manufactured look of innocence.

"Who have you upset, this time?"

"Come on Aisha, man. Look at this face. Could this face upset anyone?"

Shaft contorted his features, stuck out his tongue and Aisha shook her head in exasperation then laughed

"You look like my Mohammed when he's constipated."

"How's the little man doing?"

"He keeps asking for his uncle. When are you going to come visit?"

"Soon," Shaft said. "I promise."

Aisha held up a lanyard with Shaft's digitally rendered mug laminated and ready to be examined by overly zealous security personnel.

"Have it on you at all times or they will throw you out. Again."

"Scouts honour." Shaft said taking the ID and blowing her a kiss. "If you weren't married, I'd ..."

She brushed him away.

"Sweet!" Shaft caught himself whistling. He placed his eyes over the microfilm viewer again and brought the headlines of the 1919 Globe into focus.

Horror at the Shaftesbury Opera House.

He looked at another headline from The Observer in 1949.

Essex Gentleman's Club Burnt to the Ground. All Souls Perished.

There was a pattern. And he was sure if he went back further, he would see it play out time and time again. Every fifty years for the last two hundred years or more murders of the influential, rich and connected had taken place in Metropolitan London. Shaft also had anecdotal evidenceIt was hard to corroborate the forensic details and he could be wrong about some incidents that had nothing to do with today's perpetrator, but he was close. Their MO was mass murder, almost animalistic savagery and bloodletting and in more recent times less concern for discovery by the authorities. The modern world did not believe in the supernatural. Everything could be explained through logic and scientific investigation even when the evidence was pointing to the unexplainable. A year ago, he would be trying to disprove the existence of the esoteric to his superior, but he was way past that now. Bad II the Bone and the Darkman case had made myth so very real. Now his objective was to stop the threat, period.

Shaft's gut tightened because he knew the girls through their spooky connection with such things knew something was happening. This kind of craziness was right up their street. He would be going to see Y soon and if he could keep his hands off her, they would talk about the Platinum Exhibition Murders and what the

Guardians of the Light were planning. In the meantime, he refocused on his research.

"Detective McFarlane, you're finally here. Great meeting you in person." The Police Historian Gregory Smythson thrust out his hand and Shaft took it. His hand was cool, his shake strong. Shaft wondered if the top brass knew the talent walking through their hallowed halls. He guessed they took it for granted. Gregory wore crisp uniform ironed to within an inch of its life, the buttons on his epaulet gleaming and his boots so brilliantly black if you stared too long into them you were afraid, they would suck you in and never let go. He walked like a Benedictine monk who had swopped a Cassock for uniform. Slight with a barely noticeable curvature of the spine, almost completely bald with a ginger circumference of hair with a bald plate in the middle like Friar Tuck. His pasty white skin was hairless and his long stints without contact with the sun obvious. Shaft wondered if he had a room in the basement.

"So, where you going to set me up?" Shaft asked. "I'm not fussy as long as I've got access to what I need, I'm good."

"I have the thing for you, detective. Just the thing." Gregory laughed. "I know you were reluctant to ask for help but I thought I would anyway."

Surprised Shaft said:

"I appreciate it." He paused. "The thing."

Gregory motioned for Shaft to sit at microfilm pro-
jector 122-04.

"The best magnification of all the projectors by fifty
times."

Shaft sat.

"I use it for analysis sometimes, I tend to steer people
away from it most times. It will come in handy for a
closer inspection of these." He said sliding a box of mi-
crofilms beside his hand. Being so close to him, Shaft
smelt his woody aftershave.

"What's this?" Shaft asked.

Gregory's eyes glistened his shallow cheeks raised
appreciating the blood flow.

"I took the liberty of compiling articles going back to
eighteen hundred with a Modus Operandi that was similar in tone and method to the perp you're researching
for the Platinum Murders."

"Thanks man." Shaft said surprised. "But you didn't
have to."

"But I did Detective. I'm a fan of you work and I think
you may need a friend?"

Shaft shot out a hand. "You're a gentleman Mr.
Smythson. Just remember that I look after my friends. If
you need anything, let me know."

"It was my pleasure, detective."

"You looked at the slides?" Shaft asked.

Gregory nodded.

"What did you think?" Shaft coaxed him. "Your professional opinion."

"Are you a religious man, detective?"

"I'm a scientist foremost but yes I'm a believer."

"Then I would say you should prepare to have your beliefs tested."

Shaft shook his head. "You don't know a beautiful Chinese Jamaican girl, good with her hands called Suzy Wong, do you?"

Gregory smiled. "No."

"You sound a lot like her." Shaft said.

"I like her already," Gregory said. "I'll come back to see you in an hour, sir."

15.

The five man team made it through the traditional security system as advanced as it was but with vital intelligence they should not be privy to. It was meant to be easy access. Their skill set was not for breaking and entering but more suited for neutralizing subjects who possessed special skills.

Outside the mansion's perimeter wall in a secure copse the operative code-named Disrupt, sat cross-legged and in a deep state of meditation. This petite woman in state-of-the-art visual disruptive jumpsuit and face paint had learned the skill of psychic static in Sambor Prei Kuk, Cambodia and could generate a kind of psychic EMP pulse that could confuse and disorientate most sensitives. She would continue her onslaught until the operation was complete. The rest of the team by now would have disabled the wall security mounted on the ivy-covered red brick and were deploying modulating

EMP devices in the grounds that would fry any electronic equipment with transistors and microcircuitry, breaching the Sussex mansions security and neutralizing the targets.

The team had numerous practice runs in a custom-built kill house that represented the specifications of the three bedrooms they were focused on. They studied the interior set up of the Georgian house so they could navigate it comfortably with night scope goggles. The team leader who was in position, spoke into his local communication link.

"Team shadow. All in position." Five responses came back, clipped and eager.

"Breach in five...."

The countdown began.

"Y!"

"Sis!"

Y jumped up from her light sleep, fully awake in seconds. Her heart was pounding, and although she was fully aware, she was still looking into the darkness of her bedroom hoping to see the shape of her sister, Suzy at the foot of her bed, distorting the sparse shafts of light coming into her room, but she was alone.

Something was wrong.

Y sprang off her bed, grabbing her katana mid-flight, hitting the bedroom floor and rolling into a run. As she moved towards the door her silken PJ's ruffling, her footfalls were as light as a candle flame as she glided through the open door, the scabbard on her back and her sword trailing behind her.

Luther Vandross played in the background as Patra finished the mouthful of wine on the balcony of her room and looked out at the beauty of the garden below. Contrary to what people thought, she loved the tranquillity of her crib. She let the warmth of the wine trickle down her throat and sighed contentedly.

It didn't last.

The glow of satisfaction from the chill breeze on her skin as she stood in black bra and panties became a jarring clash of symbols like she was infusing a symphony with death metal. Her skin felt as if it was being pulled taut like a traditional drum and the beats were discordant and confusing.

It was a whole-body alert.

Just for a moment, she had lost balance, and her world had slipped the needle and jumped out of the groove. Suzy had to go heavy handed to get her psychically insensitive ass to hear.

Suzy was shouting.

Patra let the wineglass balance on the Crescent of the masonry railing. She entered her bedroom with three quick steps and on her side-table reached for a transparent gauze bag and her marbles. Taking a quick breath, she wrapped the drawstring around her wrist. For a beat of five, Patra stared at her room door her instincts guiding her away from that exit point. She turned from her room door and dashed out to the balcony her bare feet slapping on tiles and hurled herself over the railings and out into the night air. A strategy, gelling in her mind as gravity took her.

The pain in Suzy's temples exploded like miniature landmines, and if it weren't for her developing control over her nervous system, she would be on her knees. Instead, the phone that was to her ears fell to the bed.

She had been on the phone to Trevor, a nightly ritual when she was away from her boyfriend for days or weeks at a time. They both were night owls, he worked shifts and she was at her best at the witching hour. Unusually Y was asleep, and Patra was either reading or watching a film before she bedded down. Suzy needed her privacy because her X-rated telephone orgy would have Y blushing and Patra asking if she could be involved but tonight had been tame, and that was a good thing considering. Her baby had been talking about having a family in the near future, and she was picturing a beautiful little girl of mixed heritage - his African Jamaican and her Chinese Jamaican genes combined. She was basking in the glow of that possible future, when the headache struck.

"Baby, you okay?" Trevor enquired concern in his voice.

Suzy gritted her teeth and picked the phone back up

"Can I call you back T, something just came up," Suzy croaked.

"You sure everything cool?" Trevor asked again.

She licked her lips.

"Nothing I can't handle baby. I'll call you back." She licked her fingers and extinguished the single candle throwing the room into darkness. Suzy let the smartphone fall to the bed. The pain lanced into her head like molten spears, disappearing in and then out of the other side, inflict more damage to her senses. The attack had Suzy unprepared, had taken her by surprise, had shocked her even but instinctively she had begun to defend herself against whoever, or whatever was trying to disable her psychically. Her shields were mounting, and the distraction they had hoped to use to their advantage was dwindling quickly. Her sisters had been alerted and knew they were under attack and knew what must be done. First things first, though.

Eliminate the *bloodclaat* static in her head.

Suzy was not the one for sedate problem-solving. When she wanted to get something done, she was at her best when she was in motion, and her body was being tested. With her mind made up, she moved with a blur and rustle of movement. In the darkness a drawer opened and closed on oiled rails, a bedroom door opened and gently closed, leaving only the faint perfume where Suzy had been.

The battle was on.

Patra didn't know why and to be honest did not care. The compulsion was upon her, planted by Suzy and she was compelled to move unerringly to what her sister had tagged as a target. All of the non-verbal communication between herself and her sisters were being channelled through a wavelength only they could tap into. There were no voices in their head, no HD images behind her eyes. Their spooky GPS worked through feeling alone and a certainty that could override and completely dispel any sense of doubt. Letting that sense of certainty guide her Patra scurried through the estate's oriental gardens, skipping over three Koi ponds without breaking her stride. She was sprinting towards the only portion of the perimeter wall that would give you entrance or exit without using the main gates. The trick was navigating a diabolically complex hedge maze quickly and surreptitiously. She wiggled through the maze taking shortcuts and cheats only she knew existed. It was eight feet tall and a shoulder width across. It was usually lit and monitored but whoever had breached security had disabled it. In five minutes, she stepped through into the darkness of the countryside, her eyes adjusting. Patra cocked her head to one side like a fox sniffing the currents and completely blind in the darkness. Suzy's implanted compulsion forced her to charge forward through the brush with no concern for the noise she was making. Patra only depended on her preternatural senses to protect her from tripping or smashing into a tree. She came upon a small clearing and stopped.

"So, you've been the one giving Suzy shit," Patra whispered. The focus of her attention was sitting snugly in a lotus position. She was a petite white female, raven black hair dressed in army camouflage with her eyes closed. A chant emanated from barely moving lips and beside her were Night goggles, and a switched off shortwave radio. Patra kneeled in front of her almost not wanting to wake her from her trance. She had great bone structure, sexy lips. It was a shame to mess it up.

Patra grabbed her by the shoulders and shook.

"Wakey, wakey bitch!" The young woman's eyes opened with a start, and Patra noted they were a deep glacial blue. Her mouth opened but was unable to form a word of protest. She was cute Patra thought and smashed her fist into her jaw.

Suzy's headache suddenly disappeared, and relief flooded over her. She let out a stream of frustrated air through her lips and adjusted her posture. She would thank Patra later but, right now she had her part of their unspoken plan to complete. Suzy had to make her way from the second floor to the ground floor without being observed. She moved with unerring confidence, completely familiar with the layout of the mansion and the route she would take. Suzy sprang from the balcony, launching herself through the air to the ornate chandelier, that was the central feature of the rotunda-shaped main reception. Gracefully swinging from it without making a sound, Suzy positioned herself and fell the thirty feet like a leaf buoyed up by the wind. Her enhanced thigh muscles absorbed the impact, and she fluidly rolled into the shadows. The interlopers thought they were invisible, but Suzy saw them. She kept her breathing easy, and her heart maintained a controlled and steady beat. Two men in black combat fatigues carrying automatics and wearing night vision goggles strolled past her. Both covered the entrances leading into the lounge. Suzy sensed sister Y was a level above and her instincts said she would be working her way down to meet her anytime soon. There was something she could not ignore though, and that was the undercurrents that emanated from them.

It lacked maliciousness. She smelt reassuring leather, professionalism and not the coppery tang of blood or excitement of the kill. She let her thoughts percolate as she cloaked herself in darkness and watched them patrol the perimeter.

Suzy pictured the set up in her mind's eye.

One man at the bottom of the massive sweeping staircase. One man halfway up the stairs and then a team of three clearing all the bedrooms. She had left a hastily prepared surprise in three of the rooms they would enter. She wasn't worried about Y and Patra jumping the gun either. Their weird emotional wireless always got the timing right, so she waited in the shadows. She was grinning broadly when the shrill battery-powered motion detector went off with an ear-splitting shriek.

Now dem know, we know, Suzy thought.

Agent X-Ray 3 saw the movement of something quick, radioactive green from the Night Googles and petite slide into him. His assailant applied just enough pressure at the base of his ankle that if he didn't roll, it would snap. He could do nothing but collapse into the arms of whoever had checked him. Quick and strong hands tore off his goggles and added pressure to his carotid artery. Blocking blood flow to his brain and rendering him unconscious in minutes.

X-Ray 5 broke the corner confidently, her finger on the hair-trigger as she absorbed the picture of her teammate on the ground. The woman standing over who she thought was X-Ray 3 reacted immediately, and so did she. X-Ray 5 expertly swung her MP4 around, switching to auto and firing in controlled bursts. The women in dark silken PJ's, moved with incredible speed, propelling herself backward, using the wall as a springboard as if she had altered gravity. The bullets struck where she once stood.

Red dye pellets not full metal jackets.

Y kissed her teeth quietly to herself having expected to draw some blood from these intruders but unfortunately, they weren't as dangerous as she first thought. Well, at least some broken bones were justified. Y relaxed and became one with the ceiling. She formed a dark X concealed in the darkness above the men skulking below her. Her Katana was slung over her back and her breathing almost meditative. As strong as she was, even she couldn't maintain the position forever. Two men had positioned themselves beside Suzy's bedroom door. Y did not know exactly what her sister had in store, but she could feel Suzy's excitement. The anticipation is nearly making her giggle.

She held her breath with difficulty.

One of the men opened the bedroom door slowly, his teammate leveling his weapon at the darkened interior. They entered, one taking point, one immediately behind him and both tripping the rudimentary motion detector. Like a dark teardrop Y descended silently to the corridor and then entered the room, closing the door behind her.

Remember, no blood just bruises.

Patra was back into the main estate, running at breakneck speed through the ornamental gardens, skipping over Koi ponds and diving through hedge rows – Y would deal with her cuts and scratches later. She was swearing as the surprise party had started without her and she could faintly hear an alarm going off. As long as her sisters left some of the hors d'oeuvres for her Patra wouldn't be too pissed, but she had to be quick. She had a feeling this wouldn't last long.

Patra burst through the patio doors rolled twice and came up with her hands in her string bag extracting two ball-bearings the size of human gonads, very apt she thought under the circumstances and isolated the lone gunman on the steps. Without hesitation, she let both the ball-bearings fly.

X-ray 4, saw the woman in the bra and panties appearing at the bottom of the steps. She dashed towards him and let two objects fly from her hands like they were rocket-propelled missiles, giving him no time to register or take evasive action. The first projectile slammed into his night vision goggles, smashing two of the image intensifiers and twisting the panoramic array to such a degree he could see nothing. He fumbled to remove it. The second ball bearing hit his body armor below the sternum and fell to the marble step in front of him.

Uncannily the ball bearing stopped dead.

The soldier kept fumbling with his night vision goggles only to step on the ball bearing under his feet, lose his balance and fall, painfully down the steps. Patra was already on top of him before he settled, her fist balled, and a growl corkscrewed its way from her lungs to her mouth.

"You miss me dawg?"

"Exercise Alpha Delta X-Ray 696 is over!" A voice boomed the announcement, and the house lights flicked on.

All three of the women knowing this was over showed themselves. Y flew over the first-floor balcony, light as a feather she landed on the gold-plated rails of the sweeping staircase then the marble steps themselves and casually walked down towards Patra who was just standing up from the black-clad operative on the floor at her feet. Suzy strolled in from the utility room looking as if she had been interrupted. The crew met in the middle of the lounge just as the reinforced palatial doors swung open. A woman strode through with an open tablet in her right hand and in her left a small pull suitcase. She was flanked by two other men in combat gear and a medic. The woman was dressed simply, long plain skirt and buttoned gingham blouse. Her head was wrapped in a traditional Jamaican style with the material as her skirt. As much as she was trying to play it down in her sandaled feet, she moved with certainty, confidence and inner strength. They may have thought she was a white woman appropriating the style of the Jamaica peasant class of the forties from a distance, but as she drew closer, they were looking at a beautiful African albino woman.

"My name is Nanny," she said her voice resonant and rich. "I am sorry for the poppy show business, but master Spokes insisted. Him seh him need a word."

Mistrust turned to puzzlement on their faces.

Nanny was standing at arm's length from them, handing over the tablet to Y who took it tentatively. Looking at the woman more carefully Y thought of how flawless her snow-white skin was and her grey eyes.

"What's going on?" Y asked, just as the tablet screen showed the image of a face.

Spokes grinned from wherever he was in the world.

"Hey slick, whaddup?" Patra said referring to the enigmatic Jamaican millionaire, collector of the esoteric and their landlord.

"It is I," he continued with his thousand watts smile pleased with himself.

Spokes had been the catalyst to the adventure they were now a part of. His transformation from handyman and hustler to a supernatural impresario was an incredible story that was inextricably connected to them and their journey. For the foreseeable future, it seemed their fortunes would be linked.

Y shook her head.

"Why am I not surprised it's you?"

Suzy just chuckled to herself.

"Yuh could have let us know."

"Before yuh cuss me," Spokes said. "This was a test of how prepared you are and how you work as a team." His eyes clouded for a second and his grin slipped. "I wanted to be confident dis vampire threat, wouldn't catch you unprepared."

"We could have hurt them," Suzy said calmly.

"That's why I hired the best."

"How did we do?" Patra asked, always the competitive one.

"Omega Armaments gave you a ninety-three percent rating.

Patra shook her head like a badass.

"Oh, yeah." She said.

"How can we get ninety-nine percent rating," Y asked sarcastically.

"Live rounds and two Warlocks or two Witches in deh mix." Spokes said. "Dem impressed."

"And you?" Y asked. "Will you sleep better at night, knowing your investment is protected and your team battle ready."

Spokes sighed.

"Dis is business sistas Y; you girls are the custodians of a valuable and dangerous collection. And on top a dat, my snake ring has been going crazy when my mind rests on you. I'm worried about these bloodsuckers in London."

"You're not the only one," Y said.

"Where you at Slick?" Patra asked. "We could use your skills."

Spokes smiled his gold tooth gleaming.

"Yuh sweet like honey, sister P but you don't need me. You girls are more than capable of handling this. You are ordained after all. Never forget that."

Spokes adjusted his position, coming a bit closer to the camera.

"Between me and yuh," he lowered his voice conspiratorially. "I'm in the Cambodian Jungle on a research expedition with a good possibility of a hefty return on my investment."

"Got to get that paper, G," Patra said.

"No rest for deh wicked," Suzy added with an admiring nod.

"None at all," Spokes said. "And before I forget let me introduce you to our new housekeeper; Nanny. These are the girls I told you about Auntie."

Nanny bowed.

"Let me guess," the albino woman said. "Yvonne, Suzanne, and Cleopatra."

The girls nodded back to her.

"Where you from?" As if that needed to be asked but Patra did.

"My home is Africa," she smiled, flashing her white teeth. "But I have lived and fought for my second home of Jamaica."

Suzy looked at Y strangely then looked back at Nanny.

Spokes broke in quickly. Maybe too quickly.

"Nanny must be tired from her journey. Patra you can help our guest to her quarters?"

"No problem G, I'll make sure she's comfortable and give her the grand tour." Patra took Nanny's pull case and tried to help her with another plastic bag, but she declined. Patra led her away.

"We will catch up Sistah P." Spokes called after her.

Patra gave him the fist and disappeared with Nanny.

Spokes then focussed his attention on the remaining crew.

"Sister Y an Miss Wong. I know it will take time as these tings always do but take Nanny into your confidence. She is a wise and good woman and will have the mansion running like clockwork. In time of crisis, there is no better woman to have yuh back. I have a feeling you will need her guidance."

A seductive female voice called to him in the background.

"Soon come," he said to someone behind him and then looked back to the screen, his face filling its dimensions

"Duty calls daughters. Proud of you. Keep me updated with this vampire situation. Bless up yourself."

The Skype connection made a boing sound and disappeared.

16.

The gavel slammed down on the receptacle and the auctioneer Mr. Rupert Fletcher looked over his quarter glasses at the man wearing the white fedora and who nervously gripped the paddle with the number 34 stenciled on it.

"Lot 26 goes to the discerning gentleman in the corner." The auctioneer pointed to the man. "A wise purchase. Now for the lot of the evening and the much-anticipated Christian artifacts portion of our catalog."

To auctioneers' eyes almost glistened with excitement and flashed a tight thin smile at the packed Room. There were some power brokers in here that he knew of and others who were rumored to be some of the most discerning collectors on the planet. What had surprised Mr Fletcher wasn't their involvement,, after all the upcoming lot was something special. No, his surprise was how many of these names, who usually kept in the shadows preferring to use proxies to handle the bidding for them, had turned up in the flesh. The security considerations had been the most complicated he had ever had to deal with. Hence a room brim full of security personnel and their precious clients. A simmering excitement was percolating in the room. It was the kind of expectancy an audience would have when waiting for a magician to come on stage. It must have something to do with what these antiquities represented. Rupert Fletcher was not a believer but no matter how crazy these renaissance philosophers, religious fanatics and mad scientists were, their absurd ideas gave rise to objects that had an appeal they enjoyed over the centuries. He had fun describing what these creators had expected the items to be capable of. He was taken aback by how the bidders lacked a sense of humor or did they believe the stories behind what he considered to be Objet d'art? What could make you believe in the absurdity of eternal life, invisibility or entrance to nether dimensions. He laughed at the childishness of it all but if he was to be the one to encourage the eccentricities of the rich and famous for large quantities of money so be it. And his commissions from tonight's auction would be handsome.

He was looking forward to this.

The auction was ready to reconvene from a recess that gave the bidders the opportunity to catch their breath. It was lot, 126 a robe that was supposedly worn by an Ethiopian saint in the first century BC that was being sold by an Italian industrialist. Authenticity had been corroborated through historical research and Carbon fourteen testing. Its healing properties could not be so easily discerned. The church must have been desperate to acquire it because a small contingent from Addis Ababa and Rome had turned up jointly to purchase it. Money was no object as they saw off other parties with less commitment to add it to their collections.

The auctioneer had a feeling that this next lot would prove even more exciting and disappointing at the same time. Lot 127 had been a risky proposition and one which his partners were feeling nervous about. Normally, they would examine the article for sale in the auction, acquire the necessary expertise to assess its value, corroborate ownership and then promote it through their online magazine. It seemed the owner had already gone through that process and sent the required documentation instead. The item was placed in the catalogue sight unseen but what made the partners even more fidgety, the seller had pulled out last minute.

But all was not lost.

Instead of having the artifact in their warehouses waiting for prospective bids they had to settle for something not as dramatic but equally interesting. It was a note book written by the mad genius outlining the process of creating the Heart of Ares. The science, the engineering, the spells and the metaphysics that supposedly went into creating this weapon. Rupert hoped that the sale of the notebook would go so well, the client would want to sell the true prize, the Heart of Ares. The auctioneer let a smile sprout like a mushroom in the compost of his greed, parting the curtain with a pinkie finger he watched like a peeping Tom as the bidders returned to their seats. He swallowed the last mouth full of Earl Grey tea and prepared to join them on stage.

An excited hum rose up from the assembled as everyone settled back into their seats in anticipation of what was to come next. Mr Fletcher came out to the small stage and tapped the microphone for feedback. He then without further delay started his customary introduction.

"Ladies and gentlemen. Thank you for remaining with us into the night. I promise you won't be disappointed. So, without further ado let me introduce..."

The only door that led into the Private auction room outside of the fire door rattled open at the last minute. He had given strict orders for that door to be closed when the proceedings began. The private security firm were usually so efficient, but they were nowhere to be seen. The door opened gently, like a gust of wind had nudged it, allowing a man and woman through to hold it open. They were deathly pale in complexion, athletic and very well-dressed. The duo seemed to bow their heads as what felt like a force of nature entered the room. A statuesque black woman, strode in, the disconcerting energy of her character was so overwhelmingly strong, the women in attendance blanched, and the men fixed on her mesmerising glide. She wore a black couture hat with a veil that covered her eyes but were unable to contain the negative magnetism they emanated. Two men got up tripping over each other as she approached and without recognition or acknowledgement of the act of chivalry she elegantly slipped into a seat, her aides stepping to the back of the room. Mr Fletcher looked on at the new arrival, a bewildering, overwhelming sense of panic over took him like a frightened gazelle being chased by cheetahs in the prairie.

He shuddered.

Absurd, he told himself although his heart was racing. He mentally went through his list of non-attendees and surmised the woman was the high net worth Jamaican entrepreneur. He wondered what her interest was in all this and continued where he had left off, his Adam's apple bobbing nervously in his throat.

"The first lot in our series is the Heart of Ares."

A slide with images of the item appeared on the wall behind him. He continued.

"This item was created by an obscure fifteenth century German philosopher alchemist and explorer Gustaf Kholer who supposedly found the parts in the grave of a demigod in the islands of Greece. With his extensive research and an ancient manuscript, he assembled the Heart of Ares which he thought was a weapon." He pauses for effect. "Because of the request of the seller we have an extraordinary situation where the seller wants to gauge interest before delivering the item to us. Instead the seller wants to offer you the detailed note book of Herr Kholer himself, over four hundred years old, three hundred and forty-three pages, bound in dragon skin."

There were some disgruntled sighs from the audience, but he pressed on.

"If you consult your tablets, you will see the specifications and the seals of authenticity from our esteemed panel of experts. Can we begin. Bidding at two hundred and fifty thousand pounds."

There was a buzz of anticipation after the announcement like a wave of static electricity was passing between the bidders. Then the auction began in earnest. The bids were fast and furious and in moments the value was just one million pounds with paddles from different parts of the room going up and down as Mr Fletcher increased the value in increments, his verbal gymnastics providing the mirth and banter. A tipping point was reached quickly bidders were falling away and as a value surpassed the one million-pound mark only two bidders remained. Monsignor Letioni and Patriarch Abebe against the scary Jamaican woman. One of the skills that sets a good auctioneer from a great one, is your ability to remember faces, names and gestures. In an auction of this calibre, seasoned collectors had their own unique ways of indicating their bids. He never forgot a gesture. He could pick out a continuing bid from the discontinued one from a whole catalogue of body language. The clergy were unimaginative in their sign language - . Just a stern nod of the head. Miss Pheare on the other hand was downright sophisticated. She sat regally with her legs crossed, one hand on her lap and the other below the level of her chair but within his sight. She moved her fingers in a fluid intricate pattern using middle, index and thumb. He would have said her fingers signs were not just reminiscent but exactly like a Wallachian Prince who had visited his auction room a few years ago. How did a black woman understand hand gestures used by a Romanian prince? You couldn't just stumble upon something like that and to use it as fluently as she did was no accident. She sat unperturbed. Long unstocking legs crossed, on her feet were treacherously long stilettos obviously designer, her back straight, her dress form-fitting. He couldn't read much from her face especially her eyes because they were shielded but she was a study in calm.

Except...

Her full lips were a deep red and they parted every so often as if she was repeating a word to someone close. And for one heartbeat then two he was caught in the soundless exchange. Her tongue flickering in the darkness of her mouth. And then the auctioneer snapped out of it, catching himself pausing then looking over at his audience, his experience rescued a potentially embarrassing situation just as his faculties aligned again.

He cleared his throat.

"We have a one point five million bid for the Gustaf Kholer's notebook. From the lady in the back row. Do we have any more bids?"

A hand slowly rised from the religious contingent. The auctioneer sounded surprised.

"A million seven hundred and fifty thousand pounds." He said.

The Jamaican woman formed the sign with her fingers unfazed.

"Two Million Pounds!"

This had become a two-man race and the rest of the congregated buyers watched in breathless excitement and envy as the to and fro bidding elevated the value to over £2 million in minutes. The auctioneer had a duty to make this entertaining as well as profitable and he was a slave to the momentum of the bidding which had noticeably slowed from the Vatican camp. Not so from the Jamaican woman's point of view. She hadn't hesitated since all of this began. Mr Fletcher wondered what was going through that cold and calculating mind of hers.

Then again, he didn't want to.

Miranda Pheare smiled as she felt the men of God crumbling. They had started so well, she thought. But the Vatican contingent was losing focus as she filled their heads with a psychic fog of doubt and despondency. It wasn't just in their eyes but Mirandah could feel some of their spirits break and it was like music to her ears. They weren't naive, they came prepared with a plan if they came across such as her. The power of the Nazerene who the Christians worshipped was not to be scoffed at especially from the more experienced believers but like any discipline, faith required time to master.

Maintaining that bubble of belief in the Son of God, would make it difficult breach their defences.

But it only takes one.

One weak link.

The boy amongst them.

Miranda sensed that the Ethiopian Orthodox neophyte had been coached extensively before attending this event with his elders.

She would have done the same in their shoes but how do you prepare for the arrival of someone such as herself. A force unlike anything the human cattle could comprehend. Miranda waited patiently for the inevitable. The young man had controlled his curiosity all this time and maybe thought, what harm could it do? So, he checked out this person playing mind games with them. He turned, looking back at his adversary and all the discipline he had mustered went to ruin. Eye contact was all it took. Miranda trapped him like a fly in a spider's web, like a bee in honey.

She smiled again, her fangs extending as she gripped the saplings mind and entering the soft folds of his flesh.

She sighed.

Her nipples hardened, and she felt herself getting wet being around such innocence. It was intoxicating, and she almost regretted having to crush him. The vampire enjoyed his body. Explored every organ and every vessel. The blood flowing through him was whispering to her rhythmically, like the beginning of a concerto. The urge to abandon her plans, rip out the young one's throat and feel his hot virgin blood flow across her tongue was difficult.

But she was a queen and she would bring this game to an end as quickly as possible. She stroked the psychic connection like an erection and squeezed. She could feel the blood flowing through his veins but ignored the others, a practised skill she developed to reduce overwhelm when she moved amongst the cattle. But once she made that connection she was touching their unwilling minds and her urges wereere wild. Her exterior was cool but inside was turmoil.

"Ah!" She thought squeezing the young man's mind. Miranda uncrossed and crossed her legs, the heat between her thighs increasing.

"Two million, five hundred thousand pounds   is where we are at ladies and gentlemen. The group in the corner needs to respond." The auctioneer leaned into his microphone and then sipped from a glass of water.

The Vatican contingent did not respond but something was wrong. The neophyte standing beside an elder collapsed suddenly, his eyes never leaving the Jamaican woman, all the way to the ground.

Miranda squeezed the boy's mind some more.

The neophyte sat rigid, propped up by one of the elders, breathing heavily, his eyes glazing over, and blood begins to trickle down his nose. The Monseigneur in the Vatican camp raised his paddle fearfully and the auctioneer boomed out an incremental increase totally ignoring to the drama unfolding. The young seminarian began to sob gently his posture set rigid by the influence of Miranda's mental tentacles.

The corners of the vampire's lips turn up ever so slightly as she enjoyed the sport and the access to the virgin boy's body and mind. The mental manipulation of her puppy was amusing her, but she was already planning how she would kill him and acquire the book in the process. The slimy tentacles of her mental influence reached to the boys' lungs and she gleefully began to deprive him of oxygen. Blood is dripping from the young man's eyes and nose, his muscles spasming. The church elders were on their feet, making signs of the cross, saying raspy prayers, anything to help the boy. The more capable among them was administering CPU, all thoughts of the bidding had departed. Rupert Fletcher's mercenary instincts maintained the pace and continued taking Miranda's bid.

"Two million, seven hundred thousand once," he blurted out. "Two million, seven hundred thousand twice." The auctioneer slammed the hammer down on the gavel with a crack. "Sold to the determined lady in black for Two million, seven hundred thousand pounds."

A sigh whispered through Miranda's lips and she could feel the young man slip away. She had to restrain the orgasmic surge she experienced, the urge to drink him dry as his life force ebbed away.

Ah, well.

There would be more opportunities. She stood from her seat with satisfaction, gliding out of the room, the chaos around her inconsequential. Her coat bellowed behind her and the two Clan familiars fell in close step. Miranda had the Book and the Heart of Ares would be next.

17.

"Thanks Nanny." Shaft said to the quiet albino woman. "I can make my way up."

The intense woman nodded and left him to mount the sweeping staircase to the upper levels. He turned to thank her again but she was nowhere to be seen.

"Damn!" The housekeeper was stealthy as hell and not for a minute, did he believe she was a simple cook from Jamaica. That kind of movement required training and he could sense that glimmer of subdued ferocity in those pretty grey eyes. With that thought still tickling his enquiring mind he jogged up the stairs on the left and strolled the familiar route to Y's room. He could never get over how lavish this place was and how the girls just fell into this sweet deal. This 'sweet deal' as he called it was far from what it seemed. The truth was, for what they had been through and would go through they deserved it all.

Shaft padded down the hall and found himself slowing as he thought about the woman he was attracted to and intricately linked with. He wouldn't admit this to anyone but the only place he felt safe after his first true encounter with the supernatural was here. When he was here, he could take a step back and relax. No worrying about being the fearless leader, none of that hard-bastard persona he had cultivated for the cut throat environment of being a copper. This place and the women that occupied it had that effect on him. Shaft didn't visit the mansion enough, didn't visit Y enough.

She was one of the most physically attractive women he knew outside of her sisters-in-arms. Come on. Dark skin, deep brown eyes, an inch taller than him, a feminine physique to die for, a born leader and smart, scarily so. That alone was intimidating but she was a Guardian of the light, for fuck sake. An ancient force of nature gifted with abilities that even she did not fully understand. This was coming from a man who would have never believed this talk of the supernatural a year or so ago but here he was.

Damn, he missed her sometimes.

This would sound strange to most especially if you had never seen the things he'd seen but Ms Yvonne Sinclair was his touch stone. He was sure Y didn't have a clue he was feeling like that. She just thought it was the mutual attraction they had for each other. But no, it was much more, she grounded him. Thinking about her helped him when he was feeling overwhelmed. But being around her did the trick of relieving his anxiety everytime. In a crisis or relaxing together, he loved being around her. Y made the insanity of their last case 'normal'. And when you were in the bubble of their influence you began to believe it too. Shaft had to step out of her shadow and into the the 'ordinary world' and that was the challenge for his mental state. Not many people had their beleif's implode and get introduced to a world alongside your own filled with demons and sorcerers. That level of acceptance would take time and Y's calming effect helped him immeasurably.

He stood at Y's door and knocked. Always one knock and a reply.

"Hey baby. Come in I'm in the shower." Now these were the little things that freaked him out. Her voice came to him as if she was just behind the door but knowing the arrangement of her room and the fact that she was in the shower and speaking to him so clearly was impossible. He pushed the door open and entered the high ceiling large double bedroom. The crown prince of Reggae, Dennis Brown sang his classics in the background forming a cocoon of calm. The splash of water impacting on the shower curtain came from the en-suite bathroom. Shaft could only shake his head and smile. The word impossible began to lose significance around these chicks and he should know better. He gently placed the roses and apples on a chair beside her old school vanity desk and plopped himself on the double bed.

"I'll be out in a second." Y called from the shower but Shaft was trapped in the comfort of this bed. The mattress formed a man-size depression around him and he felt buoyed up on clouds.

"Take your time." Shaft called back

"Are you sure." Y asked.

"Of course. Don't rush on my account. Oh, and don't forget to wash behind your ears."

Shaft grabbed the pillow and tucked it under his head sighing contentedly. He took in a lungful of Y's scent.

Freaky, maybe.

He didn't care

Shaft let the tension of the last few days seep away. He hadn't realised how wound up he was. He was drifting and suddenly he felt a pleasurable damp weight slide onto him, with the words.

"You look so tense, Detective." He hadn't heard her leave the bathroom or approach him. What is it with these ninja women in this house?

'Umm, I am." Shaft stammered.

He preferred to be on top but wouldn't complain. Y looked into his eyes, wrapped in a fluffy terry towel, her dark skin glistening, her hair short and barbered. He could feel her nakedness, the shape of her groin, her hairless pubic area and her ample ass as she pressed on him playfully straddling his waist.

"I miss you. What can I do to make it better." She teased grinning broadly.

Your killing me, Shaft thought.

"Is that a trick question?" He asked innocently

"No." She said feigning confusion and kissed him on the forehead. "What can Miss Sinclair, the lady of the bathroom towel, do for you."

'Role-playing,' Shaft thought almost blurting out the 'S' word but Y had already beaten his response with a suggestion.

"You're so tense and gloomy. Let me give you a shoulder rub. Balance out your chakras."

"Is it that obvious?" Shaft asked.

"It is," she answered. "Now take off your shirt."

He did it without question.

"Be gentle with me." He dramatized his vulnerability, nearly laughing out loud, at on how he sounded.

"Chill." Y laughed.

Then after thinking about it, Shaft asked.

"I could take off my pants too and we could do an all over body massage." He pushed her boundaries.

Y pinched him on his arm.

"Hey!" Shaft whined. "I'm kidding.".

"You've forgotten we have a meeting?"

"No," He mumbled. "You sound like Suzy."

"Why thank you." Y bowed knowing it wasn't meant as a compliment.

Y slid off him and he hid his embarrassment by turning on his stomach before standing up and undoing his shirt.

"Straddle the chair cowboy and lower your head." Y said.

Shaft did as was requested, closing his eyes. Y came behind him and lay her hands on his shoulders. He could smell the oil she had applied to her hands and immediately he felt a dark nugget of pain dislodge and dissipate. If that felt good it was about to get better. Y leaned into his back and he could feel the material of the bath towel and her strong fingers positioning themselves on his neck. The towel that had wrapped her body slipped from between them and fell to the floor in a heap.

Shaft gulped.

The flesh of her tight stomach and portions of her breasts glanced his back as she moved. He was reacting like he'd never had a beautiful woman massage his back from behind with no clothes on before.

Just be cool.

"Comfortable?" Shaft asked unable to help himself.

"Very," Y said. "Now less talking and more groaning."

"Yes, Ma'am."

His eyes flitted to the closest reflexive surface he could find but Y eased his head back down, knowing what he was trying to do.

"No peeking, mister," she said.

Shaft did his best Whacky Races, Muttley character impersonation and was rewarded with her laughter. He sighed contentedly and swore he was ready to take on the world again. In the meantime, he let Y's expert fingers relieve the tension in his shoulders and neck.

Moments later, Shaft walked into the conservatory and was met by warm hugs from Suzy and Patra. He missed them both. Suzy had been away for months, Patra for two. They hadn't met up like this for a while and he didn't like thinking about it but amidst the laughter and warmness they felt for each other, a shadow hung ominiosly about them. At any moment something otherworldly could rear its ugly head and they had to be ready.

This was what the Guardians did.

How they processed it all was beyond him. He was a passenger and could jump off at any time. They couldn't.

"You two weren't bumping ugly, where you?" Patra asked with a straight face.

Suzy shook her head.

"And why would you ask that?" Shaft kept his cool but a prickle of embarrassment was feathering his cheeks.

"Chill, G you don't smell of booty unless you had a shower? Did you have a shower?"

"Don't encourage her, Winston." Y advised.

"Leave Winston alone gal." Suzy said. "Yuh too nosy."

"What?" Patra protested with her hands up." You bitches need to chill. I was just observing that he missed a button on his shirt."

Shaft looked quickly down at himself.

"Shit," he muttered.

"I'm practising my observation and deduction skills." Patra said her face all contrite.

"Deh only thing you are practising is poking yuh nose in other people's business."

Patra grinned.

"What are homies for, if I can't improve my skills with them?"

"You are full of shit." Y said amused at how far her sister would go for some juicy gossip.

Then somebody said.

"When you three are done embarrassing my breddrin Shaft, we can begin deh briefing."

Shaft recognised the voice immediately but couldn't see the possessor of the Jamaican accent.

"Dem love you really pardy." It said again.

That's when Shaft's ears led his eyes over to a monitor that was facing away from where they were all standing, attached to an articulated arm on a frame and wired for sound and a webcam. Spokes, their mentor looked out at him from somewhere that looked hot. The older man, seemed relaxed with a straw trilby on his head.

"Hey, didn't know you would be in on the meeting?" Shaft asked. Then said. "Why are you facing that way?"

"Dem forget me," Spokes said matter-o-factly. "But I could hear you and them mouthing off." He laughed. "Deh sound and visuals on this rig is really good."

Shaft adjusted the large monitor with the webcam on top, so Spokes could see and hear everything much better.

"You looking sharp rudie,"Shaft said delighted to see him.

"Irie, Irie," Spokes nodded. "Glad to see the sisters are looking after you,"

"Barely," Shaft quipped, lowering his voice.

"Whaddup OG?" Patra said to the transmission.

"Hey Father," Suzy said.

Y just waved at him crazily.

He beamed at them.

"Blouse an skirt. You girls looking good, like cook food." Spokes said excitedly.

The respect on both sides was obvious. Facing the screen Suzy and Y sat. Patra leaned on Suzy's chair about to light one of the aromatic Cuban cigars she favoured while Shaft stood with his arms folded. Spokes leaned into the screen from wherever he was in the world.

"It's good to see you together again, unfortunately, I wish it was under better circumstances." Spokes adjusted the trilby on his greying head.

"I heard about the terrorism attack at Westminster. My Snake ring knew the story was a rass lie from day one." He kissed the ancient looking adornment on his forefinger. "It remains my only magical possession but after a year I can't live without it. After the news, my mind settled on my daughters in the big city. Something was brewing and I wanted to know what."

"Vampires," Y said.

Shaft made awkward half turn towards the girls.

"I knew it. How are you lot involved in my case?" He asked bluntly.

"Your case?" Suzy asked. "Yuh leading deh investiga-tion?"

Shaft nodded slowly.

"We had a job." Y began, "We escorted our client to a fundraiser. Which just so happened to be ground zero for your murder scene."

"You were there?" Shaft asked knowing after his outburst he shouldn't be surprised.

"We were away with our client before shit went sideways." Patra said. "It was a hunch."

"Suzy?" Shaft asked.

Suzy nodded gravely.

"I felt someting was wrong when I was in China. Hard to explain."

"Try me." Shaft said.

Suzy dredged up the memory with her shoulders slumping and a sigh. Her words were low and wistful.

"The stink of an abattoir, a taste of blood in my mouth. The air a nasty liquid with something living in it. Something dragging you down trying to claim you, infest you."

Suzy breathed deeply.

Shaft shuddered almost sorry he had asked.

"What was the crime scene like?" Patra asked impa-tiently rolling the unlit cigar in her fingers.

Shaft shrugged.

"I wasn't there when it was hot. I got dragged into it later. But from the reports and some of the bodies I saw it was a horror house. CCTV cameras saw nothing. The entire building was thrown into darkness. All electrics burned out and if that wasn't strange enough almost the entire silver service staff have disappeared."

"Yuh check the records?" Spokes asked.

"We're In the process but we've been coming up dry."

"I don't think you're going to find anything." Y added.

"And you say that because..."

"Because Detective," Patra picked up the thought. "These were some fake ass bitches, believe me. When we looked real close, we could see the cracks in the charade. We wanted to see more but we had to get out of dodge."

"What kind of cracks?" Shaft asked.

"They were tattooed." Y said. "Carrying strange symbols as ink on their necks and wrists. They just didn't fit."

Patra shook her head in disbelief at a memory.

"One nigger had the symbol on his eyeball. You believe that shit. We talking some committed motherfuckers here."

"Check the mansions database?" Spokes said. "Use deh resources, you have. Your facilities are second to none. I'm not a multimillionaire for nothing." He paused. "An by deh way send me a drawing of one of those symbols, these duppies were sporting. I'll do a search my end."

"I'll send it to you." Patra said.

Spokes nodded.

"I'm thinking the tattoos could be some kind of rank-ing." Shaft mused. "Or just vampire tribal markings."

Shaft breathed deeply, lines on his forehead deepen-ing

"This is the UK's largest murder scene for the last fif-ty years. But it's not unique. This kind of thing has hap-pened before. They concealed it well but as far as records go back this has been happening across the country."

Suzy ran her fingers through her hair, her eyes thin slits as if she was looking inside herself at a world unlike our own. Suzy had a quiet intensity about her that made you want to listen to what she had to say.

"Dem call you in because them know this is no ordi-nary mass murder, right. We got called because some-thing or someone is making waves that I felt half way across the other side of the world."

Shaft was nodding his head in agreement

"Let us do what we do and you can make sense of this through traditional police work."

Suzy smiled and gave him a nod.

"I know our ways are alien to you brother Shaft but don't treat dis any different from you would a standard murder case." Suzy stood up. "We won't muddy deh wa-ters with our ways. Just remember, we both were called for dis."

Shaft didn't try to argue with Suzy's reasoning.

Spokes agreed with a shake of his head.

"We need to know more, an I tink I can help in dat regard. You sisters ready to do some footwork?

"We got to?" Patra asked.

"Tink of deh adventure." Suzy said.

"You may learn something Miss P." Y added.

"Yeah, manners." Suzy quipped.

Patra gave Suzy her favourite finger, giving it a twist for emphasis.

Through the monitor a scantily clad woman came into shot, showing off only her midriff She whispered something in Spokes ear.

He brightened.

"I have some business to attend to daughters but I'm sending you the contacts now. Don't wait follow dem up asap." He looked up at them with intensity.

"Keep me updated seen."

The monitor went dead.

18.

Spitalfields Market has been a place of trade for over two hundred years, providing East London's traders and consumers with everything a household would need from the reign of King George to present day. The man Spokes had advised them to see was a Mr Dave Godden Esquire. the most recent owner of a family run fruit and vegetable import export business that had been established 300 years ago.

Spokes had left it at that.

There present location may not be the top end emporium; the girls were very familiar with but obtaining honorary degrees in shopping meant they could apply their skills to any environment that used trade as its means of dialogue. The ladies walked through the market knowing they were on business but still were attracted by unique trinkets, sale items and that thing you always wanted to buy but never got around to. As they kept weaving through the stalls they became more tightly situated and the items on sale became correspondingly weirder.

"Remind me again, why we are here?" Patra asked, looking at the stall with an array of mechanical insects that were made from metal scraps and powered by watch springs.

"We've talked to a couple people, who know a lot about vampires but nothing concrete to help us with this." Y said.

"And a shopkeeper?" Patra asked confused.

"He's an old spar of Spokes." Suzy said.

"Does that nigga know any ordinary folk ? They either gangsters, hustlers or Twilight people."

"At least Spokes is never boring," Y said. "Keeping you on your toes."

"That he does." Patra agreed.

Y paused for a moment, held her head back as if she was absorbing the sigts and sounds. Then said.

"We good, Suzy?"

"We not walking into a trap if dat is what you're asking." The empath said. "I feel no chickeenee business."

"Good to know." Patra said.

They kept moving through the stalls and in moments they could sense the edges of the vast market coming to meet them. Suddenly the business premises they were looking for loomed ahead, like a huge rusting metal fortress that wasn't built but was pushed whole from out of the earth. At the front of what could have easily been a titans lair hung a cast iron sign that read Godden and sons established, 1645. The girls looked at each other.

Patra piped up.

"No way, this market is that old."

Y kept walking towards the big metal double doors.

"I think they built the market around this thing." She pointed to the leviathan building, that looked like it had been hewn from a hill of rusted Iron. "And not the other way around. It looks old with a few modern touches."

The doors were partially open, but Suzy banged on it anyway poking her head through the crack.

"Hello!" She hollered her voice echoing in the cavernous interior. "Hello!" She said again.

Patra brushed past her impatiently, locating a buzzer that looked out of place and pressed.

"When God was issuing manners gal, yuh stayed home." Suzy said.

"Ms Wong, for an empath you're just too slow," Patra teased.

Suzy kissed her teeth and the sound through her lips was like a rip of cloth.

Y stood back amused at her sister's banter but expecting a sting in the tail of their little confrontation and she wasn't disappointed. Patra saw the three sets of green luminescent eyes first, while Suzy's finely tuned ears heard the low growls at about the same time. But their reaction to the unexpected guests were polar opposites.

"Motherf......" Patra swore and backed out of the door quickly, her fists up, merging into a fight stance. "You knew didn't you." Patra hissed, glaring at Suzy as she backed up to stand beside Y. Suzy shrugged innocently still standing at the entrance. Without hesitation she walk into the darkness beyond the door. There was no sound for a moment. Then after a while Suzy's head popped around the door grinning broadly.

"Yuh tink me have all day, come meet some friends of mine."

Tentatively Y and Patra entered and suddenly a small wedge of darkness suddenly lit up in welcome from an overhead spotlight. Suzy was on her knees hugging one of three huge furry canines that sat on their haunches with their tongues out.

"Aren't they just the cutest," Suzy said. "Meet Ares, Zeus and Hades."

"Cute, yeah," Patra said uncertainly.

"I won't even ask how you knew their names." Y said.

"Me neither." Patra mumbled.

Suzy tilted her head stood up and the dogs looking like the gods of Olympus had surely split Cerberus the guardian of the underworld into three, mimicked their newfound friends' movement. A piercing whistle made them stand to attention and their ears prick up. All three dogs bounded away down a darkened aisle that seemed to disappear into eternity.

The sounds of quick steps approached, and a jovial voice accompanied the echoing march. The white man that came into view was mid height, one earing, wearing a grey flat cap and grey shopkeepers coat. hand outstretched and his eye twinkling with an unusual optimism.

"This is an absolute pleasure to meet you," the man said vigorously shaking their hands in turn. "When the boys told me, you were here I had to come down and see for myself." He shook his head and smiled. "The Guardians of the Light. As I live and breathe."

Y and Patra looked at each other.

"Mr. Godden?" Y asked.

"And Sons," he added. "In the flesh," he continued. "And at your service."

"The sons?" Patra asked.

"Funny you should ask that." A smile brightened his face and his eyes twinkled some more.

"For my sins I have four daughters and not one of them wanted anything to do with the family business. God bless em." He smiled and the corners of his eyes wrinkled. "I couldn't bring myself to turn up my nose to tradition. So, this scruffy lot are my sons." He pointed to the big canines and they whined.

"Tradition is important Mr Godden. We are testament to that." Y said.

"It is indeed and it warms my heart to see it still has its place. especially in these dangerous times."

"You heard?" Suzy asked.

"I have my little dicky birds who keep me current."

"I have a feeling dat if anyone knows what's happening on these streets, you do."

"You're too kind, Miss Young. And that's why my boys like you."

Suzy grinned nudging Patra who shook her head condescendingly.

"You know why we're here?" Y said.

Mr Godden nodded.

"Unfortunately, yes."

"How can you help us?" Asked Y.

"Let's just say over the years I've imported more than the bog-standard fruit and veg. Come on let me show you something."

As they were ushered through the vast warehouse for each step they smelt a different succulent fruit that made their mouths water. The experience was more intense because they were mainly in the dark. A dark that was impenetrable but not ominous, just vast and limitless. As they moved the squares of light seamlessly followed them.

"Conserving on energy?" Patra asked trying to peer into the murky darkness.

Mr Godden laughed heartily.

"No need Ms Jones. Here we're powered by the great city of London and its people. Once we don't run out of optimism and the old Dunkirk Spirit, I've got power to spare."

He led them to an office on the ground floor whose interior lit up when he opened the door. He ushered the girls inside and the huge dogs followed them to the threshold, sitting on their haunches looking into the surrounding darkness with darting alert eyes.

"The puppies look nervous." Suzy asked as Mr God-den encouraged the girls to sit.

"My boys are very sensitive to the changes ebbs and flows affecting our world. And they pride themselves in keeping me safe."

"Why would they be worried about you?" Suzy asked.

"Very good question, Yvonne." He said pausing. "You don't mind me calling you Yvonne, do you?"

"Of course not." Y said graciously.

"When you've been in the fruit and veg business as long as I have you acquire contacts around the world, you begin to understand how we are all connected on this plane of existence."

Patra and Suzy were nodding.

"If you look hard enough and have the years of experience as I do you can start seeing the patterns."

"No disrespect Mr G but I don't see how a business-man in a warehouse full of bananas can help us."

"Patra!" Y said exasperated. "You got somewhere to go. What's the rush?"

"I'm just saying." Patra shrugged.

"That's okay, Yvonne," Mr Gordon said. "I appreciate Cleopatra's honesty. The Guardians have work to do and I tend to waffle on with my point. But it is important for you to see this."

Mr Godden had walked over to three crates made from slats of wood and stuffed with some fibres that looked like hay, a hot brand of indeterminate design was left on the crates side. He hefted the wooden box at the top and brought it to his desk. Immediately there was a sickly-sweet smell wafting from inside. Y wrinkled her nose.

"Yuh produce is rotten Mr G. Them need refrigeration."

Mr Godden nodded grimly at Suzy.

"Nothing I do would stop this blight, ladies." He took out a screwdriver and pried off the top placing it neatly beside it. All eyes followed his into the interior.

"Damn!" Patra stepped closer to get a better look at the rotting and infested fruit.

"What was it?"

"Ambrosia," Mr Godden said. "Exceptionally rare. Thought to have been brought to Romania by a Catholic priest now a saint. It has curative properties and it is very sweet when fit but is mainly known for its arcane abilities."

"Meaning," Y asked.

"The locals ate it and also used it as an early warning system against certain types of predators."

"Predators?" Patra asked.

"The two legged, blood sucking, nocturnal variety," he said. "The undead kind."

He let that sink in.

"What I'm saying is it decays when vampires are in close proximity."

"How close?" Patra asked.

"a hundred or so metres."

"Are you saying Vampires were here?" Y asked.

He smiled grimly.

"You having a laugh! The boys would have them for supper." He sighed heavily. "This level of rot with no bloodsucker anywhere near us, says to me that London has the displeasure of hosting a nosferatu of the highest order. I am sorry to say ladies, but this looks bad."

Y frowned and asked.

"What does he want?"

Mr Godden considered the question taking off his cap and showing a full set of greying hair.

"The he is a she," Mr Godden said. "She has been here before, my grandad confirmed it."

"A vampire bitch." Patra chimed in.

"Grandad Monty told me she's from the West Indies."

"How could he know that Mr G?" Suzy asked.

For the first time Mr. Godden looked uncomfortable. He put his cap back on his head and smoothed it on his skull before replying.

"Godden & Sons is not known for its moral compass. What we are known for are the best fruit and veg in the known and unknown worlds. We don't judge our customers."

"And we won't judge you G," Patra added quickly.

Mr Godden nodded and smiled.

"Have you ever heard of the Hell Fire Club?"

"No." Y said.

"It sounds like a strip joint, but I know all of London's titty bars. Never heard that name before."

Suzy said nothing.

"If my history is correct." Mr. Godden began. "The Hell Fire Club was a name given to several exclusive clubs created for high society fiends, villains, rakes and so-called seekers of truth which was established in Britain and Ireland in the 18th century. It was said that one of their number a Rosicrucian dreamt of a club in London that would be the social hub for supernatural beings of any moral leaning." He took a breath. "A kind of neutral ground, where our kind can interact without judgement."

"A kind of Geneva for freaks." Patra said without thinking.

"A higher station of freak, that my family has been providing fruit and Veg for ever since it was established."

"Wow!" Y said. "The stories you could tell."

"Deh vampire woman is a guest at dis club, nuh true?" Suzy asked.

Mr Godden nodded.

"How do you know that for sure?" Y asked.

"Her favourite fruit is the Rwandan Blood Orange. It's a mutated tree that only fruits in fields of massacres and bloodletting. The orange fruit is riddled with human blood and an order of six boxes came from the club two weeks ago."

Y groaned.

19.

A yaro stood wishing his colleagues and drinking partners adieu to shouts of good-natured rebuke and piss taking.

"I've got work tomorrow unlike you alcoholic layabouts."

"Just admit it," someone shouted. "You drink like my tee-total granny."

"Not mine." Somebody else shot back."

Ayaro gave them the finger and guessed if they failed in architecture his friends would be world-class drunks.

"See you tomorrow?" The laughter carried with him as he left the stylish gastro pub and made his way down the quiet south London street. Ayaro hadn't driven because he knew he'd be worse for wear and would just stop in the cab office he had passed on his way to meet his colleagues. He was rummaging around in his jacket, looking for his phone when he saw the statuesque woman coming his way. Ayaro stopped to watch her more keenly and continued his search for his phone.

"Shit!" He must have left it at the pub. Swearing again he took one last look at the passing woman and turned to head back in the direction of the pub. As he took one step in that direction, he felt someone grab his shoulder and tried to force him to his knees. He tried to shrug the hand off, but it gripped his clavicle with enough power to snap it. He tried to wriggle free, but he was forced down to his knees with an overwhelming strength he couldn't overcome. He looked up and his surprise turned to horror as he recognised his assailant.

The well-dressed woman he had been ogling as she passed him.

But how did she get from where he had left her to where she was now? And more importantly why was she dragging him into the darkened space between two stores as if he weighed nothing.

Ayaro tried to reach back and pry the hand that held his shoulder fast, but it felt like a sheet of steel welded in place, unrelenting and cold. He let out a scream that in a less desperate moment he would not admit had come from his lips. In an absolutely crazy moment he was concerned about his Russell Hobbs leather boots being scraped to shit on the pavement. And then the abject horror returned, the attractive woman with the superhuman strength, launch him into the air, watching him bounce off the wall and land heavily into the detritus laden shrubs between the buildings. The space was cramped, and it stank of piss and much worst, the smell smacking him into awareness with enough force, he raised himself up, but he was in pain from the impact. He had shattered bones, he knew it and if he had any ideas of escape, they were wishful thinking.

Panic drove him to keep frantically trying to drag himself away, but the insanity needle hit the red zone and all normalcy departed to hell. From the neck down this woman could be an advertising executive but the nightmare face snarling back at him made his grip on reality totter and slip. Ayaro screamed and the creature in the woman's skin smiled an abomination of a smile. Elongated canines erupted amidst an arsenal of vicious sharp teeth bursting through her gums, eyes blazing, forehead slanted back, brow furrowed and broad. A flat snout upturned at the tip like a vampire bat as the woman-thing sniffed the air

Strolling towards him, she ran her talons across the walls with both hands teasingly, digging trails into the masonry and mocking him as he lost all composure. Then all jesting departed, and the nightmare woman lunged, teeth bared, and talons splayed.

She didn't reach her prey.

A shadow moved just a bit faster. Rebounding off both walls and smashing feet first into the creature. It screeched, flapping along the grimy ground and messing up her designer emsemble.

The shadow that was now recognisably a man stood watching the woman get to her feet. He was tall, athletic, jeans, tracksuit top, North African extraction and pale olive skin.

"How many times have you been told not to play with your food?"

"Dean Thorne!" the woman howled. "You should mind your business; the mistress will be pissed off."

Dean shook his head.

"I don't give a fuck. Just because she's in town doesn't mean you can do whatever you please. This part of London is still under my protection."

The woman made testing step towards the gibbering victim. Dean met her step with the words.

"Test me!"

The woman bellowed in frustration, a meal slapped from her slavering jaw.

"Your time will come, Thorne."

"I welcome it." Dean said.

The woman turned heel and bounded up the wall defying gravity for a moment, then scurrying along it, leaping back to the litter strewn ground and heading into the High Street.

"Women," Dean said simply and offered his hand to the man trembling on the ground.

It was cold and very strong.

Dean Thorne was walking casually down the high Street moments after the incident, when a black old-style Rolls Royce Phantom pulled up beside him. He knew who it was immediately.

The window wound down.

"DJ Faustus, that's the name you go by, nowadays right?" Dean asked.

"What's in a name?" The man in the darkened interior said.

"True," Dean agreed. "It's been a while. How can I help?"

"I may have a deterrent against Miranda Pheare. Have you ever heard of the Guardians of the Light?"

Deans smile widened, showing his unusually long canines.

20.

Y looked up at the demolition site that was Chase Estates and she shivered involuntarily. She had done her research. The Chase Estates whose concrete towers, parks, playgrounds and walkways sprawled across five acres of south London was to make way for more forward-thinking architecture. All four towers had been demolished leaving two smaller and crude looking monolithic stacks and the associated infrastructure. The two remaining high rises housed the nine rebel tenants who would not be moved until adequate homes were found for them. It was a stand against the system and caught the public's imagination. Y just thought it was the strangest place to have a meeting about a mystical artefact.

Amanda Walker had reached out to them because of their podcast. Patra had begun the email conversation but Y had decided to make the introductions in person to see if there new client wanted to do business. Ever since Spokes had been bequeathed with a vast collection of esoteric artefacts, he had gone to unbelievable lengths to keep their secrets contained and add to his mystical holdings when the opportunity arose. Through his international network of auctioneers, he got offers. Most were of historical relevance and nothing more. While some were the real deal. But what was rarer was Y and the girls finding valuable items themselves.

It was mid evening and the cacophony of hammers, drills and engines was ebbing. Y was on edge as soon as she arrived. She would have liked to have said the chaos had darkened her mood, but she knew there was more to it than that. Nanny had unintentionally passed on a viral unease that had Y, even more wary than usual.

Earlier, dressed in her bolero leather jacket, jeans and riding boots, Y pushed open the palatial double doors of the mansion to drive into London.

"Mistress!" Y had stopped immediately; the Jamaican woman had a way of throwing her voice like a ventriloquist especially when she needed your attention. Y stopped when Nanny addressed her that way. It was endearing and a stark reminder of the albino woman's traditional Jamaican upbringing. To Y the formal titles felt like some outdated hierarchical requirement, but Nanny insisted they remain in place.

Y turned towards her.

"In these times," Nanny said cryptically. "You don't want to forget dis." She handed Y her Katana, luxuriously swaddled in Louis Vuitton leather and straps, looking more like a well-cared for snooker cue than a 14th century old katana sword. They looked at each other.

Nanny took her hand and nodded, her pale features unreadable.

"Thanks," Y said slinging it around her shoulders.

"Walk good," Nanny said and turned heading for the kitchen.

Y looked up at the building in the distance and took a deep breath, reaching behind her to feel the reassuring weight of her katana on her back. She walked along the snaking path towards Wentworth Tower the memory of Nanny fading. Y needed her full attention to navigate this labyrinth not just physically but mentally. Fifteen minutes later she was at the door of flat 28 seven stories up from a fifteen-story building. The tower block was in good condition as far as Y could see, just unkempt. Dust, leaves and newspapers were strewn everywhere. It made Y think of a mass exodus of residents because of an impending natural disaster. If you listened carefully you could hear the voices or was it the wind reciting harsh stanzas through the open corridors.

Y pressed the buzzer and stood back far enough so whoever was watching her through the peephole could see her completely. Locks on the door unlatched and there were a few.

The door swung open.

The woman standing inside was smiling. Frizzy hair, freckles and light skin. She wore a jumper jeans and fluffy socks. Inside and behind her look organised and felt welcoming.

The place smelt of incense.

"I thought you'd be late finding this place?" She said. "You are right on time. Come in, come in."

Y stepped through smiling.

"You're Yvonne, right?" Amanda asked.

"For my sins," Y said. "Dad wanted something exotic while mum wanted something elegant but understated. She won out."

"Caribbean roots I take it?" Amanda asked.

Y nodded and they both laughed.

"Something to drink?"

Both womenwere gently assessing each other.

"Mint," Y said.

Amanda shook her head in a acknowledgement.

"A purest," she said smiling. "Ginger and chamomile for me. I'll go make it."

It was easy to relax here. And Y couldn't help thinking how comfortable Amanda was with the chaos that surrounded her. Her home, her attitude all spoke of someone with an abundance of patience or skilled at burying her head in the sand. Y couldn't help but wonder which it was.

Amanda came into the lounge area with two steaming cups of herbal tea on a tray. She handed the cup over and sat opposite. Y couldn't help looking out through her panoramic window. The view across south London was spectacular.

"I love it too," Amanda said watching Y relax into her seat with cup in hand

Y took a sip of her tea.

It smelt and tasted divine.

"If you don't mind me asking, why are you still here?"

Amanda sighed, leaned forward and placed both her hands on her knees.

"My mum thinks I am crazy, and my soon-to-be ex-boyfriend is subtler and thinks I am having a mild mental breakdown."

"Are you?" Y asked concerned but interested.

Amanda laughed.

"I've discovered who I am that's all."

"So, this is a new path for you then?"

Amanda nodded.

Both women knew this was a weird way of introducing themselves to business, but Y intuitively felt this was the best way, even if it was unorthodox.

"That new path you mentioned is the reason why you're here. Because of my family's legacy." Amanda said.

"I'm just surprised," Y's brows raised. "In a good way. The few times I've had to talk business about some musty old item my benefactor was interested in buying, it's usually conducted in a lawyer's office, corporate headquarters or some lavish home in the counties."

"Never eight stories up in a tower block, that is about to be destroyed," Amanda completed.

"Never," Y said.

"And then I auctioned off a book that had been in my family for over two hundred years for a six figure sum," Amanda stated. "You must think I'm crazy."

"I was thinking that too," Y said laughing. "Not the usual actions of someone coming into money. Congratulations by the way."

"Well I can explain," Amanda said. "If I'm not boring you."

"I'm interested," Y said leaning forward.

"I never could figure out what I wanted to do with my life. I went to university, did well. I worked in Canary Wharf with an investment company and I was miserable but because everyone around me was miserable too, it felt normal." The thought made her sit up from her slouch. "On my twenty-fifth birthday I was bequeathed my inheritance. It wasn't real estate or money. It was three main items with lots of different trinkets."

"Were you disappointed?" Y edged in.

"At first," Amanda said honestly. "But when I saw my ancestor had left me piece of his life I felt differently. I'm connected with these heirlooms and instead of complicating my already hectic life, it provided me with a sense of clarity that I've never felt before. Who would have thought how close I could feel to my second Great Grandfather, the monster hunter? He's such an interesting man."

"Good feeling isn't it?" Y said nodding. "Knowing what you are meant to be in the world."

"Isn't it just, "Amanda sounded less introspective as her recollections disappeared.

"I am lucky. I won't have to work ever again. I can commit to this. Make him proud."

"I can understand that," Y said. "And what about this?" Y asked. "You living here, and your present situation."

"I just don't like being taken advantage of. Scratch that," Amanda said. "I was given the right to buy this flat after years of living here. I have seen how they've handled other tenants. Now they've decided to demolish they must stick to their promises. It is a matter of principle."

"I understand. Sometimes you have to fight for what you believe in."

"So now we have that out of the way. Let me admit firstly the Heart of Ares isn't for sale at any price."

"Okay," Y said, now interested in the real reason she was here. "My contact will be disappointed but that's business. Did we have any competition?" Y asked.

Amanda thought about it.

"You did actually, one interested party was really persistent. They were the ones who bought the notebook I was telling you about. They wouldn't take no for an answer but I gave strict instructions to the auctioneers to take my records off their books."

"Why did you contact us. It seems like you had everything in hand?" Y asked.

"A second voice of reason. A trusted friend."

"Although you didn't know us."

"I love your podcast. You made me feel like I belonged to something. And Cleopatra always mentioned acquiring interesting oddities as a part of your thing."

"Yeah," Y said knowingly. "Our thing."

"Your stories are amazing and Cleopatra is a great storyteller."

"Most people think are exploits are good stories, tall tales or flights of fancy from three women with nothing better to do. You on the other hand..."

"I believe to a degree, "she said finally.

"But grandfather Ezekiel would have definitely beleived."

Y sipped more of her tea and sank a bit more into the couch.

"So, none of you family over the ages recognised the importance of what your ancestor had left behind?"

She nodded.

"There loss is my gain. Making Ezekiel Mortimer Walker Esq, freeman and vampire Hunter 1791 – 1875 a literary figure is my job. Its my destiny."

"Wow!" Y said. "Not something you come across too often. A black man in Victorian London that can be traced back to you."

"I know unbelievable right?" Amanda gushed.

"Let me get this straight. You wanted an unbaised second opinion on your family heirloom but you're not interested in selling it. I appreciate you inviting me to your home but how can me and my sisters help?"

"The Heart is showing activity for the first time since it's been in my possession. I want to know why?"

Amanda reached over to pick up her mobile phone that was perched near.

"Activity," Y asked. "What kind?"

Amanda showed Y an image on her Smartphone.

"The Heart of Ares has a moonstone in its centre that is supposed to power it. Two weeks ago, it began glowing intermittently. Grandfather Ezekiel's diaries explained a lot, but I still don't know what it means. "

"Did your grandfather say what he used it for in his diary?" Y asked.

Amanda smiled.

"Old Ezekiel went one better, not only did he document his nocturnal activities in his diaries, he made audio accounts too."

"Audio?" Y asked.

"I thought he lived in the late Eighteenth century?"

"He did," Amanda said. "But he was a man of means and foresight. He had a phonograph and recorded and stored his thoughts and adventures for posterity."

"Shit that was high tech for the time." Y mused. "So, you had to get a phonograph yourself to play it?"

"Yep." Amanda sounded pleased. "I can afford it."

"That must be creepy, listening to the voice of an ancestor who died hundreds of years ago."

"It took a bit of getting used to but his accounts of that era and his use of the Heart, changed my life."

Y took it all in. Suzy's insistence of how important this meeting with Amanda was going to be had proven to be right. Her sister couldn't read the future but as guide to how things could turn out, from her intuition, she was second to none.

She let Amanda continue.

"I'll let you look at all my notes, the voice recordings of my Grandfathers adventures and thoughts, a copy of the inventors diary and translation from old German to English. And when you have some time you can see the Heart of Ares itself. Help me figure out what it's saying."

"You have an idea," Y asked.

"Guesses , but I want to be sure."

"I hope you're prepared for what it might tell you." Y said.

"Well that's it, Amanda admitted. "I am prepared but I have to know. Do you believe in destiny Yvonne?"

Y smiled.

"I've been asked that question a lot lately. Oh yeah, I believe. I just think some of us are armed with the knowledge to tweak the results of what others think is inevitable."

"I can't help thinking, all this didn't just happen randomly. I'm helping you and you're helping me."

Y put her cup down on the coffee table, everything that had been said between them being analysed in a mish-mash of ideas and conclusions. They were meant to be involved in this, Y knew it. She just wasn't sure why.

Then Amanda said.

"Oh, and by the way. I'll cover all your expenses until I'm happy with what we find."

Y inhaled deeply and pursed her lips.

"Okay, let's do this."

An hour later Y had said her farewells and was making her way to the ground floor of Wentworth Tower. Night time had snuck up on her as she had been through the fascinating notes, mementos and one of the phonogram copper drums. She hadn't been able to examine the Heart of Ares itself, that was housed away in a secure facility in the city. But she was shown photographs. Amazing was all she could think and those thoughts occupied her mind as she walked across a concrete walkway, leading away from the imposing structure, her footfalls echoing. Suddenly the sounds of her progress was mixing with the sound of three other people walking towards her. Two women and one man. Well dressed. They smelled of a cloying violet perfume that made her think of a funeral.

They moved with purpose and a powerful economy of motion. They brushed past Y without acknowledging her presence and kept moving towards the tower. Y stopped and looked back thinking. The group had disappeared into the murky darkness. She shrugged and headed towards her car.

Knock, knock!

Pause

Knock, knock!

Amanda jumped at the first knock. The callers hard knuckles sounded as if it could shatter the door. Amanda walked out of the kitchen mumbling, her heart racing as two more knocks exploded on the other side.

She walked slowly up to it, watching the door frame.

Knock, knock!

She knew the raps were coming but she still yelped, when they did. "Can I help you?" Amanda said trying to edit the nervous spikes from her voice. With trepidation she approached her front door and squinted into the spy aperture installed at her height, magnifying a tight area of the corridor in front of her home. The grey concrete outside was empty. Amanda stepped back.

Kids.

No. She couldn't deny the sense of dread she was experiencing

Knock, knock, knock!

Amanda steeled herself and approached the door again her body tense with expectation. The front door itself was a heavy-duty beast and that fact reassured her. The decision to protest against removal by the Council while they demolished the estate, had come not just with legal considerations but with some commonsense choices and security was one of them. The door was something between store room and vault in its girth. Four copper carbide chains with sliders bolted to the wall and the door's structure, making them look like rejects from an Inquisition dungeon.

Amanda opened the door slowly with all four-chain engaged and looked through the gap. Two women and one man stood there, very intense and smartly put together.

"Hello Miss Walker." The female, pale skin, piercing grey eyes and silver blonde hair spoke. She wore a blue and grey pants suit and a geometrical tattoo, like a futuristic heiroglyph stamped on her breast.

"We represent the Black Roses holding Company and we are interested in the purchase of the Heart of Ares."

"How did you find me here?" Amanda asked, regretting she posed the question.

"We have our network." The woman said.

"Well, you need to exclude me from that network. I'm not interested in selling the Heart thank you very much."

Amanda pushed the door closed but it bumped into an immovable object halfway there. Amanda looked down and saw a designer boot blocking its closure.

How did she wedge it there so quickly? She was standing at least two steps from the door.

The woman continued.

"I have an offer you cannot refuse. Let us in and we can talk about it"

"Remove your foot," Amanda snarled. The woman smiled broadly, her teeth were usually white and canines just a touch too long. She said nothing and leaned against the door. It was as if a bear had lent its weight to it. The chain pulled taut and the door buckled from the pressure.

Amanda stepped back, eyes wide with surprise. She didn't know anyone, or anything that could do that. Soon her surprise was slowly transforming into terror.

"I am going to call the police if you don't leave." Amanda said her voice squeaky. The woman outside was laughing softly. "I mean it!" Amanda shouted.

"You need to talk to us," the woman said as if it was the safest option for her health. "We will get what we want sooner or later. Why wait for the tears of emotion later?"

The woman's smile shifted, her eyes were no longer amused but excited.

The metal brackets of the chains bolted to the wall began to twist, the concrete began to fragment, grinding away as the chain tightened. Incredibly, the woman on the other side of the door was applying increasingly consistent pressure. Either the chain would snap, or the bracket cemented into the wall would be ripped from the housing, Amanda didn't know which. She stepped back, catching herself trembling. She was hyper focussed on the carbide steel that was stretching to the limit of its malleability.

She watched it snap with a pop.

Amanda yelped, her preconceived idea of the world she occupied shattering with it. The second chain snapped and soon after the third and fourth. The door swung open. The woman with the platinum blonde hair pale skin and crimson lips smiled. Her entourage looked on impassively.

"Where are your manners?" Her voice was so soothing. "Let us in and we can talk."

Amanda couldn't find the words to say anything. She just stood there looking at the strange people with their demands.

Their eyes glinted and he world slowed

Amanda's eye lids felt heavy.

She wanted to move but they were connecting to her, their influence like slimy octopi tentacles simultaneously probing her mind and holding her in place. The distance between them had suddenly become a chasm, that only she could breach by allowing them entrance.

No, Amanda resisted.

Let us in, the voice in her head said.

You can't force me to let you in.

I can, and I will Amanda. Let us in.

Amanda was gritting her teeth and a pearl of sweat forming on her hair long. The voice in your head continued.

"I...I...won't."

"Yes, you will."

A sharp shrill whistle shattered the connection.

Y stood behind the three figures, fingers still in her mouth from the whistle.

"I don't think she wants you as her guest," Y continued, her katana case swinging loosely in her right hand. "As much as it may hurt, that's life. I think you'd better be on your way."

If they were surprised that Y had manoeuvred behind them, they didn't show it. The platinum blonde didn't bother to engage, her focus was on Amanda. The other two turned in unison to Y, there stances like snakes about to strike, their hands pulled back, metamorphosizing as they moved, razor sharp talons sprouting from their nail beds. The transformation from what seemed normal to something alien was complete when they let rip inhuman screeches then attacked at blistering speed. In a blur of motion Y danced back and spun once, her Katana pulled free singing as tempered steel bit into the leather of the scabbard on release letting out a resonating twang. It had not been summoned in anger for many months but if Y knew better it was excited. Remaining loose she absorbed the first blow from an elbow to her ribcage, keeping a keen eye on those eviscerating claws. If she hadn't positioned herself correctly, she'd be nursing a broken rib. Y could feel the power, it was raw and wielded as if it was the most natural and savage thing in the world. She compensated to match, tightening her grip on the hilt.

No reason to hold back, she thought just as the well-dressed male lunged at her, his movements fluid and precise. Y sidestepped him and lowered her centre of gravity, her Katana whipping low as his female colleague flew at her with an almost scuttling crawl, Y's blade caught the undead in the face but instead of ripping flesh from her cheeks or gorging out an eye, the blade felt as if it had hit concrete. The vibration reverberated up her arm.

Bitch!

Y adjusted.

She spun the katana from her right hand to her left, twirling it skilfully then started cutting vicious 'X's into the air along the path of her male attacker. He didn't back down and came for her. Y could feel his partner hovering behind waiting for an opportunity which came quicker than she expected. Y gathered momentum swiping the Katana from left to right with such speed it was a blur.

Once, twice then three times.

The attacker just ran into her manoeuvres without regard for the weapon or the wielder. The vampire brought up its hands parrying the blade with its toughened skin just as his partner steamed in, but Y had timed the move perfectly and with a well-timed snap kick sent her spinning to the floor. Y took the moment and pushed part of her essence into the blade. The Katana glowed pale blue and cut through the man's defences, severing three fingertips.

No blood.

No response, just annoyance.

Y feigned right, skipping a sweeping leg by launching herself into the air and coming down hard on her attacker. The blade sunk into his neck, held fast by muscle and sinew. The force of the blow put the man to his knees. Y slaps her foot on his chest to pry her weapon free and the man kicked back, shrieking. Y switched focus finding herself behind the platinum blonde still talking to Amanda. She lunged without further thought. One moment she was looking at the blonde's back and the next the woman turned or dematerialized such was her speed, grasping the swinging Katana in both palms with a slap.

Y tried to pull it free but couldn't.

Neither could the woman pull it from Y's grasp.

Y move left. The bitch moved left with her.

Y feigned the right and the woman did the same, the katana firmly clamped between her hands, but this time Y's back was pointing to the inside of Amanda's flat. A sardonic grin crept up from the muscles of the blonde's neck and her eyes blazed. Y stared her down, the blade between them took on a shimmering glow that became more intense blue.

It was Y's turn to grin.

The blonde's features switched from amusement to concern. Her swagger fell away. Then came the piercing howl as Y channelled some of her life force into her weapon. The bitch's eyes widened as the blue attempted to flow into her hands. She exploded backwards, releasing the blade like it was hot, stumbling and then correcting herself quickly.

She stared at Y from a safe distance, unused to her superiority being challenged and bested.

"We'll be prepared for you when you come calling next time," Y said. Stay away from this place, it's off limits. You got that."

Y kept the blade pointed at the trio, the warm blue glow ebbing. Platinum blonde's lap dogs stood like humans once again behind her. The beast locked away and once again they looked like passable human beings.

Y knew better.

"When you see sense, call my mistress." The blonde said reaching into her jacket. When her hand appeared, between her fingers was a gold coloured business card.

She flung it.

The metal card sliced through the air like a ninja's shuriken. Y dodged it dismissively, watching it imbed in the wooden door jamb beside her.

The blonde pointed at her with fingers that were steady, the underside of her nails grey and thick. She spun on her heels and disappeared into the shadows of the corridor, her lap dogs in hot pursuit.

21.

1839 Whitechapel, East London

"Come with me Ezekiel and together we will behold terrible wonder."

Sir Philip was right.

I should have waited, calmed myself before trying to dictate my words with quill and parchment. I'm not sure if I could and although I am not given to a nervous disposition, what I witnessed at Whitechapel tonight had set my nerves a jangle. If not for this ingenious contraption I would have no choice but to reduce my usual sterling penmanship to that of drunk but instead my words are transferred to a brass cylinder and my sounds etched into a wax disc, captured forever, my essence bent by the will of science. I am one to wonder who will ever avail themselves of my misadventures and how many years hence, one, two, three hundred years. Will the future have a more enlightened society free from the horrors of inequality, slavery and wars. With the advent of even more amazing machines of science will the supernatural threats still plague us. I may never know, I am the son of a slave born in St. Mary Jamaica, who was fortunate to have Phillip Montague as my patron and I his partner in a vendetta against the forces of darkness. Ever since his family was murdered by their unholy hands. He raised me from child plucking me from an orphanage in Jamaica, discerning in his way that I was academically gifted and had the sight. I was able to peer into the afterlife, draw back the curtain of our mundane existence and see what lies beyond. Nobody ever had faith in me, believed I was talented in any way. I was just a slave bwoy as my peers would class me. But he bought my freedom and ever since we have never been apart. I was privately tutored and obtained a gentleman's education with the more important aspects of the esoteric left for Sir Philip and his cabal of mystical experts to complete. When I was of age, we forged our association and began to rid our beloved London of supernatural vermin. These things I have written about in my other diaries are a matter of record but for an occasion such as this and on a machine that will record my voice, you will hear my pain and joy. Sir Philip was murdered two years ago and the vile creature that perpetuated that act was destroyed tonight. It was a master Strogoi, a high order vampire called Lord Byfield. Although he was originally from Wallachai in Romania over the centuries of his life he had moved within English high society and through the cunning machinations of their kind and their other-worldly kith and kin, he made himself acceptable. The irony of that was not lost on me. A creature such as this, one of the undead was able to walk amongst the creme de la creme of London's high society, hobnobbing with the best of them. And the warm-blooded man of Christian faith that I was, had to hide my features in parts of the city, taking on one of my many disguises because of the colour of my skin. But I am the adaptable sort and recognise this was the reality of these days I neither accepted it or understood it but I made it a bedfellow. I live in harsh times.

Having read my diaries, you are wondering how I came across this creature in the first place to destroy it. You will have surmised the impossibility of crossing the path of such a creature by happenstance. A master Strogoi is the ultimate strategist and survivor by its nature with an acute distrust for everything that is natural. I could not hope to grapple with it, on its own terms, it was stronger, faster, cunning and having the combined experiences of ten lifetimes at its disposal. But we humans have our advantages too and because of it we dominate our planetary orb. You see amongst our usual duties was the acquisition of resources that could help us in our campaigns and Sir Philip was a man of means and able to acquire these items for our use. One such item was the Heart of Ares. An esoteric machine that could not only track supernatural beings using portions of their tainted flesh as a metaphysical lodestone but could lead the wielder to them. Once in their sight you were equal to the creature's strength for two hundred heartbeats. All I would need to destroy it.

And tonight, is what I did. Mr Jones my trusted carriage man took instructions from me as I sensed the directions through means unknown, just strong feelings of rightness. On the seat beside me was a deadly assortment of weapons and they were charmed, blessed or simply scientifically prepared. For myself, I was ready. I had been ready for many months after Sir Philip's death, restraining my anger with patience. And tonight, that patience would bear fruit. It was in the Whitechapel area that the heart of Ares made known that the vampire Lord Byfield was close at hand. From here my senses were naturally attuned to such things, so I instructed Jones to stop. My darkened horse and carriage halted immediately. I stepped out into the foggy night, the streets gaslit, the denizens of the night unaware and I was as prepared as I would ever be. I wore my military issue trench coat woven from course black cotton fastened centrally with brass buttons that openened easily when required. The inside folds were intricately sewn with a hornet's nest of pockets required to carry my equipment. Do you think you would have recognised me on my nocturnal errands? I think not. I have a scarf about my mouth and nose and atop my head is my black bowler hat. I'm not one for fashion but I've been told my specially made gamekeepers' hat would become fashionable. Tonight, its purpose was just to protect my skull. You may be asking yourself why it had taken me so long to exact vengeance on this creature having a weapon such as the Heart of Ares at my disposal? Well it required a power source to function and a target element. The power source needed was the rare Moonstone and the target element was the flesh of the Strogoi embeded in it. These items took time to acquire. But once I did, I implemented a strategy for this formidable task quickly.

I would have two hundred heartbeats of bolstered strength and augmented senses to match the creatures own. And only then if I was to best it, I would be afforded the opportunity. As my feet struck the greasy condensation slick cobblestones, I could sense his darkness, and I followed the impulse. It was a Friday night and this part of East London was filled with ladies of the night, gentlemen, pickpockets and merriment. I walked towards the busiest quarter filled with a menagerie of curiosity, depravity and strangeness,

I fit in perfectly.

Mr Jones the carriage man tried his best to stay close enough to me amidst the humanity and fog - the enchantment concealing him needed a certain proximity to me to function. But I was focused on the task at hand giving only fleeting consideration to my comrade driving the carriage.

I was like a bloodhound, the closer I came to him, the more my sixth sense was alight and so was the Heart of Ares. Then I saw his tall figure, disappearing and reappearing in the shrouding fog. He walked casually, his cane swinging with the steps and his top hat distinguished. And I knew without shadow of a doubt that was

Lord Byfield. I realized soon after that he was not alone and a young woman was on his arm. I am not so callous as not to think of the harm that could befall this maiden from my intervention but the thought that I could be saving her from a fate worse than death spurned me on. I kept in step with them for some time waiting for an opening, praying to God from the motherland to guide my hand. Once his leisurely stroll took him beyond innocent bystanders I would strike. The final piece to arming the Heart was in both my large pockets and it was simple process of slipping my hands into the metal gantlets thus completing the circuit. In a later entry I may go into more detail about what I experienced as a demi god but suffice to say the sensation was almost indescribable and the result for those two hundred heartbeats was I felt powerful and indestructible.

It was now or never.

A normal man cannot surprise a vampire like Lord Byfield, he had ultimate control of his environment except my gift allowed me this advantage. Maybe I was meant for this very purpose.

"Lord Byefield!" I called out.

And the vampire spun around with absolute surprise on his contorting features, that was at that very moment transforming from a pallid human countenance to the slick back feral abomination, nose upturned and wrinkled at the ridges like a bat, eyes blazing slits of fury. Its mouth wider than a human face could accommodate. Gums were splitting and teeth like daggers erupting from them. He flung his head back his shoulder length hair obscuring his horrific face. He brushed his walking stick aside no longer having any use for it as his hands looked more like claws with razor sharp talons. I was in full stride at this time, anticipating a scream from his lady companion but instead she used her body to shield him and impede me. I was startled not just by her intervention but that this beautiful African woman was in the process of being fully turned.

My surprise lasted for a moment. Her snarl was cut short as I struck her savagely, my strength five times that of a normal man: sending her careening across the road, her fineries flapping about her, disappearing into the fog.

I clashed hand to hand with the master Strogoi. The arrogance of this creature beggared belief as it took for granted it had no equal and that was to be its undoing. It held my sword arm high and the secondary weapon low and away from it. A gross smile flashed across its hellish features as it squeezed my hands to disable me. It snapped at my throat and I moved with speed matching its own. It's strength and ferocity would have been overwhelming if not for magics contained in the astonishing contraption.

I will never forget the monsters breath smelling of cloves and mint, I remember the confusion in his lizard eyes when I, a human matched his strength and speed, I remember smashing my forehead into his nose and the creature seeing its own blood for the first time in many centuries. But what will never be forgotten would be its shock when I wrench my sword hand away from his, swinging in a wide arc as my silver sword cleaved his godless head from the shoulders. His head bounced on the cobblestones, his torso stumbling then hitting the ground, twitching then combusting in a bright orange flame. I will never forget the howling and screeching of the she-bitch bemoaning his death and threatening to kill me. But she remained in the shadows where she belonged and I never saw her again.

Some men say revenge is like drinking poison. Well tonight I drank from that chalice and it was like nectar to me.

End of entry.

22.

"Tonight I'd like to welcome on the Duke Ellington stage the talented vocalist known to his many online fans as the voice. Put your hands together for Mr Dean Thorne."

The MC tipped his hat and stylishly exited the stage. The intimate audience exploded into enthusiastic applause. The lights dimmed and the smoke machine was layering the stage with a wispy atmospheric mist. Y, Patra and Suzy had a table to themselves. In the middle was a silver ice bucket and snuggled comfortably between the ice cubes was a half empty bottle of Asti Spumante. All three had flute glasses with differing levels of the sparkling sweet wine inside. The girls looked relaxed and although they were enjoying great music this was still business. Y sipped from her glass, then looked at Suzy.

"Still nothing to worry about?"

"I'm sensing nothing, although it wouldn't make a difference."

"And why is that?" Y asked.

"For some reason all deh drama and grudges are left outside. It's as if they shrugged it off when they stepped in. It feels like there is an understanding here. A contract of entry."

"Ju-Ju?" Patra asked.

"I don't know," Suzy said. "I taste peppermint which usually means freedom and calm."

"Well, my ass is definitely feeling calm," Patra said. "The music, the food, it is all off the hook."

"Agreed but keep your eyes open for this possible contact. We haven't got the luxury of just enjoying the evening."

"Chill," Patra placated her sister. "We got this."

Patra raised her glass and the others followed, clinking together. A short-lived light spark erupted in the crystal of their wine glasses. A reaction they sometimes exhibited as the life energies of all three women resonated sympathetically with the molecules of the glass. No one around them showed any signs of surprise.

Y looked embarrassed.

Patra laughed.

"We still got it, bitches"

Suzy nodded and smiled too.

Moments later a hush came over the audience as a spotlight hit a lone high-stool and microphone stand in the centre of the stage. The jazz band in the background suddenly struck a languid extended note and that's when a melodious voice came out of the speakers.

"You sheltered me from harm," came the words and Y and Suzy recognised the strains of the Ken Boothe classic immediately. The voice caressed another few lines.

"You kept me warm, you kept me warm. You gave your life to me, set me free. The finest years I ever knew..."

The voice matched the original artist so closely for a moment Suzy thought Ken Boothe would step out on stage but instead the uncanny voice reproduction sauntered out in the guise of someone else. Dean Thorne moved like a boxer. Over six feet tall, North African extraction, solid frame with black curly hair pulled tight at the front and tied at the back. He had piercing brown eyes and dressed casually in jeans, cowboy boots and a white T-shirt. He brought the microphone to full red lips and pale olive skin and leaned not sit on the stool.

Suzy heard Patra gasp.

She wasn't sure if it was an echo of an emotionally charged thought or she had muttered the word unknowingly.

Suzy discounted it and smiled the memories of Jamaica cascading over her. Patra had been exposed to Jamaican music in Atlanta but her real education in the genre that birthed Hip Hop came from Suzy. Shamefully Patra had never been to a Reggea concert, so experiencing the music live was a new vibe. She began to understand why Suzy held these musicians in such high regard. Suzy and Y were swaying to the music and Patra felt as if her heart was filling up and was about to overflow with a lightness of being that took her by surprise. Dean caressed the words, expertly held the notes and with his band created a soundscape that spoke of love, struggle and redemption. Dean focussed on different parts of his audience and took turns to speak to them through his music. He ran through about six Jamaican classics in a soulful jazz style that respectfully mimicked the voice of the original artists. The audience was in awe as many of them closed their eyes as they pictured Bob Marley, John Holt, Derek Morgan, Delroy Wilson, or Dennis Brown at the microphone in their mind. But once his piercing gaze fell on Patra for the remainder of his set his eyes were only for her. And with his attention there was an intensity that transmitted between them. An intensity that had Patra deliciously uncomfortable. It wasn't just his sweet voice or those smouldering brown eyes but how he moved across the boards. A confident prowl that had him not just working the stage but ruling it like it was his kingdom. Patra held her breath in anticipation of what, she didn't know. Only when there was rapturous applause did she realize his set was complete.Patra leaned back in her chair and took a sip from her glass.

"I tink dat's our man?" Suzy said.

"No shit," Patra agreed, her voice lowered.

"Let's go talk to him." Y moved her chair back to stand butPatra put up a finger in the air as if testing for wind speed.

"Normally I'd say yeah," she said. "Have at it but this time I think a more personal approach would be more effective."

Suzy smiled.

"You okay, gal?"

"I am peachy," Patra said stiffly.

Y touched the back of her hand to Patra's forehead like a nurse would and looked over to Suzy.

"She's not running a fever?" Y said.

"Check between her legs," Suzy said. "I think all the heat is down there."

Patra shook her head and rolled her eyes.

"You bitches are pissing me off. Can I go speak to him one-on-one or not?"

"Knock yourself out." Y said.

Suzy's tone had returned to business.

"I can't discern a threat from him but Just be careful sis, I don't know exactly what he is."

Patra nodded and as soon as the interlude began, she made her way to the dressing rooms.

Patra snuck into the back of the house after faking the need to pee and ending up in a spacious area you could not imagine existed from the seats out front. It looked elaborate but she wouldn't have the time to investigate right now, her priority was to find out some more about the man who had graced the stage and connected with her. She was more D'Angelo, Usher and Maxwell but this dude gave her chills – the good kind, making her disconnect from reality for a moment.

Damn! That was special.

She snapped out of her reverie and found herself looking at a set of four doors running along the side of a sort of alcove and on the other side shelves packed with dusty stage equipment. One particular door drew her attention. A ninja's throwing star was wedged into the wooden door pinning a note to it.

"Motherfucker! So much for keeping there intentions underwraps." Patra mumbled reading the note.

The penmanship was exquisite.

So, you felt it too. I'm glad.

I wish I could stay but I have an urgent matter to attend to. Come see me any evening, I'll be waiting.

Patra couldn't help but smile.

23.

The girls sat around a massive wooden table that looked like it had been a part of the house from the seventeenth century. Thick and imposing, its sturdy legs firmly set into the floor and would have been used by the servants for their meals because they were barred the grand dining room upstairs. Since Nanny's arrival, the girls preferred eating down here anyway.

Suzy slurped on her cornmeal porridge and mused.

"How did Nanny know this was my favourite?"

Patra shrugged her mouth filled with pancakes and fruit dribbled with maple syrup.

"Yeah how did she know?"

"Amazing cook," Y commented. Her ackee and salted fish breakfast reducing significantly with every knife and fork stroke. "There's more to her than meets the eye."

The girls nodded with food in their mouths. Suzy looked in Y's plate and asked.

"Where did she get breadfruit from?"

"That's what I mean," Y said. "Mysterious, right."

After two weeks of having Nanny around, the girls began to understand what Spokes was talking about on how invaluable she was. The mansion was a huge place to keep clean for a team of people much less one-woman, but Nanny kept the place spotless. You would hardly see her doing her thing but when you did, she was usually singing melodiously to herself. She seemed shy but when she did speak it was soft and authoritative with a sweet Jamaican lilt. Suzy was even more perplexed than everyone else. She assessed people on multiple levels and described a swirling mist of uncertainty that surrounded their housekeeper. Nanny's psychics defences were strong. Nanny blew into the kitchen with a teapot in hand. The smell was exquisite. Dark chocolate, cinnamon and coconut. She adjusted a towel on her shoulder after wiping her forehead then adjusting the head wrap covering her thick white hair.

"My ears are burning." She said referring to the feeling you get when you are spoken about by people you know in your absence. Without skipping a beat, she asked. "Anyone for chocolate tea?"

"Yes please." They all chorused tumbling over each other to get their mugs filled with the piping hot beverage. Carefully she poured it into each cup.

Liquid contentment.

Y took a sip and sighed. And like it was the most natural thing in the world, she remembered her father with fondness. Mr. Sinclair separated from her mother when she was a teenager. A Jamaican boy filled with wanderlust, who wanted to explore Asia. And he did. He wrote to her about all his adventures, married a Japanese lady, gave her two brothers and gifted her the Masamune sword she wielded today. He was the one who championed her training in the ways of Kendo from she was young. Her heart warmed with the recollections and the chocolate and she promised herself to call him.

Patra used a teaspoon to stir the contents of her mug then scooped out the liquid chocolate, blew on it a few times and let it trickle on her tongue. The dark cocoa sweetened with condensed milk exploded pleasurably in her mouth. An all over feeling of safety enveloped her and she could almost feel the kiss on her cheek by her Mama at the breakfast table in Lawrenceville, Gwinnett County. With three rough and tumble brothers who thought she was a boy, faking it as a girl, Patra was reliving some of the best moments of her life sitting at the kitchen table in Sussex, England spooning chocolate tea. There was love in her home even if her preacher father wanted to deny she was bisexual. But she grew tough. Her brothers made sure of that. After being kicked one two many times in the boxing ring by their little sister they shipped her off the Mau Thai classes.

She never looked back.

Suzy slurped on her chocolate with a practised ease. Sucking air into her mouth, as her lips hovered over the rim of her cup as she sipped, cooling it before it hit her tongue. As the aroma curled into her nostrils Suzy was transported to the storage room of her parent's supermarket in downtown, Kingston Jamaica. She's doing her homework in her favourite spot. The storage room smelt of salted fish, sugar and pickled meat but for her it was perfect place to be. She could see her mom on one of the five tills all business as usual. While her dad popped his head around the door to pull faces at her. Sometimes a funny face would be followed by a hand holding her favourite baked good – spiced bun and cheese. Having spoiled her he would be away again, wowing his customers and making friends with a genuine passion that was rare. Her brother Richard got away with murder, playing his Atari upstairs in his room while she laboured away downstairs. But as soon as she was done it would be her time to practice her Chinese Boxing and gymnastics out back. Mom wasn't keen but Dad was proud of her. For Suzanne it was a passion she was extremely good at and Suzy Wong, her martial arts heroine was an alter ego a shy Chinese girl could aspire to be like.

Be careful what you wish for.

Nanny stood folding her arms amused at how the kitchen had suddenly become less chatty and more introspective. She took a moment from preparing breakfast to watch her little eagle chicks sip on the chocolate tea and reminisce. Using the old ways, she had imbued her food with the essence of their past and watched as the girls dipped their toes into the river of soothing memory. Nanny knew more than most that fully round-ed warriors didn't just master the overt arts of war but understanding why and for whom they fought. Their psyches were stronger than most but it still required tending. Her duty amongst other things was to keep them focussed on their 'Why's'. They had to remain ready, fighting fit physically and mentally. Feed them well and keep their minds right. Nanny whipped the dish cloth from around her neck and returned to her kitchen duties.

24.

All eyes were on Patra. She slowly took the cigar from her lips and dusted it in an ashtray, her eyes moving between the five community cards at the centre of the table and her two hold cards held in her hand. Opponents looked apprehensively at her and then at the fat pot in the centre of the velvet table. The Showdown Round would be interesting.

Beside her Cyrus had folded.

"I call," Patra said throwing two short piles of her chips into the pot. She felt all eyes were on her and she resisted the urge to smile or to glance at the massive pile of chips in the centre of the table. Instead, she placed the cigar back in her mouth, ruby lipstick tattooing the stogie's tip. Brandon the first aggressor showed his cards.

Straight flush.

Lame ass ... she thought.

Thomas threw down his hand with disgust at seeing Brandon's.

Three of a Kind.

All eyes were on her again as she sent a stream of smoke to the ceiling and upturned her cards.

"Drinks are on me motherfuckers!" She squealed.

Her Royal Flush winked up at everyone at the table

A litany of groans played in the background to Patra's whoops. You would think for someone gifted with the ability to distort probability, winning games of chance or strategy would come naturally to her.

Not so.

When her luck factor came to her aide it was usually in life threatening situations. Expecting a nudge from it in the right direction for the Cheltenham races or even the snooker World Cup would be appreciated, but lady luck simply smiled and kept her legs closed. Any win Patra benefited from was all on her.

"Hell yeah!" Patra pushed back her chair and stood. She was known for her flamboyance when she won at the tables. A celebratory dance or sometimes if she was in fine voice the line of an R&B classic. For this, she would do something special having lost five of her last poker games. She crawled onto the table like a cat and suggestively made her way to the hipscentre of the table. Her male opponents looked on at her well-formed rear rhythmically mimicking a prowling cat approaching a particularly tasty meal. Not surprised by her performance it was there turn to have their faces rubbed into a brutal loss. Months ago, Patra would be doing just this, in a different setting, flaunting her assets for money. Lots of money and enjoying it too. But a higher calling intervened, setting her on another path. She'd never forget it though. It's what truly prepared her for life. If this maintaining the eternal balance gig did not work out then...

"Bravo! Bravo!" Two voices punctuated her thoughts and interrupted her sexy moves. The distinct cracks of applause erupted from big hard hands. Each clap was like a gunshot. Patra stood up on the table and looked over to the two men who had entered, recognition blossomed immediately.

"Goddamn it!" She swore under her breath. "Mr Edwards and Mr Hardy," Patra said jumping down off the table.

"I see you still have the moves." The one named Mr Edwards said.

"And the curves," Mr Hardy added.

Patra strutted straight up to them as bold as brass and stood with their arms akimbo.

"Are you two for real right now?"

"We are as real as traffic congestion in London," said Mr Edwards. "Didn't you believe we existed?"

Patra blinked, the memory of meeting these two strange men coming back to her and their promises at a very low time in her life. It had been an oddly significant deal because it had made a U-turn of a gambling habit that could have become toxic. The next day she thought she might have dreamed it all. But in front of her was the evidence that she had not.

"What do you to want?" Patra snapped.

"Now is that any way..." Mr Edwards started.

"...To greet old friends." Mr Hardy completed.

"The last time I checked friends don't try to con friends."

"We weren't trying to deceive you," they said together. "We were just making sure our impressions of you were correct."

"You two are full of shit?" Patra said. "You wouldn't be here If I didn't make the dumb-ass mistake of losing to that skinny dude in the red suit and then borrowing from you two dudes in the heat of the moment. What was it? A thousand percent interest for five hours?"

"It wasn't about the money, Ms Jones," Mr Edwards said. "You had just lost to a Demon who would have you sign a contract for a part of your soul. At the time you were asleep like many on this plane, so we had to intervene." Mr Hardy shrugged. "In your case, the thousand percent interest was just a matter of principle." Mr Edwards sighed. "We aren't in the money lending game Ms. Jones. Our interest is in acquiring your services in the future."

"To be precise one year, seven months, twenty-one days, five hours..." Mr Hardy consulted his pocket watch. "...And thirty-three minutes from now you will help us."

"At the time you were still sleep walking through life, but we knew you were special, didn't we Mr Hardy?" Mr Hardy nodded.

"You woke." Mr Edwards said.

"You mean get woke." Patra couldn't help teasing them.

"You know precisely what we mean Ms. Jones," Mr Edwards said bluntly. "Your kind has been around ever since humanity walked the earth. The balance must be maintained is it not?"

Patra shook her head.

"Do you remember signing the skin, when we lent you the money?"

Patra nodded

"I thought signing my name on your arm was freaky, but money was money."

"Well that's where you are wrong, Ms. Jones," Mr Edwards said.

"In other words, you guys played me for a punk because I didn't understand my gift and the world, I would eventually end up in."

"You could say that," Mr Edwards agreed.

"If you don't want more interest on the money, I paid back to you hustlers what the fuck do you want?"

"We are brokers, dealmakers, fixers even. Our business is built on the souls of clients are willing to barter their skills for our services." Mr Hardy nodded his head in agreement.

Mr Edwards took off his jacket and handed it to Mr Hardy who pinched each shoulder and held it up to retain its shape. Patra thought for a moment that this was a way of preparing to get physical, but it wasn't their style. Patra's Luck factor was aware - that hollow sensation at the base of her spine was on standby.

So, she chilled.

Undoing his cufflinks Mr Edwards neatly rolled up the sleeves of a pristine white shirt. Patra guessed it was custom-made and matched the contours of a body that was angled and hard and could take a punch. He showed her his forearm and it was tattooed with neat runic symbols.

"You are here," he pointed, and Patra peered at the white skin riddled with blood vessels and tattoos. She could feel the temperature around him fall. Watching the ink begin to fade like the droplets were soaking into his epidermis and merging with his bloodstream. Instead of dissolving away ink molecules acted like they were being controlled and began coalescing into another tattoo that only two mystical accountants obsessed with contracts could create. The brief document was in another language Patra did not understand with her signature on the dotted line.

"Ah, man," Patra said.

"Don't worry we will make you aware when we need you," Mr Edwards said. "Right now, your purpose is more crucial in the bigger scheme of things and we wouldn't want the 'Powers that Be', getting shirty. You're going to have a lot on your plate." Mr Hardy said

"You're going to need focus, getting yourself dead is no good to anyone and that could be bad, real bad for business." Mr Edwards concluded. "An alpha vampire of the female persuasion is not to be messed with."

"Not to be messed with at all." Mr Hardy repeated.

"You must play your strength's. Together you are strong. Use it."

"I plan to," Patra said."Any other words of advice?"

Mr, Edwards nodded, completely missing the sarcasm.

""You will hear from us, from time to time. Stay alive and don't worry."

"Do I look worried?" Patra asked.

Both men smiled.

"Enjoy..." Said Mr. Hardy.

"...Your evening." completed Mr. Edwards. They both nodded crisply and departed.

25.

Y stood outside the two-bedroom maisonette in Wembley and knocked on the door. Beside her was her multi-compartment trolley with everything she needed to work the magic she was known for in the manicure and pedicure circles. In moments the front door opened, and Y was met by a smiling woman.

"Patricia?" Y asked.

The woman nodded.

She was in her mid-30s, dark skin and distinctive East African features and she was very pleased to see her.

"Come in. Come in," she said. "Did you have any problems finding me?"

"Surprisingly easy." Y said and as she was led into Patricia's lounge, that feeling of contentment reminded her of that feeling of creativity and freedom she felt working in nail art. You would think that when Y had time to herself, she would put her feet up and binge on reality television or catch up on some mindless online drama series but that was not the kind of person she was. Believe it or not, the tether to her life before all of this craziness, was making sure her old nail clients were serviced. Finding an adequate substitute nail technician in London was tough, so imagine what it was like to acquire the services of a master. In good conscience Y just couldn't leave her old clients floundering. Her nail business - Y wasn't sure she could still call it that, was a pleasant distraction from her calling. A way to catch up on the gossip and ground herself in the world outside of her own. Something she had come to understand was necessary.

Two sides to every coin.

One side is where Y had lived or occupied most of life up to this point. And the other side was a reality most would never believe existed. For Y and her sisters they had been activated by powers they may never fully understand. What was obvious London was becoming the epi-centre for strangeness and them a magnet for it. The floodgates had been opened when they had clashed with Enoch Lacombe – the Dark man months ago, the frontier of the night tribes was encroaching on her world. And not in the way she would have thought either. Even Y's client base was getting weird.

Patricia was a prime example.

She had been recommended to her by another client Y had known for many years. Patricia had been described as young woman who wanted only a special kind of nail technician to work with her nails. Y didn't consider taking on more clients as the number she was working with suited her fine but her old client had insisted.

"Go see her at least," her client and friend had said. "She's helped me out of a few binds in the past."

So, Y did.

As Y walked from the front door to the main room, lugging her equipment she found out Patricia was a qualified accountant who worked mainly from home, a home she might add was spotless, almost clinically so. Plugged in, towelled up, files in a row, clippers sharp and Y was ready Patricia sat in front of her and placed her hands on the fluffy towel. The nails of her ten fingers were like convoluted, twirling snakes frozen in place. Y imagined Patricia may never have clipped her nails in her lifetime. They were beautiful to look at. And like a two-dimensional optical illusion, if you stared long enough you couldn't tell where the twirling nails ended or began. Y blinked trying to clarify the blur that was fingers, nails and polish. It took a moment, but her eyes adjusted. Y could feel the membrane between the twilight world and the real one stretch.

She chose to ignore it.

This would be complicated work but not unfamiliar. Y lifted the drill and revved it.

Patricia stiffened, holding her breath as the bit came closer. Her client relaxed when she saw how expertly Y handled it.

"Your nails are short, Yvonne?" Patricia asked. "Does it affect your work?"

Y smiled knowingly.

"It does in a way, but I prefer to go natural, like you. I am heavy-handed. I break them at the drop of a hat."

Easier to maintain," Patricia said. "Well, for some of us that is."

Y finished moving the complicated spiral of nails on the inside with a portable drill, the dust floating in the air the smell of acetone strong as she removed the original nail polish

"I had a good feeling about you from the very beginning",

"Oh!" Y said.

"Something about you carried with Josey when she spoke about you."

"Thanks," Y said. Wondering where this conversation was going.

"You are a true professional, not once have you commented negatively about my nails."

"I am here to give you a service, it's not for me to comment on how you choose to grow your nails. If you are happy to have them then I am happy to maintain them."

Patricia sighed as if a weight that had been placed on her shoulders had been lifted.

"Can I tell you something?"

"You won't have to kill me, will you?" Y asked.

Patricia smiled tightly.

"What did you notice about them beyond their length?"

Y didn't want to talk about the energy field she sensed around her client's nails. She decided to mention something less obvious.

"The nail drill seemed to be sparking more than normal." Y knew the machinery of the drill was sound but the carbide drill bit was sparking on parts of her convoluted nails as it made contact.

"I felt something," Y said knowing where this was going

Patricia sighed again and said flatly.

"If I cut my nails I will die."

And there it was ladies and gentlemen. The supernaturalencroaching into world of the normal, no matter how you wanted to ignore it.

Y's weirdness barometer rose three notches as she took a moment to absorb her clients statement.

"Is it a gift or a curse?" Y asked.

"A bit of both," Patricia said matter-of-factly. "The curse is dealing with people's perceptions and dealing with the living day-to-day. The inconvenience of it. If I was back in my village in Kenya it would be easier."

Y nodded.

"The gift is the people I can help."

"How?" Y asked.

"My 34 years of life are all marked on my nails and with that the ability to look back to any event in the past 32 years in exact detail for any living soul on the planet."

"Wow," Y said.

"So, you don't think I'm crazy?" Patricia asked.

"I think I literally have your life in my hands." Y said.

Patricia nodded.

"No pressure then," said Y.

"I have a feeling I am in good hands," Patricia smiled it was a tight secretive smile.

"Would you consider helping me with a case I'm working on?" Y asked.

"A case?" Patricia brightened up.

"Just between me and you." Y said.

"I can keep a secret." Patricia smiled.

"Good. Doctors aren't the only ones who can enjoy doctor patient privilege." Said Y.

Both women laughed.

26.

"**S**uzy, we're having a bit of bother in the foyer. I think you better come see."

Suzy Wong was in the kitchen of the Reilly community centre, chopping carrots and potatoes. Every opportunity she got outside of work she would come down to the West London Borough and volunteer at the soup kitchen. Suzy would help in any way she could. Sometimes she would hold self-defence and meditation classes for the homeless users of the facility. Although she grew up Catholic, she wasn't an advocate of organized religion per say but she understood some of its benefits. Her parents were Christian but with her new perspective of the world she chose action over empty devotion. The permanent staff knew only that she was good natured, committed and could handle herself. With that reputation she was called on to defuse a few potentially violent situations while helping in the kitchen. If there wasas a 'spot of bother', they would come to her to negotiate a truce.

"Wha gwaan?" Suzy asked.

"It's this strange fella out front, trying to get in for food but he's pulling a trolley that stinks to high heaven." Amy made a face. "I told him to leave it outside, but he wouldn't. Instead he's abusing staff. He is a big bloke. I was thinking of calling the old bill, but ..."

Suzy sighed and placed the knives down under counter, wiped her hands and followed Amy's lead.

"Never a dull moment," Amy said.

"That's why I love it here. Yuh never know what the evening can bring."

Amy nodded grimly.

"And these evenings at this month seemed to bring the crazies and nutters out."

"We will manage," Suzy said soaking up some of Amy's concern with the calmness of her demeanour. It was only when they got to the end of the corridor that Suzy fully appreciated Amy's concern. It wasn't misplaced. Suzy controlled the breath she had taken in and allowed it to leave her in a measured exhale as she saw the man.

Hellspawn.

He was over 6 feet tall, wearing a filthy tuxedo, his white ruffled shirt grimy and his bow tie loose about his neck, shiny with grease. His eyebrows were spiky like poisonous caterpillars, his head bald and teeth unusually white. With a grubby face he looked like an iguana with a Hollywood mouth job. He stood half in and half out of the community centre, but Suzy could still smell his rancid odour and then came the smell of decomposition from the trolley. Suzy was already interpreting the kaleidoscope of dark psychic energy only she recognised, and it only confirmed her fears of the escalation of these events in London.

She shivered.

"Should I call the police?" Joe asked the only other staff member present.

"Nuh worry," Suzy said. "I think I can reason wid him."

She knew this street dweller for what it was. Thankfully the demon did not complicate the issue with the truth. If Suzy could spare her colleagues, the explanations she would.

Suzy walked over to the vagrant with her hands to her side submissively. The man made a gurgling sound as if anticipation of her arrival was too much for him to handle. Suzy began breathing through her mouth early so when she parked close to him, speech wasn't impeded by the stench.

"What's in the trolley?" Suzy asked, imagining a black bin bag filled with the neighbourhood pets or even worst. "I know what you are bwoy suh yuh can drop deh act." Suzy hissed.

The vagrants left eye rolled one way then the next like he was a chameleon.

"A fucking Guardian!" He licked his crusty lips with a prehensile muscular tongue, taken from a sloth and rammed into his perfect mouth.

"Keep your filthy voice down," Suzy said. "I have a good mind to gut yuh rass here and now."

The thing masquerading in human skin thought about it.

Then farted.

"You're bluffing. I will come back when you aren't here. Bring friends next time."

"Yuh threatening me demon?" Suzy asked.

"Do you think you bitches can protect these human cattle forever? Their time is running out."

"Not while I live and breathe. Dat won't happen."

"The path between worlds has become porous for some of our kind."

"Tell me something I don't know."

The creature glared at her.

"I will just have to have my fun someplace else tonight."

"You do that and mark this place as a no-go zone for your kind."

"Giving me orders now bitch."

"Not orders just good advice."

"Fuck you," the creature said backing out. "We will rejoice when the vampire Queen wipes her ass, with your corpses."

Suzy kissed her teeth.

"You and she don't make one. What have you heard? Is there something you want to tell me?"

His laughter was flemy but genuinely amusing for something that had crawled up from the pit, it had a keen sense of gutter humour.

"You, you..." He spluttered between gales of laughter. "Why do you think I would tell you anything wo-man?"

"Self-preservation," Suzy hazarded a guess.

The Demon backed out through the door it's words faint.

"I didn't know the guardians were so funny. Funny, funny." He disappeared into the night.

27.

Shaft was alone in his conference room in central London, his focus so intense he hadn't realised his team of three had left for a late lunch. When he resurfaced from his thoughts, he reached for a second can of red Bull, swigged down the remainder and left it amidst three other empty cans. The large table that ran central to the room was half filled with files, three laptops with associated hard drives sat around it and on the edges of the room, a photo copy machine. At the head of the table was a whiteboard and beside that an extremely large and busy cork-board. It was the focus of the room and managed to draw everyone's attention to it including his. The corkboard was a mind-map of his thought process for this case. It was filled with lots of gaps, but they were being filled with Forensic data from the scene of crime, historical facts from Police Archives and supposition from Y and the girls. At first, he felt uncomfortable letting anyone see the patterns of thought that inhabited his head. Vampirism, Immortality, the undead, vengeance, conspiracy theories and more. He sounded like a crackpot for anyone outside of Y, Suzy and Patra.

Then he was contacted by the commissioner who wanted to finally back his way of investigating this case. Shaft was left with a unique problem. Finding administrative staff who could work through the strangeness and appreciate the gravity of what they were doing without falling around the floor in laughter. It just goes to show how wrong he could be. The Commissioner had hand-picked three older women and had no problem making them sign the official secrets act and the Eridus Pact. So, the Weird Sisters – an endearing label Shaft kept to himself about the older women in his team, who were not weird or sisters, handled the repetitive, manual work. They had been asked to substantiate the authenticity of a 400-year-old document that must've blown their little minds but at least they were beginning to understand the things that go bump in the night really do exist.

While they came to terms with their new world. Shaft had turned up his creativity. That meant he slept with the virtual corkboard on his mind and was thinking about it as he walked to the corner shop from his apartment. Even when he had social engagements – of which he kept to a minimum, his subconscious and his conscious mind was working on the problem twenty-four hours a day.

Y said he was sexy when he had the fire in his belly. Strange woman.

His command centre was situated on the top floor of a Metropolitan police training facility. He had wondered many times in Black Books brief history if he would ever be given an adequate space, office or even room he could call his own. This place was ideal, but he wasn't getting his hopes up. Was Black Book finally getting the respect it deserved? It could crumble at any moment especially if he did not put this investigation to bed. The best he could do was live in the moment and let the future work itself out.

The cork board was all that mattered.

He closed his eyes, swivelled his neck until it cracked, he opened his eyes again at the coloured pins, strings connecting points, press clippings, drone symbols, Post-it-notes and crime scene photographs all arranged in a universe of information that made sense to him and the Weird Sisters.

Many of the gaps he had concerning this tableau of information required some ground work or some calls. Others needed proof and that would be difficult to come by, the rest was filled in by the Bad II the Bone ladies, which left a few unresolved points. And that's where his unique detective skills came into play. His conclusions from the information in front of him was frightening to say the least.

Vampires.

It felt strange saying it, wrong almost. What would it take for him to accept that almost anything was possible in this new world? Why was he still surprised? An organised clan headed by a female alpha that has been terrorising the UK every 50 years for the past 250 years as far as he could tell.

She was smart too.

Her atrocities have been masked over the years. A coal pit disaster, a rail disaster, a world war 2 munitions factory explosion, major fires in London and Manchester. Evidence was conveniently destroyed including bodies. And what made it more testing was the era's Shaft's investigation were looking into had little or no forensic records. He was depending on some good old-fashioned journalism of the time and anecdotal evidence.

Were vampires' perfectionists? He imagined this creature was, but at every crime scene dating back to the seventeenth Century, she left at least one exsanguinated body behind.

Hubris?

Not sure but that little fact connected ever massacre she perpetrated over history.

A calling card maybe.

London had turned out to be different. Something had thrown them off their game. They usually cause maximum carnage over two-week window and then disappear without a trace. This time something was different.

Their focus had changed.

The Clan wanted to obtain an ancient weapon that had come to the girls attention. It was owned by a young woman called Amanda Walker and it seemed they would use force to lay their undead hands on it. It turns out to be one of the few things that can definitively kill these monsters. From the notes and recordings Y had listened to, the weapon had been used successfully to destroy one of their kind in the past.

They were worried.

He had an uncomfortable feeling this was just the beginning. His superiors required solutions that fit neatly into a box. Answers that would not interfere with how the masses saw the world. A shadow narrative that ran beside the difficult truth that explained the Platinum Exhibition Murders in terms that the sleeping masses could digest. A fall guy would be great but not necessary. He had to try and contain this and could only do it with the girls help. The more he looked at it the more this felt like he was out of his depth. And he didn't like that feeling of helplessness. He didn't like that feeling one bit.

28.

Shaft arrived at Whitechapel just before midnight itching to prove his theory right. It had come to him on his drive home, in all its glory and certainty. All the information he had been exposed to throughout this investigation, from the girls, the force and his own enquirys had connected in some unusual ways in his head. In the quiet of his Jaguar, unawares to him his subconscious had finalized its mingling of ideas and uncerimonously spat out a clue.

Tonights excursion would be a shared affair; he had invited the girls to accompany him. He hadn't intended it to be anything like this, but when the spark of inspiration had lit up his tired mind he had to share his discovery with someone. He had called Y telling her what had come to him and how strongly he felt about his intuitive insight.

"I'm not going to sleep a wink if I don't check this out and if I'm right, tonight is the night."

"For what?" Patra had asked.

"Tonight, is the anniversary of a killing that started all this," Shaft said. And I wan't to see where it took place."

"Can I come?" Y had asked. "We did help you put this puzzle together."

"That you did." He said.

"Can I come too?" A soft voice in the background also asked.

"You all welcome," he capitulated. "I can't promise adventure but maybe a little history lesson instead."

"Sounds good to me boss," Suzy called out and that was that.

Shaft parked the Jaguar in a parade of shops. He shuffled out, stretched and slammed the door behind him. Whitechapel Road was quiet with a few people strolling along its length with dogs and pushbikes. Shaft had just walked past the famous Blind beggar pub. The brewery was close beside it and just across the road the girls sat in Bentley GTi feigning impatience. The broke into wide cheesy grins when they realised, he was looking at them.

He came over and leaned on the window.

"The package deal," Shaft said referencing how they loved each other's company.

"You know that sugah." Patra said.

"And you know we hate secrets star." Suzy added.

Shaft grinned then yawned.

"So, what did you want to show us that had you losing sleep?" Y asked. "I can't have you getting sick over this, no matter how important it is."

"Ah!" Patra said mockingly.

Suzy shook her head.

"Thanks babe. I am good really, but this was too hot to pass up. Who doesn't like solving a mystery?" He paused. "Walk with me."

The girls left the car and followed him.

Suzy and Patra took an arm each and they strolled in a tight group down the road. They didn't have far to go.

"Isn't that the Royal London just ahead?" Y asked.

"I'm impressed," Shaft said. "You know your London landmarks. Well, we're not going that far. What we're looking for is somewhere here." Shaft gently shrugged out of the arms of his escorts. He walked ahead a few paces, stopped then stooped.

"Suzy!" Shaft called "Come over here and tell me what you see."

Suzy came over and kneeled beside him.

"What yuh got?" She asked and immediately she felt it. It was as if she had been thrown into a hair dryer. The arcane energy emanating from that spot was undeniable. Suzy could feel every flux line, see the crimson of blood behind her eyes and taste the coppery tang on her tongue. It was becoming overwhelming very quickly.

She stepped back.

"This appears here every year suddenly, magically and mysteriously in this same spot." Shaft was considering his words. "I have checked CCTV camera footage and even online video platforms of the area and it is nowhere to be seen only on this date for three or four hours."

Shaft read the words off the blue heritage plaque imbedded into the tile of the street.

"In heartfelt and loving memory of Lord Rutherford Byfield. He fell but his spawn will live forever."

Instinctively Suzy reached out to touch it, her fingers trembling as a jolt of malevolent static connected her with the plaque. Suzy's eyes slammed shut, then sprang open again, a surge of something corrupting coursed through her and knocking her down on her ass.

"Woh!" She said and sprang nimbly to her feet in moments.

"What is it?" Patra grabbed her shoulders.

"You okay?" Y asked coming up beside her.

"I think we should go," Suzy said.

"But..." Shaft attempted to share his conclusions to a willing audience but instead their eyes focused into the shadows just ahead of them.

Shaft looked too.

Three people stood there.

Two indistinct figures blending into the darkness stood two steps behind a very tall woman with head bowed. She was dressed in black. Her hands were gloved and she wore a chiffon and silk hat that resembled the petals of a large black rose. Her face was obscured.

"Speak of deh devil and he will appear," Suzy murmured. "Welcome to deh architect behind deh murders." Suzy pointed towards the tall woman.

"I knew it!" Shaft said his breathing becoming laboured with excitement. "This is where she comes to celebrate his death. Right where he fell."

Y had already taken the katana out of its sheath on her back but not before Patra began striding towards the woman. Her Nikes made squelching sounds as she made her way over. The woman alerted by the movement raised up her head. Even in the dark, her eyes blazed , the fire inside angrily stoked by the interruption.

"We've been looking for you bitch," Patra bellowed. "You been hiding?"

The two silent supplicants beside her moved to intercept the threat like machines.

Suzy and Y called out to Patra but she was already in her stride. Fear dialled down, bravado at its peak and Patra's mouth, shooting off.

Suzy started running after her and Y followed.

"You know that motherfucker Byfield is dead an he ain't coming back, right." Patra spat. "You need to move on bitch or join him."

Her insult did not elicit a response from the vampire Queen except a slight tip of her head as if what had been said was duly understood.

Her valets or guards had eaten up the distance between them in a blink. They had transformed from bipedal humans to feral hybrids who were human in form alone. Patra was angry but not stupid and she knew her probability distorting talents were working in the background. She strode over an area of pavement that was being redone and cordoned off. She did not miss a beat as her instep scooped up the piece of loose masonry that was to be her weapon. She completed her stride and propelled it like she was kicking a football. The brick struck the first assailants square in the face shattering on impact, diverting its trajectory slightly. Partially blinded the creature came at Patra, talons extended, bursting through the flesh of its fingers like flick knives hidden in sausages, its mouth weaponized from chitin daggers erupting from its gums. Patra blocked its first strike and ducked away from the second. She countered with a backhanded blow that snapped the creature's head back, causing it to stumble.

"Damn!" Its skin, Patra thought was like rhinoceros hide. In moments it regained its wits from a blow that would have incapacitated a normal human, but it hung back. Instead, it let its partner continue where it had left off. The other bloodsucker, once an attractive female attacked from Patra's blindside. The warning came to her as a compulsion to fall backwards and Patra did so without further thought. A blur of red green and yellow flashed up beside her. Suzy caught Patra, dodged the monsters snapping jaws and trapped the creature's arm in the crux of her dragon tattooed arm.

"Now you're just showing off," Patra said and Suzy grimaced at the strength of these monsters.

"You're welcome." Suzy said. "Now, let me finish dis."

Suzy came out kicking, low and high. The vampire matched her movements with uncanny reflexes. And she could understand why they were chosen to accompany their mistress. Y joined the fray before Suzy was overwhelmed, her movements precise, the Katana flashing gold in the street lights and sparking on contact with these feral killers. But the vampires were strong, skilled and relentless. ree against two and they were holding their own.

Shaft who had been side-lined by the conflicts speed and ferocity kept his eyes on the well-dressed vampire woman. She had been silently observing the struggle and then suddenly she turned her back on the conflict and was casually walking away.

A target moving at a pace he could deal with.

"Hey, where the fuck do you think you're going?" Shaft screamed at her back "We need to have words." Shaft had his Glock in his hand pointing at her.

The woman ignored him and kept moving.

"Don't make me do this. I swear I'll shoot." His voice boomed. "This is your final warning. Stop and raise your hands."

He aimed and curled his finger around the trigger, just as Patra came into view. Ms. Jones was attacking the departing vampire from behind. Patra was airborne in seconds, a classic Thai Knee strike unfurling like an origami figure but as beautiful as it was, it never got to its intended target. The Vampire queen twisted her upper body, like a Palate master and caught Patra in mid-flight by the throat and lifted her. She gagged, grabbing the vampire's forearm but she was overwhelmingly more powerful than Patra ever could be. The vampire queen peered deeply into her eyes and Patra's squirmed with the discomfort of being probed and strangled at the same time. The Vampire woman's cold hard fingers gripped tighter and Patra could feel her world slip away.

Suzy felt it too.

The power and the darkness was like a whirlwind of raw unchecked energy.

"Oh, shit!" Shaft swore, seeing Patra frantically struggling for her life he squeezed off three rounds. Two hit the vampire queen in the chest and neck the other went wide. The queen absorbed the impact, shrugging off the high calibre bullets but dropping Patra in the process. Patra fell on all fours gripping her neck, coughing and panting. She scuttled backwards on all fours to safety.

Miranda stood calmly looking at them and making patterns in the air with her hands, a kind of mystical syntax that affected the air around her. Unravelling the fabric of reality and stitching it back to her own design. She clapped her hands together in conclusion turned and walked away. Her two minions stopped fighting too and slinked back into the shadows to join her.

The temperature of the air around Shaft, Y, Suzy and Patra suddenly plummeted. All around them was a sound of hard scurrying appendages, fluttering wings and a rising rush of sewer smell that assaulted their senses.

Then bursting fourth like a biblical plague, a wall of tens of thousands of cockroaches appeared from every grate and manhole. Every bin and even under the doors of shops exploded with the insects. They scurried and flowed into each other forming a dark and disgusting hive mind construct that erected a barrier between the conjurer – the Vampire queen and everyone else.

It was as if the battle had just been called to an end. Patra was still on her ass when Suzy, Y and Shaft ran up to her.

"You okay?" Y asked breathlessly.

"Yuh can talk, gal?" Suzy was touching Patra testing for damage. Shaft hovered above them looking concerned with his gun still drawn.

"Do I look like I can't talk to you," Patra grinned rubbing her neck. "Did you see that? Son of a bitch!" She whooped. "Man, that bitch was strong."

"She could have killed you," Y said. "And you sound impressed?"

"I am. She's a beast." Patra said.

"You're telling me dat. I already know. I tink we upset her." Suzy said.

At least she knows, that we know." Y added.

Suzy nodded contemplatively. Y helped Patra to her feet.

"She handed me my ass," Patra said hopping.

"I know," Y said throwing her arms around her shoulders.

"I needed that because when we meet again it ain't gonna be fun." Patra said. "You all hear me. It ain't gonna be fun."

"Preach, sista." Suzy teased.

Shaft looked at the three of them and shook his head in disbelief.

"I'd prefer we never see her ever again but ..."

The girls laughed nervously.

"We just watched deh mass murderer, walk away." Suzy said. "Payback for the lives taken is due Mr. Mac."

"Oh, yeah sugah." Patra added hoarsely.

"Let's just make sure the next time we meet, we are a bit more prepared." Y said.

"Next time?" Shaft asked. "I swear you three are fucking, crazy.

29.

Kew Gardens, Richmond

Miranda Pheare stood naked, head held back arms outstretched as the moon's light bathed her dark skin through the glass. The greenhouse was spaciously built to her specifications and although it was off-limits to the viewing public and hidden from the prying eyes of most of the Board of Trustees, she could freely roam here undisturbed. Miranda had extraordinary privileges, and that was how it should be. In various guises, over the years she has been a trustee and a major contributor to the Botanical Gardens since its inception in the seventeen hundreds. In life she had an affinity for plants but now being undead it had only increased her passions.

After two hundred years, she had not completely shrugged off the shackles of humanity. She loved being here. It was the antithesis of everything she represented before the majesty of her vampirism. Her garden, a place of solitude and a place of solace was a reminder to her of how much this world was as much hers and vampire kind as it was for the humans. The greenhouse nurtured the most poisonous, toxic and dangerous plants on the planet. Many of these wonders of dark nature were not naturally occurring species of the planet but through her funding and the acquisition of the best and the brightest in genetically engineering and vampire science they had created some truly breath-taking specimens.

Her favorite was the Triffidium.

She lowered herself to a lotus position and allowed her hyper-acute senses to discover the intricacies of the environment around her. She could feel the panic, the breathing and pounding heart of someone she had invited to have an audience with her. She could sense Night Shade pollen being buffeted in the air by the warm currents; then there were the spores of the mutated Venus Flytrap, the nectar from Pitcher Plants and the giant Sink Flowers which she could taste on her lizard-like tongue.

As she basked in the fauna, reveling in this dangerous ecosystem, she felt something tickle her consciousness. A touch like a young child would to alert an adult to their presence. Miranda smiled calling on her vampire essence to connect with a different kind of intelligence that was reaching out to her. Knowing what was coming and withholding her enthusiasm to see it, Miranda allowed it to present itself in its own time. Its vines came tentatively out of the darkness, first like feelers, touching her back and intertwining her ankles. When it was sure this was no trap; it stung her twice injecting its deadly venom into her. Miranda's vampire biology absorbed the toxin without due concern. There were more clicks some rapid, some spaced out, followed by slithering muscular stems, slowly approaching her in welcome like a lover. They sneaked between her legs, the plants protuberances massaging her labia.

Miranda's smile broadened.

"You miss me," she cooed. "I know you did."

Other stems encircled her stomach, and some of the smaller tendrils crept around her perfect breasts squeezing the orbs tenderly and brushing the dark areola of her nipples. Miranda closed her eyes and let the herbaceous creature stimulate her sexually. She was communicating with it in a basic format she had figure out from the last time she was here. In truth the hybrid wasn't controlled by her, she could only make suggestions in its simple psychic way. Their connection was strong because of Miranda's talents, but it made up its own mind what it would do. It was a predator like her and loved to play the murder games she was so fond of.

"Deh guest still having fun?" The hybrid bristled. Miranda interpreted that as a shrug. It was more concerned about pleasuring her than the frightened man running around the protected greenhouse.

Mr. Joseph Adams, a forensic accountant, had been in her employ for a moment, 20 years if she thought about it. Though some irregularities had come to her attention from a shell company her solicitors had created, he was incorruptible. Mr. Adams wasn't stealing from her, that would be ludicrous. But he had been a bit too free with company information. She never had to deal with him directly, but this evening called for a more hands-on approach so that he could understand the magnitude of his error. Killing employees: talented employees was not her style. There were far worse things than death, and she could wield those powers with the expertise of a conductor. So, she had him brought to her funhouse and allowed him the run of the establishment. He had been stung a few times by the Trifidium and chances are inhaled poisonous pollen from some of her beauties. If she did not administer the antivenom and question him, he would die. Languidly, she stretched her perfect figure and walked into an area that was pitch black to her eyes it was as clear as day. Thick tenebrous storks followed her obediently, positioning themselves on the odd occasion around obstacles or trip hazards. But there was no need, the hybrids mistress was as surefooted as a mountain goat and as graceful as a gazelle. In moments she was standing beside the accountant who was twitching, moaning rhythmically and had soiled himself. A stray memory dredged up by the poisons coursing through his body had him gibbering nursery rhymes. His lips trembled, and from his smell, Miranda knew how long he had left before his organs began to malfunction then liquify. He was barely lucid, and the pain he was feeling must be exquisite. Miranda's nipples hardened she kneeled beside her employee and turned him over on the side.

"Mr. Joseph," she said to him. "Yuh need to listen carefully to the questions I am about to ask you. Do yuh understand?"

The man nodded, disjointed like a discarded puppet because in a way he was. Miranda broke through his shattered mental defenses without much effort and used hypnotic suggestion on him to tell her everything he knew. If he ever was to recall this memory, Miranda had left behind a psychic booby-trap, that would wipe it from his memory completely.

"Three weeks ago, you were contacted by a Jamaican gentleman called Spokes. A businessman," she asked.

"Yes," Mr. Joseph said.

"What did he want and what did you tell him?"

30.

Patra flipped the kickstand out and switched off the Suzuki. She pulled the Nazi helmet off her head and gripped it under her arm. She tried to be cool with what she was about to do but not being a hundred percent honest with her sisters did not sit well with her. It wasn't the fact of them knowing, they would know eventually. There would be the teasing and the usual good-natured jibes. And if anyone was resistant to taunts it was her. She could take as good as she gave but this meeting was a bit unusual.

Shit, this must have been the first time, she didn't openly flaunt her relationship exploits with her sisters. Maybe she was worried her actions could compromise what was turning out to be a big deal.

Fuck it, she would follow her instincts even if some sexual tension was bungled up into it.

Patra knew of the vampire threat and the powerful and resourceful creatures that they were by reading some of the ancient texts at the mansion. When Dean's name came up and his unusual departure from the predatory lifestyle of his kin, Patra more than the rest of her sisters was intrigued. They had an obvious connection at the club. Then there was the fact of his escape from Miranda's clutches something it seems no one had ever done before. The supernatural grapevine they were now a part of, had reached out to him and had invited them to the Jazz Club. Dean had been keen to talk to them but on his own terms.

This was it.

She came prepared.

Her favorite perfume, and a revealing outfit that was comfortable; but showed her form and would not restrict her if she needed to move quickly. The Jazz Club looked different out of hours. Patra was uncomfortable walking to the back of the establishment between the wall and intervening mesh fence. Kicking down doors physically and metaphorically was her thing, but this felt like she was stepping over a boundary.

The reinforced door into the kitchen must have been the only way through. Strangely Patra was wondering where the fire escapes were. The back door was open when she came around to the back. Rap music was playing in the background, Jay-Z of all people and two guys were cleaning the kitchen surfaces to a gleaming shine. They acknowledge her as she passed with a nod of heads that Patra ticked off as being normal. Not that anything about this was normal. She kept walking to a hidden living area attached to the Club. It was cleverly concealed using the interior architecture like an optical illusion depending on the angle you approached the hallway. Dean had described it well and if it was possible to put someone at ease through text messages, he did. Patra, had not expressed her excitement with the idea of meeting a real-life vampire. Especially one who didn't want to rip her throat out and a fan too.

Dean had listened to her podcast.

This was just nuts.

A year ago, the idea of what she was doing would be fantastic enough for a book or film, not real life. But here she was at the back of the jazz club in a secret section, standing at the door considering how many times she should knock.

"Come in," the voice said pre-empting her. "I don't bite."

Patra glided in past her host who was holding the door open. He smelt of Ylang, Ylang and her heart raced.

"What kind of bike do you ride?" Dean asked.

Patra stopped and turned to look at him.

"How did you know?"

Dean opened his arms magnanimously, his torso showing the definition of his chest and abs in a snugly fitting wifebeater. Patra's eyes slid over his fine figure.

"That's what we do Princess. Apex predators and our enhanced senses. I can't help it." He seemed to apologize.

"I feel you," Patra said. She was almost certain he heard her heart fluttering. Shit!

"I think you really do," Dean answered staring at her with soft eyes that had seen so much. "The best fuel on the market too," he continued. "What do you have?"

"Oh," Patra said dismissively. "Ain't nothing special, Suzuki GZ nine thousand."

"You're being modest. That's a beast."

Patra grinned touching her nose with her thumb.

"I have ridden wilder beasts."

It was his turn to smirk.

"I believe that too."

"Funny," Patra said smiling. "You've got jokes."

He took her hand before she could react. His movement was incredibly fast, precise and gentle. It was like a cool breeze that transformed into cool flesh. He led her toward a small table covered in a gingham cloth and two chairs tucked under it. Dean pulled one out.

"Sit, sit. Have you eaten?"

Patra wanted to decline, but the smell of cooking was divine.

"A dude who can cook?"

He nodded.

"I have had more time than most to perfect it."

Patra sat.

"I guess you have."

Deans cheek was close to hers and she could feel the cold leeching from his skin. It was like standing in front of the chill compartment of a refrigerator.

"You can learn a lot when you have time on your hands." He said suggestively.

Patra shook her head, her face feeling suddenly warm.

"How did you hear about me?" He asked.

"It seems in our hood, there are OG's, who know top tier mystical niggas, who are concerned with London and the kind of gangbangers who are taking up residence here. My sisters and I are supposed to be hot shit, so when we have a problem the word gets put out."

"Stupid question," Dean said shrugging. "Your order is a legend. In my many years of existence, I have never had the privilege. I just thought I was buried deeper than anyone could ever find me, and I was right. But when I heard you ladies were looking for an advantage against a monster I knew well, I made myself available."

"Sugah, you're not that deep. You on YouTube."

He laughed.

"It's not a myth about vampires lack of reflection in a mirror. You'll hear my music, but you'll never see a physical or digital image of me."

"Who needs an image, you're doing crazy numbers. Your fanbase is broad." Patra said.

"It's a part of the mystique and replacing one need for another." His eyes dimmed for a moment as he went inside himself.

"Why do you want to stay underground anyway? Your kind isn't known for keeping a low profile. And from the history books, we tend to want you dead." She paused. "But you are survivors."

Dean shook his head.

"That we are." He said.

"Your reputation proceeds you though. The only man to have left the Miranda Pheare's family with the head still on his shoulders."

He grinned broadly and almost humanly, but Patra kept reminding herself that he wasn't.

Patra shook her head; the smile remained on her lips.

"Wouldn't it have been easier to keep running with your big homie Miranda, raising all kind of hell?"

"Leaving that psycho was the best thing I ever did." He walked over to the kitchenette and opened a small but spotless looking cupboard and took out a plate. With a towel over his arm, he walked back to Patra's table. "The thing that is usually missing from any expert opinion or study on vampires is our ability to fall in love with a human after being turned. It's rare and sometimes when it does happen not everyone will heed the call." He placed the plate in front of her.

"But you did, right?" Patra asked.

He nodded.

"I did." Dean was heading back into the mouth-watering and savoury smells. His back to her, the sounds of rattling pots and pans weirdly transporting Patra back to Atlanta, Georgia.

"Human love or connection doesn't change who I am fundamentally," he said.

"I still crave human blood, it just not an all-consuming need as it was before. The need to murder for my sustenance and to enjoy the fear in the process is a thing of the past. Not my style."

"I've got to be real with you sugah; I am on razor blades. Your family's reputation ain't to be trifled with."

"You sure your nervous? Your heartbeat is normal. It only seems to change when I'm really close to you. Fear or something else?"

"Spooky Guardian shit." Patra dismissed it too quickly, her cheeks flushing. "It makes me good at poker."

"I can bet."

Patra thought carefully about asking the next question.

"Why now. What will be different this time around?"

"You're the difference." He said. "I've tried to prevent this madness myself a few times. I felt almost responsible for what Miranda was doing." Dean shook his head. "She's much too powerful for me but together..."

"... we may have a chance." Patra completed.

"It's not going tobe easy. She's got fingers in every section of society. You'd be surprised what people will do for immortality. I have a bounty on my head from vampires and her familiars. Even if the mistress is not around her dogs are looking for me."

"So, the bitch is connected?" Patra rubbed her throat absently.

He shook his head.

"More than you will believe. The last time we tangled I was injured. Miranda sent her dogs of war to finish me off. I was backed in a corner until I found out about the Jazz Club."

"My sister says this place was protected. Sacred ground or some such thing."

Dean put his hand in his jean's pockets, his biceps bulging.

"That's right. This place was built on intersecting ley lines. Only a few places in the whole of London are like this. Once I am in here, she can't touch me. I was lucky."

Patra didn't realize she had sighed at the story's conclusion.

"You said there were two places like the Jazz club in London."

"And there lies the problem," Dean said. "The second place is a VIP only Establishment called the Hellfire Club." He paused. "That's where Miranda stays amongst the other midnight tribes, who have the means and the connections."

"We know," Patra said sourly. "We found out that's where her bolt-hole was. Untouchable right."

He nods.

"Motherfucker!" Patra drawled. "We can't get to her in her crib."

"That's what I'm saying."

"So upfront and personal it's going to be then," Patra murmured. "We gonna have to find another way."

"I don't know how prepared you and your sisters are. The information on the Guardians is sparse but to take on Miranda you're going to need everything you've got. And I mean everything." His voice trailed into the kitchen for a moment.

Dean came back to her little table with two pots in hand and a set of condiments under his arm. Patra couldn't get enough of how he moved. She wondered if he had any black ancestors. Dean let the condiment fall from under his arm, the superior control of his body evident, using his hip like a slope to guide the cheese, pepper, and parsley to wobbly stop on the table.

Nothing spilled.

He then placed two pots on the ceramic rings. Patra applauded his skill. He came back with servings utensils and a bottle of wine.

"Tagliatelle and prawns in a creamy cheese sauce," he announced as he served her. Patra squirmed in her seat while he filled her plate and poured sweet Greek wine.

"I am getting a vibe you've done this before," Patra said.

"Only for friends."

"So, we homies now?" Patra asked.

"I hope so," Dean said confidently. "I really hope so."

31.

Hellfire Club, Central London

The Wiltshire smoking room kept the name and the function for over three hundred years but has served many purposes in its time. Tonight, it seemed that overwhelming function was an evening of networking amidst the paneled walls, oil paintings and ruby red plush leather chairs set up in groups of three. The bar looked like a gnarly outgrowth from the far wall. An abscess that had been summoned from the building and that had fossilized over the centuries. It was a feature managed by male and female bartenders expertly replenishing brandies, sherries and champagne. Above and around them were lost vintages, ancient tipples shrouded in mystery and dust. Exotic blends made for a discerning clientele that had existed for centuries. There were many orders of vodka from a distillery founded by Rasputin and some orders of tequila from worshippers of the Aztec God Tezcatlipoca. But only one order of a three-hundred-year-old Jamaican rum with a half measure of virgin male blood. A bartender with a tray in hand and a lightness of step deftly maneuvered his way through the Hellfire members to a darkened corner of the Wiltshire room. It seemed like the dimensions of the space trapped a kind of primordial darkness, that the bar staff shivered at because they were human after all and this despondent corner was not for humankind to enjoy. The roving bartender placed both drinks down and played with the idea of trying to see the faces in the deep-set seats. It was impossible. The enchantment performed its function, and the barkeep turned to leave them in peace.

Anancy took in the swirling powers, potentialities, mystical energies that not just resided in this room but the entire building. He had become a part of the scene, quietly observing and listening. The Hell Fire Club was one of the seven buildings on the planet built on the intersection of seven key ley lines - mystical conduits that manifested in the physical and spiritual world simultaneously. Most were temples and shrines.

There was nothing like this anywhere.

A member's club of neutral ground, where saints, monsters, men, and Gods rub shoulders. All bound by untenable laws woven into the tapestry of the universe itself that not even Anancy's kind could not bend to their will. But he was uniquely resourceful amongst his inviolable and stuck up peers, who could only think inside the box. The Spider God was an enigma.

Take this omission for instance. None of the immortals could circumvent the universal laws more subtly, than he could. None would even think about turning up on the earth plane, in his purple pinstripe suit, tangerine shirt and his feathered trilby searching for information. The ancient edicts stated he was not supposed to directly interact with humans, and he was fulfilling that part of the bargain. This place housed only the connected beings who were far from human by design, divine conception or birth. So, he was contravening no laws other than being here in the first place. He didn't like committees anyway.

Anancy had positioned himself about three tables away from the corner booth that the vampire Queen Miranda Pheare was holding court. Two of her little lieutenants had come and gone. But the gentleman sitting with her commanded a portion of her attention. Anancy having assumed a corporeal form his powers were somewhat limited but those limitations among the humans made him Superman. He lit the end of his Cuban cigar sucked on it in rapid succession making the tip flare red. He then released a stream of smoke from Havana's finest. He cocked his ear in the direction of the vampire's conversation and even though the enchantment surrounding them was meant to block prying eyes and ears, he took in everything they said.

"Your fashion line Nasty Gal won at Gratuit de Prinz at London's fashion week today. Who do you want to represent you at the press conference?" Mr. Opoku asked his mistress. "I like Miss Simmons; she is doing a good job."

Miranda sat with a perfect posture, in a black and white Karl Lagerfeld outfit, her voice was smoky and sensual.

"She can continue in her post. I like how organized she is. I respect confident women."

Mr. Opoku nodded.

Miranda's confidante hesitated, his body language unsure of how to broach a question.

"Mistress," he paused. "The issue of the Heart of Ares remains unresolved."

"And why do you presume that situation hasn't been dealt with?"

Mr. Opoku hesitated.

"I didn't mean to presume..."

She nods, the closest gesture of understanding you would ever receive from her.

"Did you know when a master vampire is destroyed – their immortality may have ended, but all their knowledge and experiences are passed down to the next in line to lead the Clan. Uploaded to the Vampire consciousness?"

Miranda picked up her glass and sipped from it. She was not expecting an answer from him.

"Of course, you didn't. I see everyting around me, forget nothing and plan every eventuality. Then I place redundancies against what could be. It is my nature. That is why Mr. Opoku, my confidante and as close to a friend my kind can accommodate, I will survive. Because that is what I do."

Mr. Opoku knew that statement could not be truer. Her kind was like gods walking amongst men, apex predators and ultimate survivors all rolled into one. If you believed in such things, the creative force had a sense of humor. As splendid as the Vampire nation was its species would be extinct without humankind. The Nosferatu had found ways to make that symbiosis work over the centuries. Mr. Opoku's concern was not the ninety-five percent of humans who lived ordinary lives, but the gifted few who were touched by the higher powers and who seemed to have a purpose no one on this plane of existence would understand.

That's what worried him.

Being partially human could be a problem. And maybe that condition made Mr. Opoku susceptible to doubt and weakness. He had learned to disguise it but who knew what the consequences would be if his mistress discovered his uncertainty.

He asked, carefully.

"The Guardians are discovering too much about us mistress. How do you want me to handle them?"

"Handle them?" Miranda laughed throatily. "Mr. Opoku you do not handle the Guardians of deh Light. They are an elemental force that inhabits human vessels to do the bidding of the old Gods whose concern is balance an entropy."

She paused and brought the glass to her red lips again and sipped. Miranda smiled appreciatively at the taste of the concoction.

"I must destroy the meat sacks they are contained in but not before I enjoy dem company."

"How do we do that?" Mr. Opoku asked. "They are guided by higher powers."

Miranda's voice took on a frigid edge.

"The old Gods are fucking obsolete and need to know dem place. They are bound by the same laws as we all. When people stopped worshipping them some of the old ones ceased to exist except in musty books and manuscripts. To extinguish the light of their puppets we need to beat them as a triad. The power is in their togetherness. That would shatter their purpose Mr. Opoku, prove to the old God's once and for all. They are no longer relevant."

Anancy took a long pull on his cigar and smiled.

"Musty books and manuscripts," He repeated to Himself. "Was it Shaka Zulu, Sun Tzu or maybe even Mas

Wilbur from St. Elizabeth who said never underestimate your enemy."

He let out a stream of smoke that spread around him, trapped by the potential energies the trickster god carried with him on the corporeal plane.

"Mistress Pheare," Anancy said shaking his head to himself. "This time I think you have met your match. Oh yes!"

Having heard enough, he tipped his hat further over his eyes and relaxed into his chair.

32.

Patra wrapped her arms a little tighter around Deans waist as the bike slowed then broke right, into a 'B' Road. Patra could feel lean muscle under his leather jacket and with it a subdued power that showed in the way he carried himself. Dean wasn't a bad rider either and had insisted taking Miss Bitch – her Suzuki GZ, to this location. He wore no helmet, just shades and Patra nearly forgot who he really was. His relaxed demeanour made it easy to forget. This man she rested her helmeted head on, did not breathe and had no heartbeat but there was something endearing about him for all his strangeness. They sped down the commercial road and through the security checkpoint at an industrial estate that was eerily unmanned. Continuing through the vast complex, four blocks down and right into a cul-de-sac, Dean slowed. At the crest of the semi-circle and straight ahead was the Gibraltar Catering company. Dean pulled up in front of it. From the outside the building looked deserted but Patra wasn't so sure. She shuffled off the bikes seat and Dean pulled it onto its kickstand.

"I apologise for the drama and secrecy. But I wanted you to experience something."

"And you couldn't just tell me?" Patra asked.

Dean shook his head.

"This you need to see, the only way you will understand the stakes that are involved when Miranda comes to town."

"Sound like a Johnny Cash tune." Patra said.

Dean nodded.

"The man in black would appreciate that and the irony wouldn't be lost on him either." Dean's eyebrows arched.

"Let me introduce you to my safe house." He gestured to the door just as it swung open.

As she walked through the complex Patra could see the facility was manned by about five staff members in this area alone and she was having fun trying to figure out who was vampire kind and who was human. Patra guessed Dean must have turned some of these people himself in the early days of his vampirism. This was his way of fighting back and grabbing an advantage when he could. Patra was left in a very comfortable rest area while Dean took care of something. She couldn't properly avail herself of its inviting cushions and mood music because she was too wired. When he returned, she was brimming over with questions.

"How do you protect yourself here?" Patra asked. "This isn't the Jazz Club. Your ass is out in the open."

He thought about it.

"We're more traditional here. Old school even. We have a state-of-the-art surveillance system and around the clock security armed with light beam weapons that I developed with some interested business parties I know concerned with the vampire threat. All the weaknesses my kind have are built into the security arrangements of this place. If I had the choice of a place to hold up from a vampire onslaught outside of the Jazz Club, it would be here."

A communication device crackled in his belt making him pause. He unclipped the hand-held radio and listened.

"It's time Mr Thorne," a voice said.

Dean walked past where Patra sat, reached down and picked up a beautiful old school Persian broad bladed scimitar that was leaning in the corner. He threw it over his shoulder and tightened the strap around his chest.

"Damascus steel," he said matter-of-factly. "Five hundred years old. Never turn up to a gunfight without it."

He turned to Patra and held out his hand. She took it and stood.

"Come," he said. "You need to see this."

Wherever they were going it was below ground level and the whole section carried with it a sombre and despondent mood which was starkly different from above ground.

Patra would soon understand why.

This section was reminiscent of a prison wing with some rooms having their doors left open and she could see they were meeting rooms. The other rooms were not so easily explained especially the one they were approaching at the end of the corridor.

Dean knocked on the reinforced door.

There was a heavy electronic buzz then a clunk of high tensile rods being withdrawn out of the slab of a door into the reinforced frame surrounding it. The room she was ushered into was padded. That did not bode well. The reggae icon Peter Tosh was being piped into the room on the low volume. Crazily it seemed relevant for what she was about to see. In the centre of the room was an articulated table with a young white woman strapped to it. She was agitated, sweating and mumbling. Her skin was bruised by the straps around her wrist and ankles and neck. Her head twisted sharply from left to right, eyes bulging, saliva erupting from her mouth as she hissed and mumbled. The air was tainted with sweat and blood. Patra immediately held a breath as if the occasion demanded it and looked over to Dean with questioning eyes. Their gazes locked and a sadness transmitted between them. Dean's lips slightly parted showing his teeth as if he was going to speak. Instead he swallowed his words and focussed some more on the woman on the table. The restrained woman's discomfort became more pronounced with his presence and in seconds the petite woman was snarling and howling, sending saliva geysers into the air. Her bonds were substantial but barely kept her in check. Patra stepped forward to see not just deep change in temperament of the woman but the physical changes too. A chill radiated from her stomach and spread to her extremities as it began to dawn on her what she was witnessing.

The petite woman was like clay being roughly needed by a mad sculptor. The flesh of her feet and hands were tearing apart as talons erupted where her toenails and fingernails were. Her chest expanded, her jaw distended, and an arsenal of razor-sharp teeth burst through her gums. The woman's eyes became crimson, her pupils' pinpricks, her brows furrowed, and the true monstrosity came forward devoid of humanity.

"Damn," Patra murmured to herself not hearing when Dean came up behind her.

"You know of the Platinum Exhibition Massacre of course."

Patra nodded.

"This young lady had the privilege of being bitten by Miranda. An honour in their circles. Why?" He answered his own question. "Rebecca Swanson is a top system analyst in the city and a very good fit for Miranda's organisation. I snatched her before she could merge into the Black Roses clan."

Patra heard Dean's words but was too mesmerised at the horrible transformation of body and mind she was staring at.

"What can you do for her?" Patra asked.

"I am afraid we can do nothing for her. Rebecca's life like many ends up here on this table. Friends, family and colleagues all destroyed by Miranda and her ambition. Do you see what we're up against?"

"Man, this is bullshit." Patra's protest was a murmur, devoid of hope.

With that said Dean slung the Damascus sword from his back and in a blur, brought the big blade down with Thrack! Severing Rebecca Swanson's head from her body.

33.

Movie Premier, Red Carpet, Leicester Square

Where does Mr. Patel get his contacts from? He gets access to these movers and shakers without breaking a sweat. And when Bad II the Bone broached the question to their mysterious business partner, he simply played down his powerhouse connections with a humble bow. The ladies slow-walked down the red carpet with their client and co-star of the Mission impossible spin-off in their sights.

The starlet Nicole Hemmings was beginning to make waves in her acting career, and this role would help to cement her position as a rising star. Mr. Patel surmised in his way that Miss Hemmings needed their protection as she was experiencing some pronounced bad luck issues. The idea that these entertainment types believed in the metaphysical to such a degree that Mr. Patel could sell them or sway them to use their service was a mysterious process someday they would understand. Until then multimillionaire property developer, multiple gym owner and business partner kept the lucrative work rolling in.

Suzy stood in striking distance from the starlet as she was accosted by a roving TV crew. Suzy watched the young woman intently for a moment and made eye contact with Y who was the closest to the cinema's entrance stairs. Patra who was furthest away was watching the cordoned crowds scrambling for autographs. As the young actress dislodged and floated over to the throng of fans on both sides of the red carpet, Bad II the Bone converged on the area around her, just in case.

Autograph books, programs, flyers and scraps of paper were thrust at her with good-natured enthusiasm. She signed them all with a smile and a flick of her wrist. She quickly manufactured grins, grimaces and a look of shock for numerous selfies. The crowd was genuinely glad to be around her. She was emanating similar good feelings, and Suzy was satisfied she was in no danger. Inside the cinema would have a different set of challenges namely the frenemies and the disguised spite Hollywood nurtured. Anyone could wish the young woman ill but not follow through with action.

Still, they had a job to do.

Patra was getting ready to filter the cinema-goers as they entered the eight decades old, world famous cinema. Checking for anyone her senses felt were hinky.

The girls were looking glamorous in evening dresses and heels, blending in perfectly with the night. Y always looked uncomfortable without a sword when she was at events like this. Patra's unique gifts made her environment a catalog of weapons, so she was in her element anyway. Suzy was comfortable just as she was with her clutch bag containing her kitoben tactical pen and her mobile phone. They were about to usher the actress into the busy foyer, when Suzy suddenly stopped in her tracks, a heavy sense of foreboding slammed into her. She bit into her lower lip.

Her mobile phone rang soon after.

Y and Patra looked over to her, Suzy's concern radiated out to them like a radio wave, and they were the reception towers. They kept walking into the foyer anyway. Suzy unclipped her clutch bag, reached in and brought the phone to ears while walking behind her sisters. They didn't need to make eye contact to know something was really wrong. Suzy spoke once in rapid fashion, her voice raised slightly, her expression hard, eyes cold like Flint.

"How did you get my rass number?" Suzy spat.

There was a pause.

Then a female voice with a Jamaican accent deep and sensual delivered its words with absolute confidence.

"Is that any way to speak to a fellow Jamaican." Miranda Pheare's voice was silky smooth with a husky edge that tried to mask the vicious predator that she was but couldn't. Suzy kept it contained, but her psychic warnings were going berserk.

"What deh fuck do you want?"

The vampire chuckled. Someone screamed at the other end of the line.

Suzy shuddered.

"Let mi see now," Miranda pondered. "I would love to see iron spikes through your hands and feet, chained to my dungeon walls in my estate in Montego Bay. I'd like to lick that tight pussy of yours and drink you dry one drop at a time. Ah!"

Suzy could hear the creature smacking her lips in anticipation of the thought while the sobbing in the background got louder.

"Maybe some other time," Suzy said sarcastically.

"Maybe," Miranda cooed. "In the meantime, I need to speak to Yvonne. This is a life and death situation." Miranda laughed throatily. "Y's life and her friend's death." Suzy hesitated, taking the phone from her ears and pressed it to her shoulder. The world suddenly felt smaller and so much more dangerous. Suzy caught up with her sisters in the foyer and signaled Y to come over. Patra watched the activity with interest, her eyes questioning but she kept close to their client.

Y came over moving in so close no one could overhear their conversation. A virtual cold wind made Y shiver, hoping Suzy's complex body language would give away more of their dilemma.

It was serious but not an immediate threat to them. This crisis felt different.

"What's up?" Y asked. Suzy took Y's hand and planted her phone into it. The Jamaican kept her hand covering Y's own and gripped it. Her voice was harsh.

"Keep it simple, do not engage with her, do not tell her anyting about us, do not tell her where we are and what we are doing. Listen, she will try to get into your head, just be careful."

Suzy relinquished her phone and Y put it to her ear, knowing but not believing what was at the other end of this call.

"Please don't; please don't!" A voice shrieked. There were crunching wet sounds and a scream fuelled by horror, pain, and hopelessness. Another voice came into play, dark and syrupy like molasses spiked with shards of glass.

"That Yvonne is the sound of Sandy Brewster losing two fingers," Miranda stated. "Yuh remember Sandy don't yuh, your former boss."

"What are you doing?" Y asked. The relief that it wasn't her mother on the other end of the phone made her almost lose stability. But disgust replaced that vacuum quickly. "I swear you don't want me looking for you more than I already am. Making this personal is not a good idea. It is something you don't want to sign up for."

Miranda laughed again.

"But that is where you're wrong sister Y. I want you to take this personally because I want the best version of you in this game." Miranda said. "I've been away from London for some time now so think of my surprise when I find myself among Guardians who have some-thing I want. That challenge is just too much to ignore."

"This is no game," Y said. "Don't do this."

"Everything is a game sister and you humans need to know how I play."

Y shivered.

Miranda's lingering chuckle was disquieting to her ears and seemed to go on forever.

Then suddenly the line went dead.

34.

Y Knew this was a trap but she didn't care. She stood alone on the High Street in West London and stared at the darkened nail salon. Her heart was pounding in her chest, but she maintained her warrior breathing, like her sensei's past and present, believed that 'your power was your breath.' Her reflection in the plate glass window of the shop front made her wince at her blatant contravention of fashion laws was self-evident. Long shimmering red evening gown with a split, she had ripped further for freedom. Garishly green sneakers she stored in the booth of her car and her Katana slung around her shoulders. She girded herself, Suzy's words of warning ringing in her head.

"Take it careful, an kill anyting dat look pan yuh sideways. Remove deh head or pierce deh heart."

Y approached the door her Katana in hand humming with anticipation. The door was closed but not locked as she turned the handle and it swung open easily. Memories of working here flooded back to her. The difference a year can make. Eighteen months ago, she was an employee here under the tyrannical ownership of Sandy Brewster. Now she had been ordained with the duty to save the cantankerous bitch from God knows what. Funny, it didn't feel like retribution. She felt no satisfaction because this wasn't personal. This was what she did.

It was her destiny.

Y opened the door a touch more, and a cockroach scurried out, disappearing into the cracks in the pavement. Y froze, the hilt of her Katana was pressing into her palm like gravity had localized itself at that one spot. The blade hummed some more, a discordant tune, that vibrated along its length, into the hilt. She had taught herself to recognize some of its utterings.

It too was wary.

Forewarned is forearmed but knowing she was in danger did not feel like an advantage. She questioned her gifts, questioned this course of action. Her analytical mind was trying to explain why all of this was impossible, improbable and dangerous. Without effort, a skill that took a lifetime to master, Y switched off the mental chatter.

Click!

Her mind became an infinite sheet of ice, calm and cold. With one quick look around the door frame, she rushed in, her Katana trailing behind her. Her eyes adapted quickly to the darkness and the smell of acetone assaulted her. The place hadn't changed much. The reception desk was on the right, and it looked unused. An Apple Mac looked pristine atop the prefabricated unit. Everything else after that was in disarray. Nail tables and chairs were overturned, posters and merchandise were scattered all over. Blood and red nail polish were mixed. Cockroaches were scurrying everywhere. Stealth was impossible with broken bottles of nail polish on the floor and the walls, so she didn't even bother to try. Instead, her focus was painfully sharp, eyes, ears and touch pushing on the boundaries of the environment she was moving through.

The floorboards upstairs creaked.

Y looked up.

A circular wet spot spread like fungus above her head. She couldn't discern color she didn't want to. Forcing the thought out of her head she kept moving. Three rooms on the ground floor were unchecked, and Y went through them quickly. She saw only destruction and a pattern — breadcrumbs whose purpose was to rush her into making mistakes.

Drive her upstairs quickly.

It worked.

Y rushed the stairs, too confident in her talents, regretting her brashness immediately. Her hyper senses isolated a single ping sound, from the silence.

Like a guitar string snapping.

Then a cloud of harsh whispers hurtled towards her.

A trap.

Y's nervous system lit up like an explosion, slowing her perception and ramping up her reflexes.

A swarm of projectiles sliced through the air towards her.

Y let go completely, sensing the air like a liquid being disturbed from a school of deadly fish. She crouched making herself a much smaller target, contorting her body in tight controlled combat routines, her blade a blistering tornado of movement in the darkness. The darts that came at her from every angle impacted on the forged steel ricocheting into ceiling wall and floor. Y couldn't believe she hadn't been hit. She crouched against the wall her skin tingling from the adrenaline rush, both her pedestrian senses and her extrasensory perception were still sharp. Y's eyes located the mechanisms that had spat the darts. They looked old school mechanical like golden beetles with ornate designs on their housings.

She needed to be more careful.

Standing, Y moved to the top of the stairs and headed for the largest of the rooms. She put her ear to the door and listened intently before pushing it open with the tip of her Katana.

She stepped back moving smoothly into a samurai battle posture, ready for what could come.

Nothing came.

Silence met her at first. The room was unbelievably dark every possible light source was blocked, smeared by something she couldn't quite recognize.

It had a smell to it.

Y stepped in and heard the sobbing and then there was light. A dark curtain that had covered the room from floor-to-ceiling animated suddenly and all at once departed along the floor in a sheet of night. The street light from the uncovered window shone through revealing thousands of black bodied roaches, heeding a call only they could hear.

Y stifled a squeal and shuddered but held her ground and let them pass over her feet and through her legs. What was left in the room was a blur, as Y's eyes immediately filled with tears.

"Miranda, you bitch!" Y spat.

Four bodies were heaped in the middle of the room in a broken macabre form looking fallow and drained, customers she guessed. Her eyes fixed on a squirming shadow to her left and recognized Sandy Brewster's prone body; both hands nailed to the floorboards and a stricken look of pain in her eyes. Y ran over to her side, the sounds of police sirens building in the distance, scrapping on the blackboard of the London night. Beyond the sorrow and anger, she was feeling right now was a relief. Shaft was coming with the cavalry and the warmth of knowing he had her back felt good. Her attention focused on her former boss, losing blood and in shock. Standing alone in a macabre gallery of blood, Y looked at the main exhibit. There were words scrawled on the wall in blood by a vampire.

"Let the hunt begin."

Suzy stood outside the Odeon cinema at Leicester Square and kept looking at her clutch bag. A macabre thought of another chilling conversation with Miranda boasting about ripping Y's throat out tried to dominate her mood. A residual effect from the mind poison the vampire was trying to use to influence them

It didn't last long. The connection she had with her sisters remained strong. Everything that had happened an hour ago washing over her as she observed the details without judgment, the world around her proceeding as if it was normal. Because it was for everyone else. She had to get her mind back to business, even with Y gone; they had a job to do. Patra was with their young starlet, and in about ten minutes the Premiere would begin.

She needed to get back inside.

Just another minute in the bright lights and hustle.

Now!

Her mind shouted at her with a distinct voice of Nanny.

You need to get back inside now, gal! The voice in her head shouted.

Suzy blinked, surprised and without further ado ran back into the cinema.

Nicole Hemmings pushed the door to the toilet open. She had not pictured this aspect of the fame game when she was imagining what it would be like being a celebrity. Most people don't. Her first major role, her first red-carpet event and with it came the haters and the weirdos. Her agent had been sent a curse stone, a part of some ancient Germanic ritual and some strange correspondences after that. That's why tonight she had these ladies looking after her. She wasn't sure if they were meant to be so nice or she had just lucked out but being chaperoned wasn't as painful as she thought it would be. Ms. Jones stood outside waiting for her as the screening would begin in ten minutes. She wouldn't be long, just reapplying some lipstick and tidying her eyebrows. Two women were in here before her, sharing a joke or an observation between them. They both laughed and headed out to the atrium. The door swung shut, and she was alone, already taking out her lipstick and eyeliner. She could hear the drip of the faucet and noticed the tube of flickering incandescent light. She moved closer to the mirror and made sure the porcelain bowl was dry not wanting her white dress sporting a damp line at a waste. The door swung open again, and a squeeze of dialogue trickled through before it closed again. She began applying the lipstick. Nicole could hear the footsteps behind her and fleetingly looked up to the mirror to see who it was.

The restroom was empty.

Shrugging, she arched her eyebrows, dropping the lipstick in her bag. Bringing the compact out she applied some powder to her cheeks and used the mirror built into it to look over her shoulders. She could hear the rustling of clothes behind her as someone shifted their weight from one foot to the next. The hairs on the back of Nicole's neck stood to attention as she heard or thought she heard a murmur.

A wave of dread washed over her like a crashing wave. A primordial instinct of survival so acute it could have come directly from the collective consciousness of her cave dwelling ancestors. It took all she had to turn around and when she did her legs went weak and her bladder suddenly slackened.

The nightmare in front of her shrieked.

She opened her mouth to scream and could only muster a squeak.

The thing in heels and evening wear crouched forward on all fours its hand's grotesque talons scrapping on the tiles. Its face was primarily human, but it was an insane cross between a vampire bat and Wolf.

"Oh God! Oh God!" Nicole murmured. The things face was still in flux like a fluid portrait by an insane painter. She smiled, her mouth filled to bursting with dagger-like white fangs, eyes feral and Serpentine tongue slithering in her mouth. She stalked towards Nicole making no sound, strings of saliva swinging from her maw. The she-monster poised to pounce but then hesitated.

The toilet door slammed open tearing off its hinges, striking the vampire bitch hard and smashing it against the adjoining wall.

Suzy burst in like a human tsunami and reached out to Nicole. The young woman rushed to her side sobbing, and without a pause, Suzy spun her out of the door into Patra's waiting arms.

"I had a feeling you'd try something like dis," Suzy said darkly. The creature slid out from behind the door unscathed looking almost human again.

Almost.

"Get her ready for the start of the film, "Suzy fired the words over her shoulder at Patra, her eyes firmly set on the predator glaring at her. "I've got dis."

The door swung shut and, they were alone.

Suzy's heart was racing, and she knew the vampire bitch could feel it. And if she could feel it, she knew it wasn't panic. It was fear, excitement and consequence all rolled up into incandescence ball of controlled fury. Suzy slipped off her heels and shoved her hands into them. She slowly moved into the crane stance.

"Your mistress is a smart woman but, she's fucking wid deh wrong crew. I want you to send that to her before I rip your head off."

The creature took a step back for a moment looking frantic. Then it smiled again. Suzy rushed forward but, like a ballerina, the undead cackled, leaped up and spun into the prefab ceiling above. It smashed its way into the maintenance space and noisily scuttled away through wires and aluminum frames.

Suzy shook her head grimly.

"Keep running bitch." Suzy called out to her. "Yuh can't run forever, and when we do meet, there will be hell to pay. Yuh hear mi." She let her heels drop from her hands and slipped back into them. Checking her makeup, she walked through the doors and out into the foyer.

35.

The Bad II the Bone crew were on a war footing for the first time since creating the protocol in the first place. Miranda had fired a shot across their bows and if experience had taught them anything never second-guess your instincts. With that thought Y implemented operation Homestead - Spokes love for Westerns was obvious in the name choice. The idea was to secure all their loved ones and get them back to HQ safely under the mansion's mystical and corporeal protection. Luckily this exercise was easy to do in principle. An emergency call should get everyone's attention; then it was just a matter of logistics to pick everyone up. Shaft and Y had left the crime scene early. A Black Book team member with the standard Metropolitan Police Force had it all in hand. Shaft left his Jag and keys with one of his new analysts, and with it, copious instructions on how to treat his baby. Moments later he was comfortably seated in Y's red Peugeot as it sped towards Chase Towers.

Suzy and Patra couldn't leave their client until the job was done. Y's mum was abroad and had already received a text telling her to extend her holidays.

Trevor had dropped tools at his Network Rail job and should be in a taxi heading towards the mansion as they proceeded South.

Patra was free of any ties in the UK, and that left Amanda. They hadn't left her unprotected, Y had seen to that, and her fifth-floor flat was rendered vampire proof. So why couldn't they contact her? As they pulled into the demolition site that was Chase Estates, Shaft called Amanda's number again, and it went immediately to voicemail.

"She still not picking up," Shaft said. "It could be anything though."

"It could be," Y answered. "But it's not."

"Maybe, let's just get up there and check it out for ourselves."

"Let's do that." Y agreed, parking the car without due consideration and immediately exiting. She reached to the back seat for her Katana slung it over her shoulders and moved at a sprint Shaft close behind as both figures jogged through the silent shadows of the twin towers. Y moved unerringly through the labyrinth, making her way past the darkened concrete warrens, up steps, and along corridors. She stood at the bend of an ugly grey hallway waiting for Shaft to catch up, her hand behind

her back stroking her Katana, her breathing easy unlike
Shaft's gasps reminding him that his fitness levels needed improving. The darkness didn't seem to pose a problem for her as she confidently came up to the door along
with a little walkway, unlike many they had hurried past.

"X marks the spot." Shaft said looking at painted Si-
gel on the reinforced door. Y pressed the buzzer, long
and hard and stepped back.

"Spokes found out which vampire tribe she is affiliat-
ed with and made a Warlock friend create a spell to bind
the entrance," Y explained.

"It worked, the doors untouched." Shaft said. "So why
isn't she answering."

"I don't know," Y rang the buzzer again. "We need
Suzy," she said.

"What we need is entry, and I might be able to help
with that."

Shaft reached into his jacket and took up a leather
pouch that he unzipped to reveal an assortment of lock
picking tools.

"You came prepared," Y said.

"Oh yes," Shaft nodded. "It's a part of being a real detective. Didn't you know?"

Y shook her head unconvinced.

"Blame Harry Houdini for my love of this shit."

Shaft walked his fingers lovingly over his instru-
ments, chose one and started working on the lock. Y
took out her mobile and rang a number. She waited and
listened for it to ring.

The funky ring tone chimed in her earpiece and simultaneously sounded from inside the flat.

Y grimaced.

Shaft had 'jimmied' the barrel lock and was feeling particularly pleased with himself until he realized the door stood stubbornly closed.

"She has deadbolts and industrial night chains installed. Let me try." Y said breathing deeply. She let the intake of air charge her chakras, each pass of breath over her power points elevating her energy levels. With one more deep breath, she stepped back and fired a kick into the section of the door near the jam. It stood firm but not after four more attempts. The final kick, popping the carbide chains and ripping the deadbolts from its anchor in the wall and sending the door smashing open, spinning inside.

"Jesus!" Shaft said.

Y rushed in her Katana trailing behind her. Shaft followed with his service revolver drawn and shaking his head at the damage inflicted on the door.

"Remind me not to mess with you." He murmured. And in moments they were in the apartment checking rooms. Shaft called out to her from the sitting room.

"Y, you need to see this."

Y hurried in and was met with a coolly lit room, showing signs of struggle with the centerpiece of this crime scene glaring at her. The window that was the Vista to the spectacular view of south London was smashed open.

Amanda was nowhere to be seen.

Shaft couldn't help but scratch his head as he walked over and looked down the five stories to the ground. The section down below was well lit. Nobody lay there.

Shaft whistled then said.

"Miranda had bypassed the spell at the door and decided to defy gravity to use the window as an ingress and egress point."

Shaft stifled the 'how the fuck' question and followed Y's finger as it pointed to the newly formed sheer drop. A large reddish-brown cockroach had attached itself to a portion of the ruined window; it's anthropoid body smooth, it twitched its head towards Y then Shaft, its antenna swishing from left to right.

"She's watching us," Y said.

Shaft looked at her blankly, the cool air blowing on his face, his gonads tightening with vertigo, then it clicked. The roach was Miranda's organic surveillance device. Just as she had weaponized these disgusting sewer dwellers, the vampire had also modified them for other uses.

"If you hurt her, you get nothing." Y said to the insect. "I know what you want but only I know where it is. If you want it, let's talk."

Shaft shivered at the words and the matter-of-fact exchange between human and anthropoid. He tried to comprehend the mechanics of a system that used living things the way Miranda could, but he managed to reach the edge of his scientific knowledge very quickly. The terrain he was surveying was something far removed from science.

Shaft felt vulnerable, again.

Having heard enough the insect scurried down from the window to the edge. It rubbed its hind legs together, revolved its head and took flight in its awkward fluttering way into the south London night.

36.

Y knew when Nanny was alone in the mansion as seventies and eighties reggae music played low throughout the house. She must have decided to share her proclivity for Jamaican sounds with her guests. Tonight, the mansion was filled with the kind of activity it had not seen in a long, long time. The lounge was buzzing with an unusual energy as the different personalities and life forces mingled and repelled each other in a cosmic dance of social interaction. They had just eaten, and Nanny was clearing up and offering coffee and chocolate tea to those who wanted it. The big chunky leather sofas and sofa chairs were inviting, and some of the group had succumbed to their charms. Suzy was curled up like a cat on the massive frame of her boyfriend. She snuggled her head into his neck and looked slight in comparison to her fiancé's impressive physique.

Y stretched out with her feet on Shaft's lap. He sat up, his head flung back, and both arms propped on the voluminous headrest. It looked as if the couch was absorbing him into itself.

Patra and Dean stood together beside a world globe drink trolley. In a room filled with extraordinary people the handsome vampire was the only who could say, hand on heart, he was inhuman. The girls instinctively knew to keep that bit of information as far away from Shaft as possible. Dean had been introduced as one of the foremost authorities on vampires. He had enough on his plate to deal with without trying to explain who he truly was to the Detective Inspector.

Dealing with Nanny was not so straight-forward.

Before Patra could invite Dean into the mansion, the housekeeper stood at the big double doors ushered Patra in and stood having a quiet word with Dean on the threshold. In moments he was escorted into the lounge filled with a contemplative mood.

Suzy was relieved Trevor was here but frustrated they nearly had their client murdered. Y was disappointed Amanda was taken, and angry Miranda had the upper hand. Patra was excited and apprehensive about Dean's involvement. They all worked through their doubts in good company.

"Are you okay?" Shaft asked rubbing Y's feet, struggling himself to suppress the memories of tonight's crime scene.

"I will be fine but what about the people she murdered tonight, the people she butchered over the last
three weeks? What about Amanda?"

Shaft sighed.

There was no version of this that wouldn't be painful.

"The people that monster murdered is not on you,"
Shaft said. "Don't you dare try to blame this shitstorm
on your efforts. She's been doing this for over 200
years."

"With no one to stop her," Y said.

"Until now," Shaft corrected.

Y nodded, her lips a tight line at the bottom of her
face. Her eyes sparkled.

"We've got something she wants," Shaft continued.

"And she's got Amanda, who we want back safe." Y
said it like she was reading an item from a grocery list.

Shaft shook his head.

"If what you've been saying about the Heart of Ares is
true, we have a dilemma." He thought about it. "We can't
allow her to get her claws on it."

"And without it, we don't have a deal." Y made a
sharp intake of breath. "I can't let Amanda die. I just
can't."

"I know, I know." Shaft consoled her. "She's safe for
now. But when that bitch Miranda arranges to meet, if
she doesn't get what she wants..."

"Hell an powder house." Suzy interjected, standing
over them in her pink PJ's and slippers, her arm exposed
showing that scary dragon tattoo on it.

Shaft looked up a faraway expression on his face.

"My Mum used to say that a lot. Usually directed at me when she wanted to ring my neck. And yes, I think you're right."

"We need a plan," Y said.

"Any ideas," Shaft asked.

Suzy shrugged, then said.

"It will come. Give it time."

"Time sis," Y stated. "Is what we don't have."

Patra offered Dean a cigar, but he declined.

She lit up.

"What was that all about at the door?" Patra asked. "Did Nanny tear you a new one?"

Dean laughed.

"She did actually. But gently."

Patra smiled at the thought of a petite albino woman reading the riot act to a predator of the night.

Dean asked.

"What does she do around the house?"

"She supposed to be a housekeeper," Patra said. "But she's so much more. And man can she cook."

Dean smiled showing his white teeth.

"She's no housekeeper," he said. "She just made me recite an ancient incantation, very rare, very powerful."

"Nanny did that? You fucking with me?"

"She did." He shrugged, his powerful shoulders making him look awkward. "It's true that vampires need to be invited into a place occupied by human souls. Once they are, they can enter and leave at will. Nanny just gave me a day pass."

"Son-of-a-bitch!" Patra said. "I knew she was being coy about shit but damn."

"The last time someone sprang that clause on me was ..." He paused to think. "Over a hundred years ago. Keep her close; she is very resourceful."

"More than you will ever know," Patra said. "Me and her need to talk when this is all over."

They both settled beside the drinks trolley, and Patra looked hungrily at a bottle of Scotch and then at Dean. He read her unspoken gestures.

"I wouldn't say no." He said.

Patra nodded and smiled. She then proceeded to pour the amber nectar into two glasses.

"So, dis is what the office looks like," Trevor said.

"Dis is it, lover, in all its glory."

"It's an impressive layout. When am I going to get the tour?"

Suzy laughed.

"You just arrived. Don't you have more relevant questions to ask instead of getting into other people's business."

Trevor chuckled.

"Questions like what?"

"Like why you received a pentagram alert."

"Oh, dat." Trevor played down its significance. "I knew it must be something dangerous, but that is what you're all about, right?"

Suzy nodded.

"I knew you were okay because the call came from you. The details can wait. As far as work is concerned, it is a family emergency."

"Do you want to hear the details?" Suzy asked.

"Would it change anyting?"

"Not really, you're on lockdown with me. Just how I like it."

"Best place to be," Trevor shrugged. Suzy sat up on his lap and looked into his brown eyes.

"Why are you so understanding and supportive of me?"

He smiled that infectious smile of his and then became serious.

"Your old man was disappointed. In his head, he pictured you marrying an ambitious young Chinese bwoy with prospects. Instead, he got a dark-skinned ghetto yout."

Suzy tried to protest, but he hugged her into silence.

"He knew, he had lost deh battle for his daughter after you decided to come to stay with me in the UK. I know it hurt him, but I understand. He only wanted your happiness."

Trevor took a breath and smiled.

"Your old man said you were special and that with all your gifts there were some things you couldn't do for yourself. I needed to protect and support you. He made me promise. He didn't have to."

Suzy's eyes glistened.

"Thank you for being my man," Suzy said kissing him on the lips.

"Little did I know you are spooky special and instead of me protecting you, I am deh one being protected."

"You lover deserve everything I can give you."

The air of intimacy suddenly dissipated, and they understood why immediately.

"Are you fucking with my Mandingo brother?" Patra broke in to this tender moment unceremoniously.

"I hope your intentions are pure girl or we gonna have words."

Suzy rolled her eyes.

"Where are your manners?" Suzy asked.

Patra started searching the pockets in her outfit comically but came up short.

"Sorry," she said. "Can't find them suckers anywhere. Get your sexy Jamaican ass off him so I can make my introductions."

Suzy unfolded off Trevor's lap gracefully, and the big man stood up.

Patra motioned to Dean.

"Dean," Patra said. "This is Trevor, my sister's fiancé. Trevor, Dean."

Both men shook hands, and something darkly primal passed between them. A kind of fear that Trevor recalled when his grandmother told him duppy stories. A cold uncertainty that chilled the base of his skull and tangled in his spine. Trevor shook it off.

It was a strange sensation especially having just met the man. Trevor stored it away to revisit it later.

"Yuh get caught up in deh drama?" Trevor asked.

"In a way," Dean said. "I'm helping to contain the threat."

Trevor sighed.

"One of these days," he said without being self-conscious. "I will ask about every detail of what Suzy does. Not now, not yet."

"I understand. We live in extraordinary times, my friend. We are as good as our coping mechanisms."

"Amen to that," Patra said.

"Aren't you guys tired?" Y and Shaft had come over to join the group. Y had genuinely thought that after the meal everyone would want to bed down.

Not so.

The desperate dynamic that had been so pervasive earlier had not lasted long. After a meal that intangible bond of closeness drew them together like a force of gravity.

"Come to think of it. I am feeling a bit pooped." Shaft said unconvincingly. To reinforce the validity of his charade, he suddenly yawned. The expression on his face said it had been a struggle to manufacture. He stretched sealing his Oscar performance. "What are the sleeping arrangements anyway?"

Suzy laughed.

"Don't worry detective; you are crashing with Y."

Shaft's face lit up, and he immediately dialed down his enthusiasm.

"I will introduce Trevor to my room," Suzy said.

"I bet you will," Patra winked.

"What about you, Miss bigmouth?"

Suzy's question caught Patra off guard.

Y couldn't resist.

"She snores like a walrus." Y said to Dean.

"And farts like a trooper," Suzy added.

"No!" Dean said with mock surprise.

"You bitches need to chill. Me and Dean have got serious business to handle." Patra dug herself a deeper hole.

"Too much information," Shaft added his two pence worth barely restraining laughter. "Just keep it down some of us need our beauty sleep."

Patra gave them the finger.

"Kiss my ass!" She said realizing that too was a bad choice of words. Her dark cheeks flushed, and she grabbed Dean's hands. "They're a bad influence. Let me give you the fifty-cent tour of our crib instead."

Dean followed her lead and left the laughter behind him. For a very long time he felt a twinge of warmth in the tiny ingot of soul he had left.

The BS - Blood and Sweat gym was the most frequently visited and utilize room in the mansion. A room did not give justice to its dimensions. It was an auditorium, partitioned with dojo, boxing ring and gymnasium. As well as honing their martial arts skills here, they sometimes met, slept and ate here. Frustration was exercise, and new means of survival were experimented with and ways to kill honed as they navigated the dangerous world, they found themselves in. The floor space was spotless, the gym equipment and exotic weapons kept shiny. The auditorium was cool and ventilated but a pervading smell of blood and sweat still hung in the air absorbed into the walls almost.

Y snuck in first just after three o'clock in the morning. She was already dressed for action and needed the meditation only kendo diagrams could give her. She approached the combat mannequin bowed and raised her wooden kendo sword. With three calming breath she didn't exist anymore. She was one with her movement, with the twitching of her muscle fibers and the firing of her neurons. A balletic display of aggression and thought using her whole body. Thirty minutes later she took a breath, took a swig from her water bottle and dried her face. She felt Suzy's presence before she spoke. Her sister had come into the BS without making a sound.

"My mind is too active," Suzy said approaching a well-worn Shaolin wooden man set in a quadrant of the floor space that she trained in. "I need to think."

Y nodded continuing her moves but this time the sounds of wood on rubber was accompanied by flesh on wood as Suzy proceeded to attack the Shaolin wooden man. At first, she started slowly but soon her moves were a blur of hands and feet, the Chinese training aid violently matching her intensity. Moments later the door pushed open again. Patra walked in gloves on and towel around her neck. Her sisters were furiously focused. Y was wielding her practice sword, her movements precise and masterful. Suzy was gracefully blocking and striking the polished frame of the wooden man like a dancer on stage. Patra was eager to join them. She moved over to the speed bag and quickly built up a rhythm and let it take her.

Y and Suzy had finished their work out and were now watching Patra devastating a weighted dummy with flawless Muay Thai moves. Suddenly the Atlanta chick stopped. She wasn't tired just consumed with a question.

"Couldn't sleep either, right?" She turned to look at her sisters. "So, what's in the box?"

The girls looked at her blankly.

Y said.

"I thought you had brought it in."

"Not me honey."

Suzy shrugged.

"It wasn't me."

All three looked at the lacquered wooden box on the floor. It was more a small trunk than box. Intricately designed and carved in a style Suzy was familiar with from the craftsmen in Jamaica. It commanded their attention and its luminescence was distorting the space around it. If you looked at it long enough it gave you an uneasy impression it was hot or on fire. All three came closer, and Suzy lowered herself to the floor to observe it in more detail.

"It beautiful," Suzy whispered. "Powerful too."

"I can feel it," Patra said her voice lowered with reverence.

"How did it get in here?" Y asked.

"I tink I have an idea," Suzy said. "About the who, not the how." She touched the spider tattoo that had spontaneously appeared on her neck weeks ago.

"Deh box is covered with Anancy stories." She began. "Some I can remember from primary school, others..." Her voice trailed away.

"The tattoos and the box are related," Y mused. "Whatever this is. Whoever this is, they have a thing for spiders."

"This may sound like I am tripping but," Patra said. "What if this Anancy dude Suzy keeps talking about is doing this. Maybe all of this."

They were quiet for a moment then Y looked to Suzy.

"Can we touch it?" Y asked.

"Yeah man," Suzy said. "I sense no threat."

"Okay then," Y said. "Ms. Jones your up."

Without a whisper of complaint, Patra bent and picked up the box from one end.

"Woh!" Patra said in awe. "It's tingling. It's making my titties hard. Damn!" She teased.

The box shimmered in her hand, emanating waves of pale blue light around it.

Suzy moved forward and picked up the other end. She took in a sharp breath then smiled.

"Didn't I tell you," Patra said grinning. "Titties."

The box added another layer of color to its umbra.

Y came next and lay her fingers on it, and it immediately responded with a pale burst of additional color. Y's eyes lit up with the energies stimulating her. All three could feel the changes within the box as its inner workings turned, slid and ratcheted. The mechanical movement inside ended with a whirring sound as the lid cranked open. Three pairs of eyes peered into the box. A faint whiff of white rum perfumed the space between them.

"Now ain't that something," Patra said.

Suzy reached in to touch it.

"Rass! If I didn't know better, I would tink it was real."

But Y's smile was the brightest of them all.

"Whoever did this for us. Thank you." She looked up to the ceiling and paused. "I think I have a plan." She looked over at Patra.

"Get Dean back here but keep it on the low down. Miranda has eyes and ears everywhere."

Patra nodded, her eyes twinkling.

"Sure thing."

37.

St. Peter and Paul Cathedral, Central London

"**D**o you think that skank is going to show he raggedy ass in the house of the Lord?" Patra asked.

"Language!" Y said hoping not to start laughing at how her sister expressed her frustration. "Be patient. If Suzy says, this is a good place to be then it is a good place to be."

"I know, I know," Patra whispered. "But we been here for about three hours and I just know that bitch is making us sweat."

"I think you're right, but you're going to have to get used to it. We leave when Suzy say so."

"Maybe we should be looking at another angle." Patra speculated.

"What makes you think that?" Y asked

"We know she ain't coming herself. It's daytime and we in a church. She's got to send one of her human flunkies." Patra paused and looked around at some of the street dwellers and office workers seated in quiet contemplation. "These dudes don't look like they could threaten shit. The bitch ain't coming."

Y nodded.

"Okay you may be right, but however she does it, we need to talk terms with her. We have something she wants; she has something we want."

"Me and her got some unfinished business to attend to."

"I know, but let's keep it professional. Whoever turns up as her proxy let's just plan for the exchange nothing more."

Patra shrugged.

"I heard they store wine in the back of the crib," Patra asked.

Y gave her a look.

"What?" Patra protested. "I'm a Baptist."

"Why don't you pray," Y teased. "I am sure you've got a few things to be forgiven for."

"Funny," Patra said.

"Suzy has been on her knees for twenty minutes. Follow her lead."

"I grew up in the church remember, and the memories aren't good ones. When I think of the old man and his holier than though bullshit. Hating his daughter but loving his congregation, makes me want to tear shit apart."

"Do it quietly." Y said.

Patra rolled her eyes.

"I have two words for you," Patra said. "But I will wait until we are out of the church."

Y smiled and leaned back on the hard pews, closing her eyes satisfied that she had wound up her sister enough. Y for one enjoyed the solace at St. Peter and Paul. Although the Catholic Church's history was a mixed bag of slavery, wars, sex scandals and corruption it opened its doors to the weary and downtrodden, at least some of Christ's lessons had been learned. It was mid-afternoon, but the interior maintained a timeless feel that almost forced you to reflect on your life. Frankincense and myrrh were burning somewhere in the building, and Y took the opportunity to drift away.

She wasn't sure how long she had closed her eyes for, but Y could feel Suzy's intensity approaching and with it Patras impatience. In moments Suzy's hands were on Y's shoulders.

"You okay?" Y asked opening her eyes and looking up at her sister's grim features.

"She's coming," Suzy said and Y could feel it. She wasn't sure if it was Suzy's empathic gifts amplified in some way, but there was a palpable disturbance. It felt like the onset of a storm, a muggy, charged atmosphere pregnant with threat and malice. Y headed down the aisle towards a large double door at the front of the church, Suzy and Patra behind her. The door pushed open flooding parallelograms of light on the floorboards. Standing in the middle of that and taking two steps into the church was a tall, imposing female form. It was hard to discern details because the daylight hit her squarely in the back, blurring her outline and obscuring the features. All three women felt a malevolent power. If Bad II the Bone had learned anything from discovering their gifts it was fear was overrated. A primitive response that would reveal itself at the unknown.

It wasn't real.

So why did it feel real.

Suzy, Y, and Patra moved close enough to her that they could hear each other without shouting. The statuesque woman stood looking at them. She wore a fitted coat, gloves, trousers, and chic boots. Her face was completely hidden by a stylishly floppy hat, a scarf, and Gucci shades.

"Ladies." The figure nodded, her words sounding snakelike. "Mith Wong," she lisped. "Have you considered my offer. There is a dungeon in Jamaica with your name on it. We could have so much fun, fucking, and bloodletting."

Suzy silently adjusted her weight then rotated her head left to right her fists clenched. She could feel the thing in front of her probing her mind, but Suzy's barriers were up, and they were strong.

"Let's cut the shit and get down to the business at hand," Y said. "Your thing for Suzy can wait."

Patra smirked.

Suzy was stone-faced.

"Letss!" Miranda said. "I am interested to see how the Guardians can add some flavor to my stay in London. So far it's been interesting."

Patra attempted to step forward, but Y held a hand to her stomach to stop her from moving.

"I am glad we can provide you with entertainment," Y said. "We'll make it worth your while. But there is the matter of my friend."

"Ah, the ancestor of the vampire slayer. If you didn't have someting I wanted more than revenge, we wouldn't be having this discussion."

"But we are," Y said dismissively. "Deliver my friend unharmed, and you will get the item. If she is touched in any way, the deal is off."

Miranda seemed to think about this.

Y continued.

"Chase estate, ground floor car park of Wentworth Tower after midnight two nights from now. Come alone."

"Only if you do," Miranda said.

"We a package deal motherfucker." Patra blurted out.

"I can see that. By the way, how's your neck, Cleopatra?"

Patra made another step forward and this time Y turned to stare her down.

"You three are so cute, " Miranda mocked. "I welcome any plots or schemes you may think up to challenge mi. It will make or encounter that much more exciting." Her gloved hand came up to her face, adjusting something there. "Just remember if the Heart of Ares is not on my person when we meet next, I will skewer and jerk you over hot coals for my pets." She laughed lightly her shoulders bouncing with mirth and promise.

"Yuh tink we fraid a yuh," Suzy spat.

"You'd be a fool not to be." Miranda said.

"Fuck you," Patra's voice rose up, but it was controlled and measured. "Coming all up in here like your shit don't stink. You messing with the real deal bitch. Appointed by the higher powers, we will fuck your shit up."

Miranda kept laughing.

"I love your fire," she said. "Is dat a promise? If it is, I look forward to it."

"Bank on it." Patra slung back.

"Until next time then," Miranda said brightly.

And then the form that was Miranda Pheare turned away without another word. Just as she hit the threshold between the dimness of the church and the sunlight of outdoors the vampire suddenly lost form falling on the church steps as a teeming swarm of black cockroaches that had held her together skittered for cover from every item of clothing. The designer clothes lay on the floor in a pile.

Suzy sighed with relief as the last vestiges of the creature they were talking to disappeared from her mind. The girls walked out of the church and stood over the heap of clothes left behind.

"That is how she could move throughout the day. She transfers her presence into the insects from a safe distance." Suzy said looking peaky.

"That must take some doing." Y thought aloud.

Suzy nodded.

"Holy ground must have made it difficult, but she managed."

"Did she suspect anything?" Y asked.

"She tried to break through our psychic barriers, but she couldn't."

"We dealing with a boss," Patra added. "I wouldn't say it to her face, but she's gangster."

Patra pushed the toe of her boots into the heap of designer wear as if she was looking for something.

"The bitch wears no panties either," Patra said. "I could have told you."

"We have to be careful. She is top of the food chain with all the powers that position affords her." Y said thoughtfully.

"She thinks we are pushover's, poppy-show," Suzy said. "I can sense she feels walking all over us will be fun."

"Good. I like when they think of us as underdogs. That's her first mistake. Underestimating Bad II Bone is not a good idea."

"Goddamn, right it's not." Patra said.

38.

2 Days Later. The Meet, Chase Estates

Patra made herself comfortable on her perch fifteen stories up on Kentchester tower. The derelict block of flats stood dark against the light-polluted London sky. It's shattered windows empty and ominous. The wind whipped at Patras nest on the building's roof. She was much too comfortable in this precarious position. She was here instead of Suzy or Patra because of her lack of fear for heights and they wanted her out of the way when Miranda turned up. She was just too worked up about challenging the vampire Queen to keep her cool in this situation. So, she was sent to the Hill for fear of threatening the plan. And because she had a skill they did not have.

Base jumping.

She wasn't complaining. Patra was like a sniper without the high-powered rifle. Her job was to pinpoint the bloodsuckers and their positions and feedback the data to Y and Dean. She was pleasantly surprised on arriving at the top to see that it wasn't completely caked in bird shit. There were a few feathers, the acrid smell of droppings and dust but all made bearable because everything was exposed to the elements. The capital hadn't seen rain for a week or so, making the flat surface dry. Patra found a spot close to the ledge and laid out her parachute, the tablet, high luminosity torch, her blanket and food, prepared by Nanny.

Her bird's eye view allowed her to see who entered the car park of the adjoining building and give her a kind of x-ray vision thanks to Dean and his innovation. The Vampire had devised a piece of kit to handle that. He had planted hundreds of Wi-Fi enabled receivers and transmitters all over the estate, concentrating them in the areas leading into the rendezvous point. He had a software program that mapped the Wi-Fi waves being interrupted by movement. Once the numbers were crunched in the program and wirelessly fed into the tablet beside her, she could pinpoint movement.

She would be here a while, and Y's suspicions were correct very busy. In the world they had come from this would be considered overkill for even the most ruthless of gangsters. But Miranda Pheare was the most dangerous and devious adversary any Law Keeping organization would ever face. Patra knew there was no trust here just who would outsmart whom. They planned with that in mind.

Patra pulled a blanket over her shoulders and kept her eyes on the tablet screen. It was thirty-five minutes before midnight, and she was eager to get this party started.

Y and Suzy sat in the front seat of the darkened Bentley holding hands. Y leaned back into the plush seats, while Suzy sat up peering out into the darkened underground car park of Wentworth Tower. Both women were silent for a long time. Y checked her mobile for the fifth time and shuffled in her seat. Suzy did not move a muscle.

"We've got five minutes to show time." Y said. "And we have everything in place." Y crossed her fingers and tapped the case at her feet with her toes.

Suzy's eyes flickered open.

"Mek we prepare deh place."

Both women exited the car into the surrounding with bags under their arms. They were filled with luminescent tubes that they snapped and shook to activate. The underground car park began to light up, revealing some of its hidden recesses. It became even brighter as twin beams of halogen headlights momentarily replaced the morose and dingy vibe. Shaft flicked the Jaguars lights off and on grinning nervously even with the knowledge of what they were about to face tonight.

Y smiled back, her eyes longing to be somewhere else. A warm moment with Shaft formed in her mind for a moment.

Y looked around at their theatre of conflict, not for the first time and was as happy as she could be with the setup. The exit in and out was clear. There was good line of sight for Patra on the outside and for them on the inside. She could see three-quarters of Patras building without walking outside. The underground parking had potential to accommodate up to twenty cars so there was enough wiggle room if things got sticky.

"Come mek, mi check yuh," Suzy said, coming over to Y and making sure she was prepared. Her sister was in the same body-hugging reinforced Kevlar and leather jumpsuit that all of them wore. Flexible but strong. When she finished her inspection, she tightened Y's katana sheath on her back, and she slapped her ass.

"Shipshape," Suzy said smiling fleetingly.

"And you?" Y asked.

"I am good sister Y," Suzy said. "I just feel like I'm waiting for deh exam results in High School. Like mi whole life depends on deh outcome."

"How did you do?" Y asked.

"All passes A's and B's, but you know what I learned? There are more important tings to my life and in deh world. Tings I can influence and change."

Suzy took in a deep breath and on exhaling, she had materialized the Chinese butterfly knives into her hands. Such was the speed of her movements; she plucked the butterfly Knives from her lower back before normal eyes could register. Then in a brief display of her prowess, making the blades whistle through the air, spinning and thrusting them at an invisible adversary, slashing and gorging. In a blink, the blades were snugly back in the sheath on her lower back.

Y wanted to applaud the display but instead put her hand on Suzy's shoulder and squeezed. Words were not necessary.

They had five more minutes.

Dean sucked in the cigarette smoke and let his vampire lungs neutralize any adverse effects it could have on his immortal body. He was parked on the fringes of the town center just far enough away from Chase estates that Miranda could not sense him. She was cunning and heartless and would think of every eventuality. He was no slouch himself and was blocking that Vampire homing signal that allowed her to control and detect her Clan. His time in Tibet had given him some tools that even worked with his soulless kind, and he was using every one of those meditative practices now. He would do anything to scatter her ashes to the wind, but he had to be smart about it. The woman was resourceful and the survivor in the purest form. There was no telling what she would do if she knew Dean was anywhere in the vicinity when the exchange took place.

He had faith in the Guardians. And Patra warmed the cold dead, hearth of his soul with a bright ember of her personality. He wanted more time with her if it was to be.

Once the exchange took place, then he would be initiating the fun part of this plan. Dean didn't care about being detected then. By that time the trap would be sprung, and the world would be free of that monster. For a moment he considered himself not too far removed from the mass murderess who had turned him. Except for some unexplained quirk in his transformation, he would be one of her top lieutenants.

Fate, if there was such a thing had intervened.

He dropped his cigarette to the ground and crushed it with his boot. He swung the car door open slipped inside, and that's when he sensed it. They came out of the shadows like wraiths, having suppressed their vampire essence, long enough to catch Dean unaware. They moved with purpose and blistering speed. Dean tried to open the car door, but Miranda's clan swarmed in, blocking his exit. They came equipped and motivated. Just like a Grand Prix motor team, they immediately started covering all the windows with metal plates and were riveting them in place.

They were encasing him in the car.

Dean used his shoulders, and his fist, the sound; as they landed on metal was like industrial jackhammer. But every time he broke through, a new metal plate was slapped into place and welded tight. Dean felt the vibration of not just the tools but a heavy-duty vehicle that had come alive and was being driven into place.

It stank of diesel and grease.

The human familiar at the controls was excited as his heart was pumping in his chest, the blood circulating his body in spurts. Dean's anger was making him lose control. The sliver of humanity that he nurtured would disappear as his survival instincts wrestled dominance from him. At that moment, he could tear the human's throat out and drink him dry. If he were human, he would feel shame at the thought of murder for blood.

But he wasn't. He couldn't change his nature, but he could control it. Dean kept hammering his fists into the roof, thinning the metal until it tore, but the team outside was on it with hot rivets and acetylene torches. He could hear the Beep! Beep! Beep! Of the large vehicle reversing outside.

Then silence.

Suddenly his world shifted violently. The sides of his mustang buckled something powerful, something mechanical grabbed it and flipping it over on its roof.

"Dammit!" Dean snarled with frustration.

He was trapped.

A bank of fog, ankle high, that exhibited a creepy sentience drifted into the car park down the ramp and into the area where the cars sat. Suzy and Y came out from the security of their ride.

Y was carrying the case. They stood at the front of the Bentley.

"We all good?" Shaft asked from behind them, slamming the Jaguar door shut.

"Stay frosty babe," Y called back.

Shaft nodded silently.

"Any moment now," Suzy said. "I can feel her." She shuddered, even as the words left her mouth, they could both see vampire Scouts silently looming in the shadows. The advance guard used the fog to obscure their presence but they could not mask their intention. They prowled the murky darkness, red eyes glistening, heralding the approach of their mistress.

Soon she arrived in a tinted black Mercedes gliding into the parking zone with Ford panel van behind it. Both parties parked face-to-face. Immediately Y and Suzy lent off the Bentley and stood to attention focusing on the foreign vehicles that had invaded their space. The silence was permeated by the ticking engine's cooling down, and the place got decidedly colder when the elegant Miranda Pheare stepped out of the car.

Patra whistled.

Vampires showing as luminescent blips - ten on the last count, broke through the Wi-Fi net. They all converged on the car park. Some directly, others hanging back. A jolt of excitement zigzagged through her abs and an all over sensation of warmth enveloped her. Patra wasn't sure what her senses were trying to say. How things would end up was anybody's guess. Patra almost wished something would happen. She brought the night vision binoculars to her eyes.

Nothing.

That is when the black Mercedes sedan and a black van pulled into the Estate, slowly making their way to the sunken car park. Patra felt the need for a Snicker bar, but she decided to wait. The vampire homies were getting excited before the big concert. The closer the queen bitch rolled to the rendezvous point, the more animated they became. Just like crack fiends glad to see their hook-up. She looked around her perch to make sure she had everything she needed. Satisfied, she nodded her head and kept her eyes on the tablet watching this exchange take shape. This game of wills, strategy and revenge, was going to plan. Patra wondered what would be thrown into the works to mess things up.

39.

Miranda Pheare stood tall and confident. She was dressed in an elegant red sequined split evening gown, showing her long, strong legs. She wore brutally tall stilettos but moved like she was in flats. Diamond earrings glittered in her earlobes.

In her cleavage rested a blood red Ruby. She glided away from her carriage and faced Y and Suzy, eyes flashing from some infernal furnace that powered her.

"Where's Amanda?" Y asked her voice sounding hollow.

"Do you have the package?" Miranda's voice was rich and vibrant as if it was being fed through an amplifier.

Suzy patted the case with her free hand. Miranda nodded and kept watching them coldly. Y and Suzy stood patiently watching the vampire Queen's human minions busy themselves inside the black van.

In moments a hooded and struggling prisoner was guided out by two vampire wannabes on either side of her. The party moved purposefully to Miranda's side.

"Take off the hood," Y demanded.

The twitch of a smile showed on Miranda's face. A micro-expression that transferred meaning to her slaves without so much as a hand gesture or a movement of her head. But they understood. They immediately whipped the hood off the hostage's head.

Amanda scowled making Suzy smile. She looked in good shape.

"You okay?" Y asked.

Amanda nodded vigorously.

"I think so," Amanda croaked. "They threw me about a bit and made threats but other than bumps and bruises, I'm okay."

Y looked over to Suzy. The empath closed her eyes and went silent. After a moment her eyes fluttered open and then looked at Y.

"She's not under the influence of anything I can detect." Suzy stared into the middle distance for another moment then said: "I tink she's clear."

"Now dat you're satisfied," Miranda interrupted. "The package."

Suzy lifted the aluminum flight case.

Miranda smiled.

"Open it." She demanded.

Suzy Lowered her head for a beat then brought them up again. Concentrating, her lips parted as if she was about to speak then instead, she opened the latches, tipping the top back so the vampire could see the contents. The two gauntlets and the chest attachment sat snuggly in its container. Miranda reached out with more than mundane sight to the Heart of Ares enclosed in the dark foam padding, caressing and investigating it with her psychic tentacles. She nodded and let out a barely audible hiss of satisfaction. Suzy took a deep breath and closed the case, her brows furrowed in focus.

"Satisfied?" Y asked.

"Very," the vampire cooed.

Before Y could get the proceedings moving to a conclusion, two vampires peeled away from the walls on opposite sides of the darkness. Reluctantly leaving the gloom, they met up where Miranda stood. One took Amanda's arm and guided her and the other watched with intense red eyes. They cautiously approached Y and Suzy, under the watchful gaze of their mistress. The duo suddenly stopped, and Suzy stepped forward putting the case on the ground. Then stepped back. Immediately they released Amanda who ran towards the women. She hugged Y savagely, and as a group, they moved back. The vampire wannabes retrieved the flight case.

Y, Suzy, and Amanda headed straight for Shaft's Jaguar. The detective who had been witnessing everything had stood prepared with the car door open for his passenger to be released. He holstered his service weapon when the three women hurried towards him.

"Get her out of here," Y said, ushering Amanda over to Shaft who then encouraged her to quickly slide into the back seat which she did without question.

"Yuh sure about the route?" Suzy asked Shaft.

"I'm sure." He said without hesitation. "I'm heading straight to the mansion in Sussex." Shaft hurried to the driver's side his back to her for a moment. He loaded himself into the car, bulky Kevlar vest under his long coat and his Sig Saur strapped to his leg. He closed the door and slid the window down. "I didn't mention I have a police escort arranged as soon as we get onto the North Circular Road. Don't worry ladies; I got this."

Y reached in and kissed him. Her lips were soft, warm and inviting.

"Be careful."

"My middle name," he quipped. "You do the same."

He called out to Suzy.

"Look after her."

Suzy nodded.

Patra held her breath as she watched six green blips on the tablet simply disappear from the screen. There had been eleven vampire blips in all whose signature had been mapped by Deans equipment. And they had been orderly up to this point. All maintaining their positions like a well-trained army unit.

Five held the car park and six on the outskirts. But something was happening; their behavior was changing.

"Fuck!" Patra swore.

She couldn't call to find out what was happening. They had agreed on complete radio silence. All she could rely on was their spooky connection and what she could see with her two eyes. And what she was seeing made her uneasy. Patra brought the binoculars to her eyes again, looking below for anything interesting. The car park seemed quiet. The exchange must have taken place by now?

That's when Shaft's Jaguar burst out of the underground parking facility like a bat out of hell and started negotiating the road to get out of the estate to the safety of the mansion.

That was a good thing, right?

It meant Amanda was safe and the vampire bitch was happy with her acquisition. Suzy and Y would wait for the vampire crew to depart and they would leave too.

A plan well done.

Hell naw!

She had a sense of these things. A sense of how events could turn out. The likelihood of a result occurring. Patra continued to watch Shaft get out of Dodge.

Dude could drive.

Then her eyes focused on the tablet again. She pinched the screen to reduce the Wi-Fi field's image size. She was beginning to realize the vampires hadn't just disappeared but had left the area where the Wi-Fi detectors were covering.

Where were they going?

Then a light bulb moment.

"Son-of-a-bitch!" Patra spat, jumping up from her position. They were about to intercept Shaft's route out of the estate.

She reached down for the flare gun, pointed it skyward and pulled the tab letting it rip. The red trail of incandescence streamed upwards and exploded at its zenith lighting up the night sky. Patra had to get to Shaft before those things took them out. Y and Suzy would have to deal with the boss bitch while Patra would help Shaft.

They better leave a piece for her.

She scooped everything into the shockproof bag. The mat gave another layer of protection to the electronic equipment as she threw it off the building. Hurriedly Patra picked up the case and clipped it to her belt, she checked her parachute harness for the last time and without hesitation threw herself off the building.

The Jaguars lights were on full beam as Shaft negotiated the maze of streets. He was concentrating hard, making sure building material, equipment or debris wasn't lying in his path. Counterintuitively silence was not good for him. He had struck up a conversation with Amanda as he evasively drived his way through the darkness.

"I don't think she's going to let it go," Amanda said.

Shaft peered at her through his rear-view mirror.

"What makes you think that? We're heading for a safe place now."

Amanda's eyes were wide and tired.

"It's the things she said to me. How she wanted to end my bloodline, one Walker every year, starting with me." Amanda paused thoughtfully. "Have you ever met her in person?"

"I have," Shaft said. "And it is not a reunion I want to repeat."

Amanda shook her head in agreement.

"I don't think she understands sarcasm or irony. When she speaks, it is with a conviction that does not waver. If she says she's going to kill me, that is what she's going to do." Amanda's voice grew weak and tiny. "You know we've given her the only thing that we can use to destroy her."

Shaft groaned in his head.

And that is why he didn't drive with anyone in his car.

The negativity.

"She may want you dead, but Y and her team aren't going to let that happen."

"I don't think we've got a choice." Amanda hugged herself, looking small and insignificant in his back seat.

"Fret not, we got..."

Shaft just saw the digger in time as it moved across the road in front of him. He pressed hard on the brakes; the superior German engineering brought it to a stop before a collision.

"Fuck!" Shaft growled through clenched teeth. He was in reverse before he could swear again.

The Jags wheels spun wildly responding immediately to his commands, taking traction, biting into the loose soil, finding purchase and then hurtling backward. Shaft expertly guided the car in the opposite direction then violently swung the steering wheel left, dancing on the pedals as he went.

The Jaguar spun around, skidding in the process and ended up pointing in the direction they had come from. Shaft put his foot down again, and the beast of V8 engine roared.

The shadows around them came alive, and he began to understand what was going on.

Miranda had fucked them over.

But she wasn't the only one who had an eye for strategy. Y had an uncanny knack for surmising where those possibilities could manifest and preparing with that in mind. Y's instincts would prepare them, but they would have to do the heavy lifting. Shaft was hurtling through the night at sixty miles an hour in what was once twenty miles an hour zone. He would not make this easy for them; he wasn't making it easy for himself.

"What did you do?" Y snapped, her eyes leaving the red incandescence smoke trail that told her something was wrong. Miranda had the merest smile on her lips, when she shrugged. Her eyes twinkled with amusement.

"Why do you think our kind has survived over the millennia? How could I commune with the essence of my lover knowing I did not do everything in my power to avenge his taking. I will turn Amanda personally, come back and destroy you later. After all you're tonight's entertainment."

"You're mistaking me for someone who cares." Y said. "We're walking out of here."

Miranda's smile broadened.

"You can try, but I'm not done wid yuh yet. We just getting started." The vampire Queen spun into her car, leaving Y and Suzy poised with their weapons at the ready as the shadows closed in on them.

"Fuck!"

The airbag exploded open in Shaft's face as the Jaguar collided with the skip that had been drawn onto the road just as Shaft geared down. It could have been much worse if not for his driving skills. He looked back to see how Amanda was doing. She seemed dazed but otherwise unharmed.

She gave him a thumbs up.

"Stay in the car," Shaft barked and started shuffling out of the driver's seat with the urgency of a punch-drunk fighter. He shouldered the stiff door open and stumbled out into the cool night. He felt twinges of pain in his chest and arms, but he didn't let it slow him down. It felt as if the shadows were pressing down on him, surrounding the car. They were moving like apparitions, skulking in the shadows, waiting for an opportunity to strike.

Shaft hurried to the back of the car seeing the silhouette of Amanda inside and popped the boot. That primordial feeling of dread was mounting at every moment, tightening in his chest. He reached into the darkness of the boot, felt his fingers contact with what could have been grenades but were much more useful. He picked up four of the objects and twisted their tops throwing them over his shoulder. Silver reflective spheres hit the ground and exploded with a steady stream of simulated sunlight. The darkness encroaching on them fled with painful screeches as the exposed vampires that had surrounded them scuttled for the safety of the darkness. Shaft dug a little deeper and felt the heft and stock of a carbine. He pulled it to his chest reassuringly with a box of ammunition and chambered cartridges. The things in the darkness where unhappy with the light from how the screeched and snarled. Shaft shuddered but kept the shotgun steady.

"Jesus!"

They were everywhere. They blended perfectly into the darkness with only those otherworldly glowing red eyes that reacted to the light. Shaft wondered how long he could keep them at bay before he was overrun.

He had nine more incandescence bombs and 15 shotgun cartridges.

Not long at all.

So why did he get the impression that they were holding back, waiting?

Patra had plummeted for about a hundred feet before she pulled the ripcord on her base jump. She was heavy but not dangerously so. The night was still, a current manageable. Controlling her fall in the urban sprawl below was hazardous because of the manmade landscape and buildings, demolition equipment and the darkness. What she was doing well was following the path Shaft had taken with the undead bogies not far behind. As she adjusted the surface area of the aerofoil, tweaking her angle of descent with the directional chords in both her hands. The ground was coming up to meet her quickly, and she was preparing her landing. Patra made a hard right, seeing the possibility of landing on what seemed like a driveway. She braced for impact, her muscle memory preparing her for a routine she had done many, many times before.

She relaxed.

Then suddenly tensed.

A line appeared out of nowhere hurtling towards her throat and decapitation. The tingle in the base of her skull activated, the threads in her harness popping, making her body shift lopsidedly. The garrotte missed her neck, the defunct Power-line that stretched from one side of the road to the other, making a demonic smiley face in the air. Patra twisted and loosened the pull on her directional chords.

She gasped and swore.

The parachute slammed into the wire and tangled immediately, jerking and spinning her to a stop. Patra hung like she had been trapped in a giant spider's web, slowly turning in the breeze, ten feet from the ground. Cursing again she reached for one of the two push daggers sheathed on the right and left breast of her combat suit. She easily cut through the straps and chords around her shoulders and then her crotch. She wiggled out of the harness and fell the ten feet to the ground, silent as a cat.

Now she had to get to Shaft, but first, she had to pick up something on the way.

"Divide and conquer." Y said under her breath. "But stay in my orbit. We leave here together or not at all.

Y needn't have said anything more.

Suzy's butterfly knives were already in her hands as she strode towards the ramps leading into the parking space, goading them to try and stop her. The vampires knew what they had to do, and anything short of death was acceptable. Suzy's strides got longer, and soon she was running instead of walking. The entrance loomed ahead. At the mouth of the entrance, something that had been attached to the ceiling silently dropped to the floor on all fours.

It fixed her with blazing red eyes and then stood erect.

Suzy kept going.

The vampire crouched and roared out a blood-curdling screech, flexed its extended talons and attacked. This was its primal form, and they were truly monstrous. More bat than human, blazing red eyes, muscular jaws and a mouth filled with a jagged array of razor-sharp teeth. Their hunger for blood maybe all-consuming but it did not interfere with their calling as warriors. Suzy braced herself, trotting to a stand. The vampire launched itself at her and Suzy with incredible dexterity, leaned backwards, her two blades flashing as the bloodsucker flew over. Springing back to her feet, she turned to see the monster sizzling and grunting with its guts hanging loose, her holy water dipped blades doing their job.

She resumed running.

Another taker sauntered forward from the shadows, his tie slightly askew but his fight posture perfect. Another came bounding from Suzy right, defying gravity for a moment as it scuttled along the wall, bouncing off it with inhuman speed. The pincer movement did not make Suzy slow down or hesitate for a moment. She saw the gap between them and realized it was closing quickly. She sprang forward taking to the air her powerful legs shooting her through claws that slashed at her torso, twisting like a corkscrew, her blades flashing. She landed on her shoulders and tumbled. The howls and the thunk, thunk of severed limbs were like background sounds she quickly forgot. Suzy knew she couldn't outrun them, but she would be ahead, and that was an advantage. The remainder of her momentum carried Suzy gracefully back to her feet. The two ominous shadows ahead would not be so easily dispatched, and Suzy would not be so easily stopped.

40.

A t the other side of the underground parking bay under Wentworth tower, Y was attacked by three vampires at once. She knew how difficult that was for her attackers. Coordinating your assault in sync so they would have the most potential for damage, required practice or an uncanny intuitive ability between them.

Y guessed these creatures had the latter.

One was striking at her low, the other two concentrated on her right and left side. She spun her Katana sweeping from left to right, her blade like a lightning bolt blocking the razor-sharp claws attempting to rip her gut open and tear her face off. The two vampire women to her left and right stumbled back making the third in the group lunge for her crotch. Y thrust the blade down with all the power she could muster, skewering both its hands through the wrist and anchoring her mystical sword into the concrete. The creature screamed, viciously pulling as if it was willing to tear its arms through the sword. Y executed a low whip kick, snapping its neck back from the force. Its eyes blazed with fury, and its mouth snapped at her like sentient steel traps.

Y pulled the sword free and rolled backward, brushing aside the attacks from above with a flash of her blade. She held an almost interactive construct of her battlefield in her head and with her back to the slope of the exit she could sense something behind her. Instead of turning to see and exposing herself she placed her back to the gritty exit wall where she could see up and down the ramp. The three she had countered to her right were regrouping, the person she was yet to come to grips with still shrouded in shadow above. Y moved quickly towards the exit, the three other vampires snapping at her heels. Y's Katana vibrated in her grip, warmth emanated from her palm, her weapon was beginning to feel like an extension of herself and that felt good. The good vibes disappeared quickly when she saw who or what stood guarding the exit. Before being undead, he was a muscular and athletic man, and from his preparations, at Y's arrival, he was also a proficient boxer. He shadow-boxed filling the time, his face monstrous, obscenely sharp fangs seemed to be rammed into his mouth, and a macabre smile gave you goose flesh looking at the nightmare he represented.

"You ready Guardian bitch." He bellowed.

The vampire beckoned her forward, still hooking and jabbing the air.

"Ms. Bitch to you, fuck face. And yeah I am always ready." Y grimaced charging towards him her Katana humming in the gloom as it trailed a blue light stream behind her.

Patra ran a mile in under five minutes, with her back-pack and without breaking a sweat. Dean had buried the case at a pre-agreed location, that was indelibly stamped into her mind. In the darkness, she uncovered the buried and tightly packed titanium case. Checking the contents and confident everything was in order. Patra's mind unraveled the remainder of the plan.

Dean had not made contact.

He was the cavalry if things went sideways and if he couldn't handle it, shit would get real very quickly. Patra hefted the bag and began jogging towards Shaft's loca-tion. She thought of Dean and rammed her concern deep inside. She ran in the middle of the winding road the broken and crumbling buildings leering at her steady progress. She was in a rhythm, her senses leading her to Shaft's location and the danger he would be facing. Her sisters were engaged that much she knew. Their spooky comm. network was blowing up. The lines were busy, controlled and frantic.

That was good.

Refocussing from her musing, the sound of car en-gines, made her flinch. Patra broke right and slid behind a broken wall that once skirted the perimeter of a grass verge. She quickly shrugged out of the bag around her shoulders and straddled the case between her legs, keeping low and watching carefully as big black Mercedes and a similarly colored Ford van flew past.

"Miranda! I'm coming for you bitch." She said.

Patra hurriedly picked up her backup, the case and started running slowly picking up speed as she disappeared into the darkness.

Dean had moments left before he would be entombed in his car. The survival force that drove his species was taking over, transforming him into his natural form, the form that the human legends loved to whisper about in ghost stories. It was far worse than they could imagine and not something he reveled in, but tonight it would be his friend, saving him or dooming him. He let the transformation, amidst the noise of the rivet guns and the stench of acetylene torches, take hold. He slid over to the back seat and used his substantial strength and his talons to tear away at the upholstery. Whatever metal or veneered plywood between the seat and the car boot was ripped to shreds. The car was being jostled and banged but not with as much energy.

They were finishing their work.

Dean pushed his feet first into a hole he had made and forced himself into the cramped space of the boot. He contorted his body easily; vampire infected muscle and sinew compounding traditional science. He squatted like a weightlifter. Both feet apart and flat, his backside touching the flooring his broad shoulders propped up against the top of the confined metal box. In the darkness infernal energy flashed behind his eyes, he smiled an awful smile and began standing, his powerful legs pushing his unbreakable skin against the metal. The boot buckled, the metal distorting against his raw power. The lock popped first, but it did not fly open. He could sense they had reinforced that area in the process. He shifted his squat position and pushed up again. Whatever they had used to bind him faltered and tore. With a guttural roar, Dean tore back the booth like a tuna tin and squeezed out into the night air an angry welcoming party greeting him.

Shaft wasn't fooled into thinking it was his efforts alone that were keeping these monsters at bay. They were waiting, and he had a good idea who for. How prepared could he be? These things could shrug off twelve-gauge rounds, their ferocity was astonishing and their strength unbelievable.

The facts should interfere with what he had to do, but he couldn't let it overwhelm him. Shaft's senses were straining in the darkness. He was on his third set of high-intensity daylight spheres, the creatures skulking in the ever-encroaching shadows, perfectly blending into the night, waiting. Sometimes only their glowing eyes and snarls giving away their presence.

And that was the unnerving thing.

Shaft paced the small area around the car, Mossberg in his hand and his fingers slick with cold perspiration.

Every movement jangling his nerves, every sound imagined or real made him lift the shotgun and point. He cleared his throat, and the grits of dust and a rotting organic tang irritated him. He tried to reign in his imagination but thoughts of how this would all end reared like a demented jack in the box.

He was still processing the fact that vampires existed.

Hands curled around his shoulders, and he spun around wildly. His eyes met Amanda's who had left the security of the car to join him outside.

"Fuck!" He sighed, relieved. "You almost gave me a heart attack."

Shaft hadn't forgotten her; he was more concerned with protecting the diminishing oasis of light they occupied. Amanda stood in an unflattering light. The shifting shadows from the spheres adding years to her life. She had been through so much and now this. Stress was taking her apart, bit by bit; the slow-burning terror was disfiguring her features; she looked at him. Eyes wide, lips trembling. Shaft wondered what he was looking like himself.

No mirrors to see.

Would he want to?

"Amanda," he said softly. "I know how you feel, but I can't protect you as well here as I could if you were inside. Please."

She looked at him eyes suddenly glistening, showing a flicker of determination or tears, he wasn't sure which. She slid back into the damaged Jaguar and shut the door. And not a moment too soon. Something carried through the air like negative static electricity, the minions felt it and responded with an excited caterwauling that rose up from all around them in a discordant chorus. That's when Shaft saw the headlights piercing the gaps in the building as it negotiated a corner and his gut told him, they were welcoming their mistress.

Miranda Pheare and arrived.

Shaft felt as if his heart was about to exit his chest, that's how violently it was beating. No more than a minute had passed in real-time since the black van and Miranda's luxury ride had parked some hundred meters from his disabled Jag. For a queen, he wasn't important enough for her to show herself. She could orchestrate this massacre from the comfort of her back seat. Strangely he felt put out by this.

Who the fuck does she think she is? He asked himself. Immediately he felt stupid as he made a case for his disembowelment at her hands. The answer came back terrible and unflinching in his own voice.

She a centuries-old vampire Queen, dip shit, who was about to send her Clan to rip your balls off.

Instinctively he looked down at them for what could be the last time. From above, a blur spat from the black inky pool of night, a roar trailing with it. Shaft reacted by swinging the shotgun up and around, trying to track its motion, but it was just too fast, too fuzzy. It landed on the roof of his Jaguar, exploding windows and sink-ing the shocks and the chassis with the force of the impact.

Shaft's eyes narrowed to view the inside, and thankfully, Amanda was okay but shook. Steadying himself his eyes settled on what was left of the roof of his car. What he saw next made his blood chill.

The man he knew as Dean grinned back at him.

On what was left of his cars roof, Dean had a thrashing and snarling vampire under him, pinning it in place with his knees and free hand. He then proceeded to detach the creature's head from its body with a very sharp, Arabian Nights looking scimitar.

"You ready to fight for your life?" Dean bellowed.

Shaft couldn't speak, his throat was too dry. Dean lifted the decapitated head by its hair and flung it into the darkness.

The detective just shook his head in disbelief and the irony, lifted his shotgun and chambered a round.

41.

"What do you wish, mistress?" Mr. Opuko asked. Miranda sat in the back of her carriage beside her trusted familiar, posture perfect, the plush leather was soft and supple, exuding a faint but beautiful smell of abattoirs and fear only her hyper senses could appreciate. From the pitch-black comfort of her luxurious back seat, she had reached out to her driver, compelling her to stop while her Mistress deliberated on the most satisfying course of action. This pilgrimage to London had been filled with surprise and uncertainty. For an immortal such as herself, uncertainty was a precious gift. She was never disappointed coming to the great city every fifty years, shedding precious blood in the name of her lover. But finding the ancestor of the slayer of Lord Byfield and the tool responsible for ripping him from this earth plane was a prospect too delicious to ignore. If it was at all possible, her pilgrimage had become even more exciting. London was under the stewardship of the Guardians of the Light. She could not have asked for a more thrilling development especially as her wayward child Dean Thorn had been recruited into their camp.

She smiled to herself.

Her exploits would be chronicled in the great vampire consciousness. An object lesson for her kind to learn from. She felt nothing at this. No pride, no excitement, just an overwhelming need to give her kind the advantages to survive and thrive in this world. At her feet was the Heart of Ares, the only thing that could have been a cause for concern. She had neutralized that cause.

"Your wishes?" Mr. Opuko asked again.

"Kill the lawman and bring the gal to me."

The tires screamed, and the V8 engine roared as the car reversed out of the underground car park at speed it, vampires clinging to the bonnet and the roof. Y was sure the Bentley had never been driven in this fashion before, but she knew the superior German engineering could take it. The undercarriage sparked, as metal hit concrete and Y locked the steering wheel left gritting her teeth, making the machine spin in the direction she wanted it to go. It came to a dead stop, and in a heartbeat, Y was changing gears. The bloodsucker that was attached to the bonnet didn't have a good enough handhold as it had thought. Brake force tore him off and sent him tumbling away into the gloom. His sister in blood, had her metamorphosized talons partially shearing through the metal of the roof.

The female vamp was going nowhere.

"She hanging on like a tick, "Suzy hollered at the un-invited guest still attached to their roof. Y looked back to see the shadows streaming up from below the car park still pursuing them.

They would follow she knew it.

The creature above them was unrelenting. It was slowly tearing and pounding away at the rooftop. The Bentley accelerated, and a bruised Suzy looked up at the guttural snarls and rending sounds above them.

An unspoken message passed between the two sisters. Suzy grabbed the steering wheel and with an impressive degree of flexibility, she contorted herself, so Y could slip out of the driving seat replacing her sisters' smaller feet on the pedals. The surreal game of swap ended, and the car rocketed forward its movements uninterrupted, but this time Suzy was driving, and Y sat shotgun. The darkness squeezed at them from all sides, and Suzy was able to keep them on an even keel, her reflexes acute. Y sat quietly beside her; eyes closed Katana in hand. Suzy didn't want to rush her sister, but the thing on the roof was slowly peeling it away and forcing its way in, its jaws snapping, saliva dripping onto the plush leather in its excitement.

Suddenly Y opened her eyes, whatever she had been looking for in her altered state, she had found. That key to an elusive power they were all coming to grips with but once recognized they could turn on. The Katana glowed a pale blue as Y gripped it two-handed. Her eyes flicked up and then she thrust it through the roof. The blade melted the metal, and a stink of burning leather wafted into the interior. The shriek was ear-splitting but abrupt as the blade bucked at its hilt. Y twisted it savagely and withdrew.

"Job done," she said wiping the gore off the steel.

"Not yet Mama," Suzy said her hooded eyes on the road. "One down but plenty more feh go."

This was neither the time nor the place for a mutual admiration society, but Dean and that old looking short sword was a goddamn force of nature. As soon as he arrived the shadows had come to life and the vampire horde attacked in numbers, but he was more than ready. Believe it or not, they settled into a violent groove. Shaft was leaning on the bonnet with Amanda beside him; he could swing from left to right with his shotgun, she could swing her tire iron. Dean had everything else.

Shaft could feel the perspiration trickle down his back, and the muscles of his shoulders and arms ached from the repetition of racking the pump action and the kickback of the stock on his shoulders. A repetitive strain injury was in the cards of which he didn't care. His ammunition wasn't killing these bastards just making this exchange as painful and uncomfortable as possible. He was reloading regularly, and under normal circumstances, he would be a sitting duck to these monsters, but Dean had his back at those moments, like he was reading his fear and shifting landscape of this battle. Ready again, his weapon breach full, Dean's blade was needed elsewhere.

Shaft chambered a round, and at the corner of his eyes, something was pulling itself out of the gloom as if he was coated in it. The man's tailored suit was expensive, his Clarkes shoes comfortable and Shaft couldn't help himself nervously cataloging the humdrum aspects of the undead. The vampire hurtled towards him on all fours. If he didn't know better, he would have thought this well-dressed monstrosity had left his investment banker friends in the Docklands to head towards Miranda's call. Some crazy reticence shored up in Shaft panic-stricken mind, concerns about ruining the suit.

What the fuck!

End this wanker, he chatted to himself and pumped several twelve-gauge rounds into its head. The impact dumped it to the ground like a charging rhino would if hit by a large caliber weapon.

He did not stay down. They never did.

The damage was superficial. It shook off the eighty-two-grain shot and charged him again. Shafts shoulders drooped, a blanket of weariness enveloping him. The stink of sweat and hopelessness could be what made the Docklands vampire lunge at him with gleeful expectation. His world slowed to a snail pace, its way of telling him his reaction time was lagging.

He lifted the shotgun that suddenly weighed a ton in his sweat-slick hands and swung it. The monster screeched not in a weird triumph but pain. Docklands was caught skewered in mid-flight, impaled on a steel pipe that had swung into its trajectory. Shaft shook his head in confusion then saw what happened. Amanda stood dreamlike beside him, the length of broken pipe she had levered upwards on her shoulders. The vampire struggled, thrashing and smiling, inching its way off its skewer but not before Dean swooped down like a vengeful angel separating its head from his body.

42.

M r. Opuko loved to watch his mistress work. Every expression she made whether she was scheming, or some imbecile was challenging her authority, it revealed something about the inner depth of his Queen. He could never make his practice obvious or sexualize his fascination although she would encourage it because they were expected to show their adoration for her. No, his interest was in her beautiful mind. Her dark and scheming mind. Mr. Opuko would not dare to give it a title because that would make his pastime a formal memory in his head. That would be testing fate. Her mental capabilities were formidable. Her talents unfathomable

What if she took offense?

Instead, he preferred to bathe in her ruthlessness and maybe learn a thing or two. Mr. Opuko would not be disappointed with tonight; he could feel it. He sat stiller than he ever had beside his mistress, after the last of the clan were extinguished by the traitor Dean Thorne.

What would her next move be?

Tremors of anticipation pin balled around his nervous system. He wanted to squeeze the armrest and stiffen in his seat, but he did none of this. The Queen never got angry not really. He preferred to think of it as righteous indignation. A wave of coldness emanated from her body, making him shiver slightly. He had experienced this a few times in his history with her, and it never got stale. He waited with interest for her to make her move and wondered what was on her mind. What unusual tell would she exhibit when she had made the decision. She drummed her long-nailed fingers, once and then twice. Mr. Opoku's eyes twinkled in the coffin darkness of the sumptuous back seat. He held his breath as long as he could - he was not immortal yet, then exhaled. Three beats from a heart that one day he wished would have no need to sustain his human form. Three beats that's all it was before the Queen spoke.

"Keep deh engine running; I have some business to attend to."

Like a Spectre, she had left her seat and let herself out of the car before Mr. Opoku could register her movement. As the door slammed shut, only her perfume remained.

The air on the darkened battlefield was murky and felt heavy with death but also dreaded expectancy that eluded your ability to pinpoint. You knew something was coming and only if you were unfortunate enough to be in the loop would you know what it was. The light globes were dying not even the vampire bodies spontaneously disintegrating in a brief light show leaving behind their black residue could stop the encroaching darkness. Soon this scene of carnage and scorched earth would be devoured as if it never happened. Shaft didn't want to be here for that.

Dean agreed.

The vampire hurried over, looking more human than he was in battle. Shaft stepped back from him, an immediate reaction of fear that should have been gratitude. He cursed himself for being human.

Dean ignored the slight.

"You need to leave here now."

"I think I figured that out myself." Shaft said. "But where do we go? And on foot."

"Anywhere," Dean rasped. "I can't protect you from what is coming. The girls will be looking for you both, but you need to get as far away from here as possible."

"What about you?" Amanda asked. A smile broke the surface of Dean's features for a moment but sank back into the depths.

"I will be doing what I was meant to do." His eyes shot away from them to the Mercedes in the distance. The passenger door opened. He dug in his zipped pocket and fished out an oval yellow amethyst stone and another wrapped package. He handed them to Amanda.

"Your machine needs these two items to work right?"

Amanda looked at them and mumbled.

"Moonstone and vampire flesh."

"That's right," Dean said. "It was hard to come by. Make sure the girls get it. They're going to need every advantage they can get. Now go!"

Amanda carefully placed the items in her pocket and squared her shoulders.

"Let's get out of her." Shaft said looking painfully at his wrecked car and grabbing Amanda's hands as they ran towards the shadows.

Stumbling over the debris-strewn landscape the duo didn't get very far before Patra came jogging out of the shadows ahead of them.

"You two aight?" She asked breathing evenly.

"We're good," Shaft said. "It was touch and go for a moment." His words trailed off.

She nodded.

"Those bitches not arrived yet?" Patra asked. "They want me to finish this on my lonesome? Shit, why didn't they just say?"

"You're not alone," Amanda said. "Dean needs you."

Patra brightened.

"She's not going to stop." Amanda continued sounding tired defeated and scared. "That monster is going to keep coming. I don't think anything can stop her."

To Patra's thinking there was no such thing as unstoppable.

"She gonna keep coming and we gonna keep fighting." Patra said. "Something's got to give."

Patra shrugged out of her backpack and set the case she was carrying down. Amanda's eyes fell on the large aluminium flight case. Patra looked at Amanda for a moment.

"Did you think we were dumb enough to give Miranda the real Heart of Ares?" Patra said winking mischievously. "We may look dumb but give us some credit."

"But how?" Amanda asked.

"A tale for another time. Take my backpack and the Heart and get to the main road," Patra said. "Get as far away from here as you can. You two need to survive or Y will fuck my shit up." Patra turned away from them looking over to where the action began.

"Get going!"

She took in a deep breath.

"The champ is here," Patra said more to herself than to anyone else. "The champ is here!" she repeated beginning to walk away from Amanda and Shaft. "The champ is here!" By this, she sounded like a young Muhammad Ali jogging towards the hell Shaft and Amanda had just left behind.

"No! No! No!" Patra screamed her natural night vision making this stark scene even harder to process. Patra was sprinting through the debris her lungs were oxygenating her muscles at a rate Usain Bolt would be proud of as she skimmed across the ground into a scene she did not want to admit was happening. The picture was a shattered pane of glass, destroyed by a maniac in her mind, the shards distorting the reality she did not want to accept, but which glared at her anyway.

Miranda.

Dean.

The vampire Queen held up Dean by his chest; she was tall enough and strong enough to have him dangling off the ground, her talons piercing his skin.

Patra was pushing herself. Her reflexes responding to the obstacle course of the broken landscape that was in front of her. She was moving unbelievably quickly across the scarred terrain. Her leaps were precise, her steps a study in dexterity as she sprinted ever closer to save him.

Miranda's right hand held the vicious looking scimitar – Dean's preferred weapon, stained and dripping with gore. Without pause, she plunged the sword into Dean's chest with a slow and purposeful thrust. The vampire queen then tossed him away from her with the sword still skewering him as if he was tainted. Patra screamed in frustration and was so close to her she could hear the rustling of her clothes. Patra leapt the remainder of the distance, her lips pulled back in a snarl, willing herself forward. Miranda turned her torso, both arms outstretched, palms flat and that is what Patra barrelled into. It was like hitting the trunk of a tree, rooted and ancient. Patra bounced off and rolled away, coming to her feet.

Patra came at her again.

Miranda moved gracefully, and with a controlled power the human eye could not track. Before Patra could react, the vampire queen slammed both her fist into her shoulders.

Home girl grunted as she heard and felt the clavicle snap. A red haze filled her field of vision; she rolled away and bumped into Dean's inert body. She levered herself up on hands and knees, looking into his face. Whatever supernatural anti-force that flowed through these creatures had not departed Dean just yet. He recognized her and smiled.

"Patra," His voice was croaky and broke when he spoke. "Take the sword. It has some special properties." He swallowed. "Don't give her the fucking satisfaction of killing me with it."

The pain in her shoulder and now the pain in her heart throbbed in unison. She lowered her face to his and kissed his lips.

They were cold.

She grabbed the hilt of the sword pulled it free and heard him groan. Patra looked up to see the vampire queen standing in the distance then in a blink Miranda was beside her. Traversing the distance between them as if she had bent space-time. She came with gifts. A back-hand that connected to Patra's jaw with such force it catapulted her away, flinging her body spinning into the street.

Dazed Patra sat up with the sword still in hand.

"Son of a bitch," she drawled, saliva and blood, pooling in her mouth. She spat and jumped back to her feet. "You hit like my grandma?" Patra bellowed. "You've done enough. Let him die in peace."

Miranda shook her head at the comment as if it was meant to be funny and placed her foot on Dean's neck. The real Miranda, the monster hidden behind the veneer of humanity emerged as horrific and savage as your worst nightmare could conjure. With eyes blazing she looked at Patra then at Dean and roared. Patras' eyes widened, her jaw slack. The Miranda thing reached for a metal pipe sticking up from the ground, snapping off a length. The vampire queen spun it in her hand stylishly and thrust the pipe through Dean's neck. She withdrew it and thrust it in again.

And again.

Dean's severed head rolled Patra's way, his handsome face a mask of pain, shock, and disbelief. The image would be seared into Patra's memory and so would her friends' words. Patra stood frozen and did not hear the car skid to a halt behind her. She was lost to shock and grief to hear the footfalls approaching in a hurry. Her head was filled with the amplified sounds of the rush of blood. Patra was preparing herself in her head. She tensed and stepped forward only to be stopped with a firm hand on her shoulder.

"Yuh alright, sis?" Suzy's voice was soothing.

Patra turned to look at them then beyond at their fucked-up ride.

"What took you bitches so long?" Patra's voice was toneless.

"Traffic," Y said, and they all hugged in a tight scrum, Patra winced her shoulder grinding the bone and tissue.

"Where's Dean?" Y asked.

Patra shook her head angrily. Her lips a tight line across her face. She pointed to the head

"Jesas!" Suzy said. "I'm sorry, baby."

Y closed her eyes.

"I want that bitch in pain." Patra said.

A pause.

"It's time we send her back whence she came," Y said.

"Whence?" Patra was kicking the word around in her head.

"I've always wanted to say that." Y said.

"Good word," Suzy said. "Biblical."

"Yeah," Y agreed. "Let's fuck her shit up."

They unclenched and side-by-side, the ancient power of the light crackling around and through them, they rounded on the focus of their attention.

Miranda was striding towards them, her voice like a cosmic ventriloquist as it seemed to be behind them and in front of them like a labyrinth echo. She moved with a barely contained fury that was laser focused.

"You sisters are as resilient as the legends say. But mi have no further time to play. Deh gal a come with me, her family have a debt to pay."

"I can't let that happen," Y commanded quietly. "Not on my watch."

All need for conversation was unnecessary and inadequate after that. The vampire queen beckoned them forward then made a grand gesture as she approached them. Like a conductor orchestrating, arcane forces only she could sense and manipulate. Her talons made complex diagrams in the air while the red lips on that horrific face recited an incantation or a command, and the air around them became electric. The girls crashed into thin air, blades flashing, Miranda nowhere to be seen. In her wake was a familiar sound and even more familiar smell.

"Son of a ..."

"Ambush!" Y spat.

"Her friends are coming," Suzy shouted over the din.

The trio tightened, weapons ready. Just as the skittering, scampering tsunami wall of cockroaches enclosed them.

43.

Miranda was not exactly where she should have been; her trans-migration spell had relocated her physical presence beyond the barrier of her anthropoid children who were now forming a dividing wall between her and the annoying adversaries. She would deal with them at her leisure. Right now, she wanted the girl, then she would dispatch the Guardians.

She lifted her head like a canine and sniffed the air. Her eyes blazed with an inner fire fanned with the winds of recognition. Miranda's muscles bunched in readiness for the chase only to be forced to hesitate.

Nothing could force her to do anything, but this did. For an instant, Miranda felt like her vampiric senses had switched off and she was weak and human again. She hadn't forgotten – she remembered every moment of her life, but her vampire nature kept her human experiences relegated to a dull, forgettable patch in the collective. The unfamiliar emotion of panic welled up in her, snatching her sense of balance with it. Miranda rocked from side to side the Earth moved underfoot. Then it was gone. Her formal power snapped back into place.

"I heard you were looking for me?"

Miranda didn't hear the person approach and as worrying as that was, what she saw next made that fact pale into insignificance.

Amanda Walker stood staring at her, resplendent in the Heart of Ares, the moonstone bathing her chest and face with a throbbing yellow light.

Miranda took a halting step backward. Instantly all the connections and conclusions that led to this very moment mushroomed in her black mind.

This was the real Heart of Ares wasn't it?

The Guardians had given her a fraud.

Somehow, they were able to mislead her vampire senses into believing it was genuine. The real Heart of Ares was standing before her, manipulated by an inexperienced child. And instead of a glorious morning of abduction and torture, she would be defending herself against the one thing that could end her. It had cut short the existence of her precious Byfield. But forewarned is forearmed.

She could turn this around.

She knew she could.

Then she was not so sure, and the uncertainty tasted like a bitter pill being forced down her throat.

Amanda vaulted over the wreckage that once was Spokes car, landing into a short sprint and then barrelling into the vampire queen like a runaway freight train. The impact was like a clap of thunder. Two spiritual forces colliding. Amanda was knocked back, skidding along the ground but maintaining her balance by lowering her center of gravity. Miranda was knocked off her feet too but executed a graceful somersault landing expertly meters away. When she turned to face Amanda again, she had transformed to her savage alter ego. The insatiable beast who wanted blood and revenge.

Amanda was no fighter unless you consider her rebellious streak in Grade Seven, but she was no pushover either. How could she be when this incredible power the Heart of Ares was able to channel was coursing through her body. The power was an intoxicating feeling that not just made you feel invincible like a cocaine hit but rendered you invincible.

And strong.

She was beginning to understand how her great, great, great grandfather felt.

Amanda's perception narrowed. It was if she was burning with a cold fire from the inside out. The hairs on her body stood to attention. Every breath she took was fanning the flame.

Amanda could feel the level ramping up at the site of the monster that was Miranda Pheare. The Heart is preparing for what came next.

Her adversary was preparing too.

Amanda sprinted towards the vampire and then in mid-charge struck out at her head. The Queen blocked her, but the force that Amanda carried from the blow was undeniable. She rocked back but returned her blow with a swipe of her talons which Amanda stepped away from with blistering speed. She attacked again seeing an opening in the vampire's defenses and began raining blows down on her. The Queen looked shocked as a human was delivering a beating unlike anything she had ever experienced in her very long history. But Amanda was not done. The ticker was timing down and once it hit zero the power of the Heart would have depleted. She would use every second to inflict as much damage on the monster as she could.

But would it be enough?

Amanda gritted her teeth, absorbing a snap kick from Miranda. The vampire queen was experienced, precise, graceful and athletic. Amanda was determined and clumsy, but she was causing pain. Yet, grace was winning out. Miranda held a grotesque smile knowing the tide was turning.

Inexperience would be her downfall.

For now, Amanda was holding her own against a flurry of slashing blows to her body and face, using her forearms to parry them. She was close to the zero point as the internal countdown was preparing her Amanda imagined it would slowly wind itself down until there was nothing left.

Not so, for the otherworldly forces that powered the Heart.

It would run at its full capacity.

Two.

One.

Zero.

Amanda felt the power suddenly drain from her and the Heart of Ares was dead

They were suffocating.

The cockroaches weren't just circling them in a wild tornado, crashing into them, crawling all over their bodies but sucking the air out of the confined space they were trapped in. It was becoming more difficult to breathe. The sisters were saying nothing, how could they? A battle was raging, and it seemed nothing they could do was making a dent in the sheer weight of numbers these insects were brought to bare. They wished for an adversary they could reach out and touch. Fighting against this enemy was like shadowboxing a waterfall and just as exhausting.

Suzy was the first to stop fighting as wave upon wave of bugs surrounded them. It took all her effort to short-circuit her instinct to fight. But she quashed it, her heart racing and reached out to hold Patra's hand. The rudimentary nature of her plan was transmitted with her touch, and Patra slowed down too. Moving closer to her sister, Patra reached out to Y grabbed her arm in mid-swing. Y stopped immediately and was pulled in close to her sisters. All three focused, channel their energies from Suzy through Patra into Y and then into her Katana. She held it up like an antenna, and they continued to focus. The cockroaches did not relent, tightening their circle of movements.

At first.

The katana started to glow a pale blue, and there was an immediate hitch in the stream of insects. The blade of the katana cycled up to a brilliant blinding white, and the effect was immediate. The roaches lost coherence in an explosive parting of ways that destroyed the swirling tornado of insect bodies. The girls looked around thankfully, taking in a lungful of sweet air, hugging each other but the congratulations did not last.

Patra was far from done.

"let's go show this bitch what time it is!" Patra said.

44

"The real Heart of Ares." Miranda whispered the words as she bent down to the woman who had used and was still wearing the impressive weapon. Amanda was pinned to the ground under the vampire queen's foot. The human was thrashing and squirming, but Miranda paid her no heed. She lovingly ran the tip of one talon over the metal form of the Heart.

"Exquisite workmanship, don't you think?" She said adding more pressure to the woman underfoot and hearing a satisfying snap.

Amanda screamed, and Miranda smiled. The vampire trailed her talons across the depleted crystal, and suddenly her grin turned crooked.

The Moonstone was not as dead as it seemed.

Her whole world slipped.

The supernatural control she had over her environment, herself and the many resources she marshaled, flatlined. Her head spun, and her hand snapped back from the crystal, stumbling backward, releasing her connection with her children, watching helplessly as they scurried back to the embrace of the darkness, the thorn's in her side free! Her omniscient awareness of her kingdom and players had disappeared for an instant.

Static.

"We back bitch how you like me now?" Patra flew out of the shadows flashing the Damascus steel blade, Y and Suzy close behind. Miranda was disorientated but still dangerous. She flew backward clear of the slashing metal, landing on all fours, ending in a low crouch like a lizard.

Patra kept coming.

The thought of Dean's head rolling end over end at her feet fuelled her rage. The plan was to attack simultaneously, and for the most part, they were, but Patra was just ahead, wielding the sword with more ferocity, more intent than they had planned. Miranda's calculating smile was slipping. The battle was hyper-frenetic. A gorgeous ballet of the martial arts. Miranda moved like a gymnast, sometimes evading slicing blades, other times deflecting metal from her almost invincible skin. But one blade would break through, and when it did, it hurt.

She bellowed in frustration, Y's Katana still channeled some of her life force. She came back with even more ferocity lashing out with her feet and arms simultaneously, catching Y and Suzy off guard. Patra took up the slack and moved in but received the back of Miranda's hand for her trouble. Patra spun and tumbled away. V8 engines roared, and Patra could see the vampire queen's black Mercedes pulling up to a spot in the clearing, closer to the battle.

Miranda spotted it and turned to escape. It was Patras time to scream.

"No fucking way!"

Patra jumped up, holding the Damascus sword with both hands and with a cry of grief anger and exhaustion she flung it with all her strength. It flew through the air spinning like a discus, ricocheting off a concrete block almost picking up velocity. Miranda moved like liquid electricity leaping over a pile of rubble, letting gravity take her. As she started to descend to the ground the sword's trajectory suddenly changed, glancing off a rebar matching the vampires' movements perfectly.

Miranda sensed something had changed.

Patra felt not a tingle at the base of her skull but a punch.

Probability had altered.

Miranda turned to glance at the projectiles course correction, but not even her legendary reflexes could stop it. The scimitar embedded itself in her shoulder knocking her off balance. In mid-air she righted herself landing agilely. Her scream echoed off the fractured buildings, a cry of frustration more than pain at first. She stumbled to her knees and then back to her feet again. Slowly she reached over grabbed the hilt of the blade and pulled it out, letting it clatter to the ground. She found herself genuflecting from the exotic explosions of pain throbbing through her. Miranda kneeled there, unfamiliar with this sensation. A vampire queen, an apex predator did not kneel for anyone. The spell in the sword acted quickly but her own defences were countermanding its powers. Miranda was weak and needed a moment. And that moment came in the guise her car backing up beside her. Miranda looked up languidly as the big black doors of the Mercedes opened like the wing of a giant beetle accepting her into its embrace. The vampire queen hesitated and looked back at the three women battered but not broken, her eyes blazing, her now human face twisted into a snarl. With the nod of her head and dredging up a bitter respect for her opponents. She shakily entered the car and sped away.

45.

"Kiss mi Muma! You did it." Spokes was jubilant and relieved all at once. His dark skin was flushed and his teeth white as he grinned with his gold incisor glinting. "Bwoy, I was worried this would end before it began."

"No faith in our potential then?" Y asked hoping to see him squirm, but their benefactor was too sure of his purpose to be perturbed by Y's barbs. He would have made a legendary car salesman on some intergalactic car lot.

"If anyone have faith in yuh sisters, it's me." He paused still smiling. "I'm a gambling man. Yuh know dat and I would still put money on you, even against the odds."

"Figuratively speaking right?" Y asked.

There was a twinkle in Spokes eyes.

"Of course, sister, of course." He laughed.

"She's going to come back to London. I just know it." Suzy said her voice almost distant.

"Mek she come. We will be prepared." Spokes said his jovial demeanor turning grim. "She may not be so lucky next time."

"Amen to that," Patra chorused. "She'll come correct the next time she steps up to fuck with London or us."

"And that could be the problem." Y pondered.

"Let me worry about dat." Spokes raised his right hand showing them the enchanted signet ring he wore; It could discern the truth in any situation. And he was obviously happy with its observations. "She's never wrong."

"How's your shoulder, Miss P." Shaft asked.

Suzy rolled her eyes.

Y shook her head.

"These bitches don't realize I took one for the team, but that's aight." She lifted her arm in a sling and revolved her bandaged shoulders. "We heal quick."

"I know," Shaft said. "It still hurts to see..." He lowered his eyes in thought then changed the subject. "Any updates on the box and who produced the replica Heart of Ares, how they knew our plans on how they got it into the mansion in the first place."

Spokes lifted his Panama hat revealing a crown of peppercorn white and black Afro. He scratched his head under it.

"Nothing but the spontaneous tattoo formation on all of our bodies." Y said.

"Crazy shit," Patra said.

"You sent over the symbols, didn't you?" Spokes asked more to himself than the girls.

"Yuh said you would check them out." Suzy reminded him.

"And I did sister Wong," Spokes slapped his head. "Pinkie, baby," he called out. "Check in the recent research file, and the Anancy cult tab." In moments of svelte well-dressed dark-skinned woman approached him. Her high heels were clicking on the tiles as she handed him the file. Comically all three women lowered their heads as if doing that would give them a better view of the sexy PA, but it didn't. The webcam on Spokes end remained at waist height. The only saw the well-proportioned rear and the long legs of a woman with enviable dress sense leave the room.

"I don't know what I'd do without her." Shaft murmured, opening the file. "Now, oh yes, here we go." He cleared his throat and read snippets from the papers in the file. "These are eternity symbols used by an obscure cult in Ghana who worshipped Anancy the Spider God. The high priestess had that Mark on their bodies."

"It mek sense," Suzy mused. "I picked up snatches of the jungle, the sounds of drums, the heat, the taste of Palm oil, and the excitement of the worshippers from deh box. The rituals felt old, ancient."

"It seems, and Anancy is one of the most accessible of African deities. Legend says him have a special love for the Earth plane and his worshippers."

"A God?" Y asked.

"It looks like you have a fan." Spokes said as if it was the most natural thing in the world.

The girls looked at each other. When they thought their lives couldn't get any stranger it did. Spokes let that fact sink in with an all-knowing smile on his face.

He was back to his excitable self again.

"Right now, after that ordeal yuh need rest, some good food and family around you."

They all agreed.

"Talking about family G," Patra asked. "When are you swinging back to London?"

"Miss me?" Spokes asked.

"Come on man; you know I do," Patra said unabashed.

"Unfortunately, I have plenty left to do sister P. The world is a strange and wonderful place with so much to do and see. In time," he philosophized. "Meanwhile you have my back and London's too. The city is in good hands. The powers know dat."

"Why thank you," Y said. "You're beginning to understand being the Guardians of the Light is one thing. Try being three diverse women in a world that misunderstands who you are and what you're about. We're fighting on multiple levels." Y paused. "I'm just saying."

Spokes looked at all three of them in turn. He adjusted his chair and sat up straighter as if he was on a military parade

"I respect dat." He said. "Just remember you're not alone. We all know there are much bigger tings at play.

Tings we will never completely understand. I may have found you, but I am not the only one looking out for you."

"We love you same way." Suzy said.

"I can feel you Ms. Wong," Shaft said, his voice breaking slightly. He gathered himself. "Go chill. And congrats again on this huge win. I will pray to whoever will listen, to not make your journey easy but make you stronger." He paused. "Give my best to Nanny and drink a pint of Guinness for I."

He touched the screen with the palm of his hand and kept it there for a moment. The girls followed suit from their side of the communication.

"See yah."

"Later."

"Peace my breddah."

When they took their hands away from the monitor, he was gone.

Tonight, the long form oak table was full of mouth-watering treats. They usually spurned the dining room - the girls preferred to eat in the kitchen with Nanny but this time they made an effort.

Shaft had left Amanda and Trevor talking while he made his way to refill his plate. He was bent over the table helping himself to cocktail patties, when a pleasant shadow in a cloud of Issey Miyake perfume stood behind him. Shaft smiled, welcoming what came next.

"Hey lover, what you doing?" Y gripped him from behind with her strong arms around his waist and rested her head on his neck.

"Don't tease me," Shaft said. "I'm a sex-starved man at the moment, and I'm dangerous." He placed his plate of goodies down and reached back to grab her ass.

"Who is teasing now?" Y laughed with such gaiety and carefreeness you would be forgiven thinking she held no responsibilities. Shaft's level of respect rose a notch and if it was at all possible so did her sexiness quotient.

"How do you do that?" Shaft asked turning to face her. He was eye to eye with her, and she came even closer, rubbing her nose on his, her breath faintly peppermint.

"Do what?" She asked.

"Detach from what we just went through."

"I don't know," she said more seriously. "I never thought about it. I just guessed it was normal."

"Trust me it's not. But I have a theory." Shaft said but before he could elaborate Y put a finger to his lips.

"Boring," she said. "Enough about me. How are you?"
Shaft sighed.

"I am as good as I can be. I am still getting my head around what we are doing, and that doesn't get easier."

"Have you told your people about us?" Y asked.

"Not in so many words. The Commissioner of Police would prefer not to know about the details. He's even staying away from my department for that matter. He was glad the threat was over but pissed off I couldn't bring him a collar."

"Vampires don't do well incarcerated and neither do their fellow inmates." Y said.

Shaft laughed.

"A point I tried to explain to the Commissioner myself. Explaining all this to the government overlords was one thing but telling them they would be rubbing shoulders with the supernatural on a more regular basis, did not go down well."

"I hope it gets better but I have a feeling it won't."

"Yeah," Shaft said. "Me too." He twisted his lips in that weird way that he carried with him from a child to an adult.

"A year ago, my department was unrecognized by the Met. I was like the embarrassing secret they kept in the attic. The weird shit they couldn't get their heads around or didn't want to risk their careers looking into came across my desk. You ladies changed all that for me. Now the wankers are beginning to understand how important it is. Black Book is official." He bowed with a royal flurry of his hands. "I have an open plan office in Pimlico and three full-time analysts."

Y squealed and hugged him.

"Congratulations, your hard work is finally paying off."

Shaft shook his head.

"I feel like I'm looking at a boiling cannibal pot not knowing the pot is boiling with me in it."

"Think about the money."

"More money, more problems." He murmured.

"It comes with the territory. You know that." Y said.

Shaft nodded.

"You sound stressed?" Y asked.

"I am, I am." Shaft lied eagerly.

"What can I do to make it better?" Y's voice lowered.

Shaft shook his head as if the question caught him by surprise. It didn't take long for the cobwebs to clear. The question required his full concentration.

"I have a few ideas," Shaft said hugging her closer.

"Just a few?" Y asked and whispered some kinky preferences in his ear. Shaft suddenly stood to attention, his eyes bright, a wry smile blossomed on his lips.

"Keep your head in the game mister." Y said masterfully. "That prospect could be in your future if you're a good boy."

Laughing like a maniac, Shaft grabbed his food and they both sauntered over arm in arm to Nanny who was diligently wiping down a table.

Amanda hobbled over to Patra, her skill with the crutches needing work but at least she was wearing a smile after everything they had been through, and that was a win. Patra had been talking to Nanny who excused herself when she approached.

"The warrior queen has arrived, all hail the warrior queen," Patra teased. "You were badass A. We were ordained into this, but you dived into this vampire slaying shit like a duck to water. You're a natural sugah."

"Look who's talking. I still can't believe what you did. How you did it." Amanda looked at Patra carefully. "Are you for real?"

"I'm as real as a heart attack, baby."

Amanda lost her smile, her sparkling eyes diminished.

"If it weren't for your friend Dean, I wouldn't be sitting here talking to you."

Patra cleared her throat and lowered her head then raised it again. The tears were trapped in the ring of her eyes, and the slightest move would take them over on her cheeks. She looked straight ahead unmoving. Amanda put her arm gently on Patra's wounded shoulder.

"He was a stubborn motherfucker, talented and a good person. He didn't deserve to go out like that." Patra said.

Amanda's voice was low.

"I think he made a choice. Maybe he felt his sacrifice was worth it."

"Maybe," Patra said wistfully. "But do you know what the worse thing is? I didn't trust him. I couldn't get over the fact that he was a vampire. And still, he sacrificed his life for my punk ass."

Patra shook her head.

"I don't think he cared," Amanda said. "They say vampires don't have souls, but Dean showed that the soul might not be that important to be an honorable man."

"Damn straight," Patra said. "Damn straight."

A silence materialized between them that was comfortable but profound. Both women wrapped themselves in it without question and let it inform them of who they were.

Amanda sighed breaking the spell; her eyes widened at the sight of something on the dinner table. She reached over to pick it up. It was a steaming roasted corn

"My grandfather had a restaurant in Jamaica, and he used to do roasted corns. My God, smells just like him." She paused and took a bite eyes closed. "It tastes like Papa Derek's too." A dribble of butter trailed down her chin. "How can one person cook so well?"

"That is a mystery; we may never solve. Not sure we want to; the food is too damn good."

Amanda smiled and awkwardly shuffled in her seat a question struggling to emerge.

"What next?" Amanda asked.

Patra sighed.

"Hell, if I know." She said honestly. "The podcast will keep playing. It's important. We will do what we got to do to keep the balance." she paused to think. "This bullshit is going to keep coming, and when it does, we have to be ready. The fucked-up thing about it all is it feels natural. As natural as anything I've done in my life. Can you believe that shit?"

"I can," Amanda said. "I should be scared out of my mind. But I want to get more involved.

"You think that's a good idea?" Patra asked

"I want to research my ancestor, write about his life, his exploits and share it."

"You know they will think it is fiction," Patra said. "And the ones who don't will have their eyes on you."

"Maybe but I don't care."

"Can we get signed copies?" Patra asked. "An interview."

"Of course, but how about being in the book?" Amanda said.

"Hell yeah! Just promise me one thing," Patra said. "You leave the vampire gang banging to the professionals."

"I promise," Amanda said with a playfully devious smile on her face. "No warrior princess stuff."

"A vampire?" Trevor asked, the peppered shrimp that was clamped between his fingers fell back into the plate. "From Jamaica?" He paused. "Bomboclaat!" The Jamaican swear word resonated with incredulity.

He kept looking at the face of his unblinking girlfriend, waiting for a smile to appear but none came. He had been patient over the months when Suzy had met Patra and Y. The connection they shared was uncanny, and strangely it strengthened their relationship, it just threw up some questions he couldn't answer. The physical damage Suzy sustained was worrying. What man could stand by and see his woman get hurt, but Suzy was no shrinking violet. It took a special man or woman to inflict damage on her. And what she took she could give back in spades. So, what was that all about?

His girl was superhuman.

How quickly she healed was incredible. Jah know, he'd seen nothing like it and may never again.

Don't get him started.

How was it soon after they met their fortunes changed almost overnight? One day she was a security guard and the next celebrity bodyguard. The money challenges vanished soon after and an opportunity for him to leave his job - it was hard work, but he loved the railways. She never asked him to make that decision or implied it was a good idea. Whatever made him happy made her happy. Suzy was a special woman in ways he may never fully understand. Even with his patience, his inquisitive mind required answers. The search for these answers had been stifled for the better part of seven months, but he wasn't sure he could do that anymore. He didn't want to force anything; he wanted it to come in its own time.

An old romantic, he was. He blamed his father for that.

What he hadn't realized was Suzy felt now was the time.

"I couldn't keep it from you any longer," Suzy said kissing him on his forehead. "Yuh more open to suggestion when yuh belly full." She smiled.

"Thanks, baby," the big man sounded dejected, swallowing and crunching on some more shrimp. He paused as if he couldn't chew and think at the same time.

"Dis is real?"

"As real as life and death, baby."

Trevor thought about living without her and a hollowness formed in his chest. Not having her in his bed made him sick to his stomach.

Was that healthy?

He thought about not sharing in this crazy adventure with this woman who was like his heartbeat, no matter how short-lived it could be. The idea was too much to bare.

Fuck it.

"Ride or die," he whispered to her, his voice deep and soothing.

"Ride or die, baby," Suzy said with tears in her eyes.

The lights dimmed in the dining hall without warning and candles that no one realized had been lit were burning in the background. Immediately everyone became silent as if it was a queue for something special.

It was.

Nanny came out from the kitchen, gripping to her chest what looked like a small cabinet. Everyone watched her come over, her white skin translucent as she placed the old-fashioned cabinet on the table. The woman drummed her hands on the top of the cabinet focusing the attention of her audience.

"In Jamaica when one of our own has fallen in battle we celebrate the life, the contribution for nine nights. We believe at the end of this period the souls will find peace, helped by our merriment, our energy." She drummed hands on the top of the cabinet, the rhythm pattern like a heartbeat. Her fingers were making cross beats symbolizing struggle from the sound. The drumming was replacing words. Without really noticing, everyone huddled together listening to this powerful woman talk and play.

"We had one such warrior, who's soul many thought was damned, his sacrifice for our sisters will not be forgotten. He will soon realize redemption is open to all."

Her fingers and palms rhythmically fell on what was slowly feeling like a drum more than a cabinet. A basal tone vibrated from it, the notes were resonant, having an authority that not only influenced your emotion but matter itself. She stopped suddenly, lowering her head looking tired.

Then Nanny announced.

"We will remember him, preserve his essence." Nanny pointed over their heads and what looked like a luminescent butterfly was fluttering above them. "Dean bobo! Dean Thorne come to me." And the butterfly came to her. Nanny reached down to the cabinet and opened the doors. Everyone at the table held a breath looking at her glowing face then at the interior of the cabinet that was busy with other dancing points of light. A chromatic orchestra extended inwards beyond the boundaries of the cabinet like its own universe.

A world within a world.

The butterfly could not wait to embark on its new adventure.

"You are with us, and we are with you." Nanny said.

The butterfly flew inside, Nanny smiled and gently closed the Cabinet.

46.

Hellfire Club, Central London

Mr. Opuko stood with his hands behind his back in the loading area watching the forklift gently maneuver the ornately designed sarcophagus of his mistress into the black Mercedes van. The Hell Fire Club staff were thorough and very professional, and his stay here was pleasant. But most importantly his mistress had everything she needed, and beyond the unfortunate affair with the Guardians of the Light, her stay was exemplary.

London for him was very memorable; he learned a lot about himself and his Mistress. He always did but this time was different. Mr. Opuko would not say Mistress Pheare was angry. That was a human trait. He chose to think she was passionately involved in a learning experience that was complete and taught her what she needed to know about the Guardians of the Light. If he knew anything about his Queen, whoever comes in contact with her when she returns to London in fifty years will have a less pleasant experience than the Guardians of today. Vampire kind were the ultimate survivors; that is why he thought the humble cockroach was her creature of choice. No vampire bats, timber wolves, or black cats.

The cockroach, like his Mistress in its diminutive way was the ultimate survivor. This insect from his research had ancestors that scurried on the planet before human-kind arrived. He hoped to be in her employ for another hundred years. Mr. Opuko could not imagine himself doing anything else. To his mind, he had done an exem-plary job in London. Even learning from her ways and planning ahead at every juncture. That smooth extrac-tion from the battlefield was a consequence of her ex-ample. That situation could have turned out for the worst.

Not that it was likely but possible.

He folded his arms contentedly.

The economic statistics say job satisfaction was fall-ing. He counted himself lucky to be so fulfilled.

The Mercedes S class pulled up beside him and the door silently opened. He looked in at the back seat, at the vast, luxurious space and all the modern convenienc-es for this journey to the Southampton Port.

Mr. Opoku nodded to himself.

He didn't want this adventure to end.

Being a vampire familiar was the best calling in the world.

Hands down.

THE END

<u>Don't Forget to Review</u>

A review is like oxygen for my books. I live for them; I love them and I'm so appreciative of readers when they take the time to share their opinions and support my work. Thank you for finishing the book, I hope you enjoyed it and if you did, help me to spread the love.

Please leave a review.

ABOUT THE AUTHOR

Anton Marks first novel began a trend of bestsellers that would transport readers to the ghettoes of Kingston Jamaica in **Dancehall**, futuristic London – **In the Days of Dread**, government agents in **Bushman** and the futuristic world of vice in – **69**.

His next offering will be a young adult fantasy novel entitled – **The Last Prince of Alkebulahn** and the second in the *Bad II the Bone series* – **Good II be Bad**. Expect great things as the Marksman continues writing the most creative and exciting novels in the new Urban Fantastic genre.

Come visit him at:

www.antonmarks.com

Printed in Great Britain
by Amazon